"You're shivering. Do you want my jacket?"

When Hadley shook her head, Gabe shifted closer to her and tucked in the blanket more tightly. Even through the thick wool, his touch made her dizzy.

Gabe leaned closer to her. "It's your call. Do we go on, or do we stop here?"

She needed to tell him to go back. But when he reached out to trace his fingertips up the line of her jaw and curl them around the nape of her neck, it was already far too late.

She was sinking slowly. There was every reason to avoid this, and she couldn't make herself even try. She felt his breath before she ever felt a touch. When his mouth fused to hers it seemed inevitable. His lips were cool at first from the frozen night, and then she felt the heat. She could have held out against demand, but his touch was more an invitation.

And it made her want more.

Dear Reader,

If you're eagerly anticipating holiday gifts we can start you off on the right foot, with six compelling reads by authors established and new. Consider it a somewhat early Christmas, Chanukah or Kwanzaa present!

The gifting begins with another in *USA TODAY* bestselling author Susan Mallery's DESERT ROGUES series. In *The Sheik and the Virgin Secretary* a spurned assistant decides the only way to get over a soured romance is to start a new one—with her prince of a boss (literally). Crystal Green offers the last installment of MOST LIKELY TO… with *Past Imperfect*, in which we finally learn the identity of the secret benefactor—as well as Rachel James's parentage. Could the two be linked? In *Under the Mistletoe*, Kristin Hardy's next HOLIDAY HEARTS offering, a by-the-book numbers cruncher is determined to liquidate a grand New England hotel…until she meets the handsome hotel manager determined to restore it to its glory days—and capture her heart in the process! Don't miss *Her Special Charm*, next up in Marie Ferrarella's miniseries THE CAMEO. This time the finder of the necklace is a gruff New York police detective—surely he can't be destined to find love with its Southern belle of an owner, can he? In *Diary of a Domestic Goddess* by Elizabeth Harbison, a woman who is close to losing her job, her dream house and her livelihood finds she might be able to keep all three—*if* she can get close to her hotshot new boss who's annoyingly irresistible. And please welcome brand-new author Loralee Lillibridge—her debut book, *Accidental Hero*, features a bad boy come home, this time with scars, an apology—and a determination to win back the woman he left behind!

So celebrate! We wish all the best of everything this holiday season and in the New Year to come.

Happy reading,

Gail Chasan
Senior Editor

Please address questions and book requests to:
Silhouette Reader Service
U.S.: 3010 Walden Ave., P.O. Box 1325, Buffalo, NY 14269
Canadian: P.O. Box 609, Fort Erie, Ont. L2A 5X3

UNDER *the* MISTLETOE

KRISTIN HARDY

Silhouette®

SPECIAL EDITION®

Published by Silhouette Books

America's Publisher of Contemporary Romance

To Paul Ronty Jr. and Martha Wilson
of the Mount Washington Hotel
for their time and generosity
and
to Stephen—
this love will last

SILHOUETTE BOOKS

ISBN 0-373-24725-7

UNDER THE MISTLETOE

This edition published by arrangement with Harlequin Books S.A.

® and TM are trademarks of Harlequin Books S.A., used under license.
Trademarks indicated with ® are registered in the United States Patent
and Trademark Office, the Canadian Trade Marks Office and in other
countries.

Visit Silhouette Books at www.eHarlequin.com

Printed in U.S.A.

Books by Kristin Hardy

Silhouette Special Edition

‡*Where There's Smoke* #1720
‡*Under the Mistletoe* #1725

Harlequin Blaze

My Sexiest Mistake #44
*Scoring #78
*As Bad as Can Be #86
**Slippery When Wet* #94
†*Turn Me On* #148
†*Cutting Loose* #156
†*Nothing but the Best* #164
§*Certified Male* #187
§*U.S. Male* #199

‡Holiday Hearts
*Under the Covers
†Sex & the Supper Club
§Sealed with a Kiss

KRISTIN HARDY

has always wanted to write, starting her first novel while still in grade school. Although she became a laser engineer by training, she never gave up her dream of being an author. In 2002, her first completed manuscript, *My Sexiest Mistake,* debuted in Harlequin's Blaze line; it was subsequently made into a movie by the Oxygen network. The author of nine books to date, Kristin lives in New Hampshire with her husband and collaborator.

Dear Reader,

I first got the idea for *Under the Mistletoe* a couple of years ago while taking my parents on a leaf-peeping trip through northern New Hampshire. I brought them to one of my favorite places, the Mount Washington Hotel, a hundred-year-old grand resort hotel in the White Mountains. One night, I was walking through the lobby past the walk-in granite fireplace and I had this flash of a couple in love, waltzing before the fireplace on Christmas Eve— and *Under the Mistletoe* was born.

I modeled the Hotel Mount Jefferson in *Under the Mistletoe* on the Mount Washington. You can see for yourself, if you're lucky. Please see my Web site—www.kristinhardy.com— for details about an exciting contest I'm holding!

I'd love to hear what you think of Hadley and Gabe's story, so please drop me a line at kristin@kristinhardy.com. And stop by my Web site for future contests, details on upcoming books, recipes and more.

Happy holidays.

Kristin Hardy

Prologue

"Because I didn't meet the Wall Street number?" Hadley Stone stared at her father incredulously.

Robert Stone looked back with the same mix of dispassionate censure he'd offered her most of her life. "The stock price of Stone Enterprises has dropped two dollars since the earnings release for Becheron Minerals. That division was the highest profile buy we made last year. Your job was to turn it around."

"I *did* turn it around," she protested. "We beat our in-house earnings target."

"But Wall Street expected you to do better."

What the hell did a bunch of Wall Street analysts know about the inside dealings of their company? Hadley thought furiously, remembering the hours she'd spent flying halfway around the world to various Becheron facilities, the countless jet-lagged meetings while she struggled to bring the shaky mining company back from the brink of bankruptcy to meet the punishingly high profit margins demanded by Stone Enterprises. And now, to be told that the division was being taken out of her hands because she hadn't met the inflated expectations of Wall Street analysts?

Grimly, she shoved the frustration down. Showing emotion to Robert Stone was an invitation to be totally discounted. "I know Becheron inside out," she said instead. "You put someone else in there, it'll take them a month just to get up to speed."

"Eliot Ketchum's taking over. I'm sure he'll be quite capable."

"So I'm demoted?"

"Think of it as a reassignment. It was my error to push you too far, too fast."

Protesting that it wasn't fair would fall on deaf ears, she knew from experience. Her big opportunity, she'd delivered the goods and all she'd earned was a smack down.

The frown on Robert's face softened. "It's not your last chance, Hadley. You know I have big plans for you at Stone. I always have."

Since toddlerhood, to be exact. For as long as she could remember, he'd orchestrated her life—her school, her friends, her career. Relentless standards, unyielding discipline and occasional and unpredictable praise, doled out just often enough to make her knock herself out to earn more. Another child might have rebelled. Hadley only worked harder to be the heir Robert wanted, a stand-in for the son he'd never had.

To be what he wanted? For the umpteenth time of late, she wondered if that were even possible. She didn't want to go there, though—couldn't, not after spending twenty-eight years of her life trying to please him.

Robert's intercom buzzed. "Who is it, Ruth?" he asked.

"Justin Palmer, to talk with you about the W. S. Industries restructuring."

"Send him in." Robert clicked off the intercom and looked at Hadley. "I'll be with you in just a minute. WSI takes precedence."

Indeed. Everyone at Stone Enterprises was dying to know just what Robert Stone planned to do with the company of Whit Stone, his bitterest rival—and the father he'd been estranged from since childhood. Robert had labored all his professional life to outdo Whit and to destroy him financially. In the end, he'd been unequal to the task. Whit had died with his holdings stronger than ever. To have the point rammed home by Whit leaving him the entire conglomerate had to be burning her father up.

Not that Hadley was about to ask.

The graying, hawk-faced legal counsel of Stone Enterprises handed a bound report to Robert and took a seat in one of the plush leather client chairs. "WSI, in a nutshell. You've got the preliminary assessment of holdings, value, et cetera. It's all in agreement with the estate declaration, though slightly overvalued by my estimate." He smiled faintly.

"Any surprises?"

"Not really. Most of it is a matter of public record."

"The list of underperformers is longer than I'd expected." An expression of satisfaction spread across Robert's face. "Do you think they were cooking the books?"

"Unlikely. If you flip to the page of overall holdings, you'll see that those are a minority."

Robert nodded. "I don't care. We need rid of them."

"I'll notify mergers and acquisitions to get on it."

"You misunderstand me. I don't want them sold off whole. Take them apart and sell them off piecemeal."

Palmer stared at him. "Robert, about seventy percent of the

companies on that list are running in the black and another twenty are looking at profitability within a five-year time horizon. You run them all through a chop shop, you're going to lose value and revenue."

"It'll lower the hit from the estate taxes." Stone flipped closed the briefing book. "Get our salvage specialists to work on it. I want those companies to be history within the month."

"I don't think we can entirely execute on that."

Robert's brows lowered. The only occasions Hadley had ever seen him lose an iota of his iron control involved his father. "I don't want to hear arguments, Justin. I want to hear 'yes.'"

"How about 'the terms of the will won't allow it'?"

"Explain."

"Your father's will identifies one holding that cannot be sold or dismantled. It has to be held by the Stone family and run in good faith or else the entire estate reverts to charity."

Hadley watched, fascinated. After years of being the puppet master, Robert was now a puppet himself. And not even he could walk away from thirty billion dollars for the sake of principle.

"What is the business?"

"An old hotel up in New Hampshire."

"What the hell would he want with a hotel?" Robert demanded. "He specialized in high tech and industrial manufacturing, not hospitality."

"I get the impression he dealt in whatever he wanted to."

"And Stone Enterprises deals in what *I* want to," Stone said icily. "Find a way to break the terms."

Palmer shook his head. "We've been over and over it. It's ironclad. You can do what you want with the rest, Robert, but this one has to stay in the family."

Robert's jaw tightened visibly. Long seconds passed while Hadley waited for the explosion. Finally, he relaxed a fraction, the struggle for control won yet again. "All right. If we can't unload it, then we need to turn around the earnings. I won't have this kind of an operation showing up on our financials."

"We'll need to put someone else on it in a hurry."

"I know." Robert turned to Hadley. "Well, it looks like that new opportunity I was telling you about has cropped up sooner than I expected. Get the Becheron transfer rolling. You're going to New Hampshire."

Chapter One

New Hampshire, December 2005

Opportunity, her father had said. More like banishment, Hadley thought, as she swung into a curve on the narrow road that threaded through the White Mountains of New Hampshire. From vice president of one of the most high profile divisions at Stone to triage specialist for an antiquated hotel out in the sticks with the squirrels and chipmunks. Forget the flights to Zurich, Cape Town and Buenos Aires. Now it was Montpelier, Vermont, which was still nearly an hour and a half from the hotel. No direct flights there, of course, which had meant cooling her heels in Boston while she'd waited for a connection on some crop duster.

After all, demoted V.P.s didn't rate the corporate jet.

Her cell phone rang and she answered it absently. "Hello?"

"Good morning, sweetheart," said a voice filled with perfume and gardenias and air kisses.

"Hello, Mother."

"Can you stop by the house before you leave so we can talk about the holidays?"

Hadley resisted the urge to roll her eyes. "Too late. I'm already here."

"The wilds of Maine?"

"New Hampshire."

"Ah. And how is New Hampshire?"

"Cold," she answered. "Lots of trees and snow."

"Sounds wonderfully rustic. Your father seems to think you'll be gone for a while. At least through the holidays."

Nice that he had such faith in her. "We'll see how it goes. I should be able to take a day or two over Christmas, anyway."

"Actually, that was why I called." Irene hesitated. "You see, we're going to Gstaad over the holidays. The twins are mad for the idea."

Eight hours of flying each way, not counting time spent on the ground. "Sounds great," Hadley said slowly, "but I don't think I can take that much time off right now. Any chance of going after Christmas?"

"Well, the twins really want to be there for the holiday. A bunch of their friends are planning a big party and they don't want to miss it." Hadley could imagine the spark in her mother's eyes on the other end of the phone. "And next year the girls will be in their debutante season, so we can't possibly go then. This is really our only chance."

Debutante season? "Sure, the debutante season," Hadley said, biting back a sigh. "No problem."

"Oh, and if you're trying to think of something to get them, they've been absolutely crazed for those new Louis Vuitton bags, the ones with the cherries."

Hadley looked at the pine covered mountains around her. "I'll see what I can come up with."

"Wonderful. Anyway, I should let you go—I know you're busy. I'll call you before we leave."

"All right. Love you, Mom."

"Love you, too, dear."

And the line went silent, leaving Hadley with another unsettling reminder that when it came to the Stone girls, there were her mother's twins and her father's daughter. They shared the same wheat-colored hair and gray eyes, the same delicate features that Hadley often thought put her at a disadvantage in business. They'd grown up in the same household.

And yet not. Robert had taken command of Hadley's life early. Perhaps it was only human nature that when Irene Stone finally gave birth to the twins, she'd made them hers. It became more apparent each time Hadley saw them that her mother and the twins inhabited an entirely different world than the one she lived in. Theirs revolved around shopping and hairstyles and parties, all the things Hadley had never had time for. All the things her mother loved.

And every time she talked with her mother, that world seemed farther and farther away.

Enough! It wasn't a crisis. They had plans for Christmas and she was a grown woman with a job to get done.

Checking her directions, she turned onto the highway that led to the hotel—if you could call the pockmarked asphalt that threaded through even denser forest a highway.

She could tell the first problem with the Hotel Mount Jefferson sight unseen—location. Skiers and hikers, the people most likely to go to the mountains for recreation, were not the kinds of people to pay a bundle for a glorified bed-and-breakfast. They were far more likely to camp out or, if they had the kind of money that the hotel hoped to attract, choose the stylish condos she'd passed a couple of miles back. How, then, was she supposed to meet her father's astronomical expectations?

Hadley's hands tightened on the wheel. Instead of running a division with seven locations, three business units and a head count of more than two thousand, she was now responsible for turning around a superannuated hotel with a few hundred employees, most of whom were probably missing teeth.

Evaluate, set a strategy and implement it, her father had directed her. Double the profit margin within six months, quadruple it within twelve.

If she had any sense, she'd tell him to go jump in a lake. After all, she had choices. She could update her résumé and shop it around. But who out there would hire her without worrying she was a mole for Stone Enterprises? And Robert Stone was a jealous god. When you left his world, he made sure the departure was permanent—home would be home to her no longer. Did she want that? Could she give that up?

Hadley sighed. She didn't want to be in this car, on this road, heading for oblivion. But she didn't really have a choice, not when she thought about it. No, her only real option was to do the job, give Robert what he wanted. So she kept driving to the Hotel Mount Jefferson, a place in all likelihood few people other than the misbegotten souls who worked there cared about, she was sure.

Misbegotten souls who were about to get a big surprise.

"You're kidding." Gabriel Trask stared at Mona Landry, his head of housekeeping. "No water in the entire laundry room?"

The stout woman glowered. "Burst pipe. Apparently laundry wasn't a priority when they redid the plumbing last spring."

"Burke?" Gabe turned to his head of facilities.

He spread his hands. "We only have so many months to work with. Guests come first. I was planning to run new pipe out to the facilities building this spring."

"And what are the guests going to say when they don't have any clean sheets or towels?" Mona asked tartly.

"Mona." Gabe raised his hand. "We've got a problem to address. Let's fix it. Burke, have you isolated the break?"

"I've dug a couple of sample holes. As near as I can tell, the pipe out to the laundry plant is split. Frost heaves."

"As near as you can tell?"

"We're still trying to dig down to it."

Gabe frowned. "It shouldn't be that hard."

"Frozen ground. Winter staffing levels. Plus it's ten degrees out there and dropping. We can only keep the guys outside for short stretches."

Gabe nodded. If he cursed a blue streak in his head, it was nobody's business but his own. "How long?"

"We're working on it. No later than tomorrow afternoon. I'd like to repair the whole line while we're at it. Otherwise, it's just a matter of time until this happens again."

Not what Gabe wanted to hear at the start of a heavily booked weekend. "Mona, how's our linen supply look?"

"Enough for today and maybe half of the rooms tomorrow. After that…" She shrugged. "I keep telling you we need more."

New linens, new plumbing, new pillars to replace the rotting ones on the west porch, new carpeting in the ballroom.

Old budget. When his coal-dark hair eventually turned gray, he'd know where to place the blame. Gabe suppressed a sigh. "All right, we go to the laundry in Montpelier. Mona, get the number from Susan. One of the grounds guys can truck it over."

"Not if you want that trench dug," Burke reminded him.

Gabe closed his eyes a second. "Right. Okay, find a bellhop but get on it now. We need the laundry to turn the job around by the end of the day." Pulling from the bell staff would leave them short up front during checkout, but they'd manage.

If necessary, he'd drive the damn truck himself.

* * *

Trees, unending trees. Hadley yawned. No wonder she was in a bad mood. Taking the morning flight out had sounded good when she'd bought the ticket. It had only been when the alarm sounded at five that she'd realized she'd been out of her mind to book it. When she got to the hotel she could give them their first test—how they dealt with grumpy early arrivals.

She swung the sporty little rental car into another curve, and the line of trees fell away, revealing the valley ahead.

And her jaw dropped.

The Hotel Mount Jefferson perched on the hillside like a white castle, a sprawling fantasy of turrets and porticos. The roof glowed red under the rays of the winter sun. Flags atop the towers snapped in the breeze. Hadley could practically see women in pale Victorian gowns and parasols promenading along the veranda that ran the length of the building. A snow-covered hillside rolled away from the hotel. It would be green in summer, she thought, green and magical.

The pictures hadn't done it justice. She'd done her homework, of course. She knew the financials by heart, understood that it wasn't just a little mountain lodge. But she hadn't been at all prepared for a place that looked as though stepping through the doors would be to walk back in time. For a place that instantly made her think of ball gowns and afternoon teas, of hot toddies sipped by a roaring fire.

She hadn't been prepared to be enchanted.

This isn't about enchantment, she could practically hear Robert saying. *It's about business.*

And with that the enchantment dropped away. How did they heat that many rooms, no doubt drafty after withstanding nearly a hundred winters? Radiators, probably. Radiators installed by Civil War veterans. How often did the radiators break down? Hadley sighed. However enchanting the hotel was on the outside, she had to meet her numbers or else she'd be

in exile a whole lot longer than she'd like. And even enchantment got old.

She considered her strategy. Come in like an ordinary guest
and spend the weekend looking for ways to economize, ways
to increase occupancy. Shameless romance was one angle to
play, she mused as she drove past the white, Victorian-style
lampposts that marched up the access road to the hotel. Hope-
fully, they had an in-house consultant for that part, because that
one she was going to have to delegate.

At the pillared portico of the hotel, Hadley paused for a moment. Up close, the Hotel Mount Jefferson was all her first
glimpse had promised. The front facade of the building
gleamed with broad windows. Marble steps led up to a green-
carpeted porch where a small fleet of shiny brass luggage racks
held the bags of departing guests. To one side sat an antique
sleigh, painted gleaming red. Christmas was drawing near and
whoever ran the place was laying it on just right, she admitted.

The valet opened her door. "Welcome to the Hotel Mount
Jefferson. May I get your bags?"

"In the trunk."

"Very good." He passed her a green ticket in trade for her
keys. "If you'll just call this number when you get to your
room, we'll have your bags brought right up for you."

Hadley walked up the steps and over to the sleigh. The cut
glass lamps reflected the daylight, the brass fittings gleamed.
Someone at the hotel paid attention to detail, she thought, trac-
ing the graceful curve of the front panel. Someone knew the
little things counted.

A smiling doorman in a caped greatcoat opened the wide
white front door with its curling brass handles. "Welcome,
miss," he said, tipping his cap. Hadley stepped through the door
and straight back to the turn of the previous century.

For a moment, she simply stopped and stared, carried back

to a time when the world was a slower, more graceful place. Nineteen oh three, or so her research said. From where she stood, the lobby seemed to stretch the entire length of the east wing of the building, all space and light, airy and open. Ornate white pillars soared to the coffered ceiling twenty feet overhead, their inset panels gleaming with gold luster, capitals at the top curling elegantly. Overhead, bronze-and-crystal chandeliers threw a warm glow that competed with the sunlight spilling in the enormous picture windows.

And yes, there was a carved granite fireplace with a leaping blaze. All she needed was a fancy-dress ball and a hot toddy before bed to make the fantasy complete.

Shaking her head, Hadley approached the front desk.

"Welcome to the Hotel Mount Jefferson." The young, auburn-haired and obviously pregnant clerk gave her a friendly smile. Angie from Albany, or so her badge said.

"Checking in, name of Stone," Hadley said, sliding her credit card over the polished wood. "I know I'm early but I was hoping you might have something ready."

Angie looked at her apologetically. "I can take your card and get you signed in, but we won't have any rooms ready in your class until at least two-thirty. I'm sorry, but we just had a big group check out. We were full up last night."

Impressed despite herself, Hadley raised a brow. "Full?"

"Oh yes. A big corporate meeting."

Hundred percent occupancy, Hadley mused. Perhaps things weren't quite hopeless. Maybe it was just a matter of making some cuts to control costs, and things would be fine.

"All right, you're all set." Angie handed her card back. "If you'll just come by at two-thirty, we should be able to get you in. In the meantime, Cortland's downstairs is open for lunch, and we have a complimentary afternoon tea at two. We also have changing rooms if you want to go ski. The shuttle runs to the slopes about every fifteen minutes."

Balls. Afternoon tea. Hot toddies by the fire. "Thank you so much," Hadley said. "It's perfect."

Afternoon tea was set up in the semicircular conservatory that arched off the lobby, a fantasy of white wicker and greenery. Hadley poured a cup of Earl Grey and picked up a pair of the pretty little tea sandwiches. Gorgonzola and pear on rye, watercress on white, no crusts. Balancing plates, she settled in a chair near one of the enormous floor-to-ceiling windows. The view was breathtaking, the snow-topped mountains across the valley practically sitting in her lap.

A burst of laughter had her glancing over at a couple settled side by side on a wicker love seat. And for a sudden, lost moment, she imagined herself as the pretty young blonde, sitting next to the handsome man who looked at her with love.

Hadley's pleasure fizzled as her imagination suddenly failed her. She stared at the couple as though they were exotic creatures at the zoo. Were they really happy? How long would it last? "You have too much money," her father reminded her often. "You have to be cautious." Which was an easy thing to do with the men she ran into, who either feared her or pursued her for the thrill of getting near Robert Stone.

Anyway, what was she really missing? An icy détente like her parents' marriage? Any of the countless paths to divorce that she'd seen her relatives and acquaintances follow? Acquaintances, because she hadn't become friends with anyone since she'd left school, her classmates scattered to whatever ports of luxury or business they or their families fancied. There had never been time. It was hard to hook up for dinner when you were always on a plane somewhere or staying in the office late for a telecon with the Tokyo office.

It was easy to fall into the trap of wishing for love, here in a place outfitted like a movie set. For wasn't that what love was—a movie fantasy? Among real people, infatuation waned and affection was always conditional; she'd learned that lesson long ago. It depended on what you could do for people. Far safer to remain on her own.

Even though she always had had a soft spot for the movies…

Setting aside her teacup, Hadley rose. It was just the demotion, that was all. A walk would get her out of this funk. A walk and a chance for some fresh air would make her stop taking stock of her life and coming up wanting.

Gabe pulled the truck into its parking place at the side of the hotel and turned off the engine, rolling his shoulders to relax them. He hadn't really meant the part about driving the laundry himself, but who'd have figured that he didn't have anyone in the place with a Class A truck license? He definitely wasn't crazy about being away from the hotel for several hours in the middle of the day. Cell phone reception was so bad in the mountains that he could hardly connect most of the time.

If he had to be away, at least he had the staff for it. He'd never understood managers who preferred to surround themselves with ineffectual subordinates. He wanted people who knew how to think, who could act without direction when necessary. Management held challenges enough without setting up a brainless ant colony that fell apart when you weren't around.

As a result, he'd been able to mostly enjoy what was a gorgeous day, with a sky so brilliantly blue it hurt the eyes, and a snow-covered landscape still new enough to be charming. It had felt kind of like playing hooky. The brightly clad figures whizzing down the slopes of the ski area opposite the hotel reminded him that working Saturday wasn't normal for everybody. One of these days he needed to find time for the slopes.

For now, he climbed down out of the truck, slipping on his bomber jacket to ward off the outside chill. A quick stop at the manager's house to put his suit on again and he'd be back in business. Gabe skirted the rear of the hotel, heading toward the path that led to the three-story farmhouse that predated the hotel. Free on-site housing in very plush digs, one of the bennies of the job. Of course, it worked for the ownership, given that he was around 24/7 in case of crisis.

Ownership, he thought, and felt the familiar tug of regret.

It wasn't going to be the same without Whit Stone. Lost friends, new challenges. Still, the hotel was a constant. He turned to look at it in all its palatial whiteness.

It wasn't the view of the hotel that made his footsteps slow then, but the figure on the little loading dock outside the employee entrance. A woman, standing with her arms wrapped around herself in the winter cold, strands of her pale hair shifting in the breeze. She wasn't staff. He knew the face and name of every person who worked for him. It was a point of pride. This woman he'd never seen before.

He'd have remembered.

She gazed at the sweep of the Presidential Range behind him, her face angled a little away. She looked like a faerie come down from the mountain, all silvery-blond hair and pale skin, wrapped about in a cape of dark green. There was a magic there that drew him, something compelling in the tilt of her eyes, the temptation of her lips.

Then she turned her head a bit and he saw the faint air of wistfulness that hovered around her mouth and shadowed her eyes.

Without conscious decision, he headed toward her.

She probably wasn't supposed to be in this area of the hotel, but it was the only place Hadley had found that had the view she wanted and an absence of people. She'd get over her funk as soon as she started working. It was just the unfamiliar experience of having time to herself that was throwing her off.

The air was crisp and cold enough that her breath created a

white plume each time she exhaled. So beautiful, the sweep of valley, the rise of the mountains, the snow-iced trees. She stared out at the panorama, wishing she knew how to draw, to capture that sweeping vista, that soaring openness in practiced, flowing strokes.

"Beautiful view, isn't it?" a voice said.

Hadley jumped and stared at the man who approached her on the flagstone path. Beautiful view? Beautiful man, more like it. It was almost bad form to be that gorgeous outside of a movie or a magazine. Tall, dark and handsome was such a cliché, she wanted to tell him. Maybe she would.

If she could get her tongue to work.

"Sorry I startled you."

She moved her head, the desire to avoid attention immediate. "You shouldn't sneak up on people. It isn't polite." Which was a good thing; after all, there had to be something wrong with anyone who was that perfect looking, all cheekbones and honed jaw, dark hair flopping down over his forehead.

The humor in his eyes only made him more attractive. "Well, I can't have that said of me. Please accept my apologies."

"Maybe." She hadn't heard him approach; he'd just been there, long and lean in his charcoal crewneck and expensive leather jacket. Not a staff member, not with that kind of clothing. She recognized designer quality when she saw it.

"So are you blowing off the Employees Only sign?"

"I wanted to see the mountains."

"I don't blame you. But I'm betting there are better places to do it here. Places where the heat's on, for example." His feet crunched on the flagstone path as he crossed it and came to a stop before the railing behind which she stood.

"You're outside."

He looked up at her, one corner of his mouth turning up. "Only for as long as it takes me to find a door."

If he'd stepped just a bit closer she could have moved her hands from the railing and pushed his dark hair back off his forehead. She stared at him, wondering if his eyes were really that green or they just looked that way because of the backdrop of pines. The sudden pull that she felt caught her by surprise. "I'm fine," Hadley said, putting her hands in her pockets. "It was just too crowded inside."

"A loner." He nodded as though confirming something to himself.

"Or choosy."

"Is that a polite way of telling me to get lost?"

Not yet. She wasn't ready for this to end. "It's a public place. You pay the rates, you ought to be able to go anywhere you want, I guess."

"Well, it is pretty here. I like the view."

"But you're not even looking at the mountains."

He grinned. "You noticed that?"

Hadley felt the flush creeping across her cheekbones and, dammit, she couldn't help smiling back. She could just imagine what Robert would say. She was on assignment. She was supposed to be working, not flirting.

Flirting was foolish, anyway. There was a girlfriend somewhere, had to be. Men who looked like him didn't come to places like the Mount Jefferson solo. She had no business looking at his mouth and wondering just how it tasted. She had no business talking to him at all.

She belonged in a winter landscape, Gabe thought, with her white-blond hair and those gray eyes. The soft, wistful gaze was gone now, replaced by a guarded expression he felt an illogical urge to wipe away. He'd seen the startled look flash across her face a few seconds before, though, had seen her eyes darken. As hotel manager, Gabe was always talking to guests, but his interest in her was far from professional.

Down, boy.

Okay, he was a grown-up. He could chat with her a little bit without drooling all over her. After all, charming the guests was his job. "Well, I guess you're right to enjoy the blue skies while you can. I hear it's supposed to snow tonight," he said.

Her expression brightened. "Really? I love winter, it's my favorite time of year. I envy anyone who gets to live here."

"Of course, *you* don't have to shovel snow for five months running."

She laughed, and Gabe felt the jolt right down to his toes. Forget all the foolish stuff about faeries and pixies. With her eyes dancing as she looked down at him, she was flat-out beautiful. "Spoken like someone who lives in snow country. Look at it as a cheap way to get in shape. Some people spend money on health clubs."

He shook his head. "I grew up on a farm. I always swore I'd never pay good money to lift weights." He had grown up on a farm, and he'd left it as soon as he decently could. If he could point to any one character flaw, it would be an unreasonable affection for luxury. He was happy to work hard, as long as it was on his own terms. The Hotel Mount Jefferson suited him like a comfortable pair of shoes.

"Where I live," she said, "snow's rare enough to be fun."

"Where's that?"

"Manhattan."

He wouldn't have picked her for a city girl. She belonged in this kind of setting, among mountains and snow. "It's not that rare there. It's just that the city clears it away as quickly as they can."

She opened her mouth to speak, then looked beyond him, her eyes widening in alarm. "Oh God, there's a fire. Look." She pointed at the plume of smoke that rose from the distant slope.

Gabe peered at it. "That's not a fire, that's the engine from the cog railway."

"The cog railway?"

"There's an old railway up there. It's open now for skiers."

"A train goes up the side of that mountain?" she asked, staring at the steep slope that rose from the forested valley.

"All the way to the top, in summer. You can only ride it halfway this time of year. Ski down, too, if you want to. Do you ski?"

"I've never found the time to learn."

"Maybe while you're visiting. Either way, you definitely shouldn't miss the railway." In his pocket, his combination walkie-talkie/cell phone chirped. Gabe frowned at himself. Getting distracted chatting with a guest—however lovely—when he should be inside wasn't like him. He'd already been gone too much that afternoon.

"Something wrong?"

"I've got to take this call. Excuse me." He flipped open the phone and walked a few paces away. A consultation with the chef before dinner. Another crisis to deal with. The twinge of regret he felt surprised him. He turned back to his mystery girl. "Duty calls. Are you staying here long?"

She hesitated. "I'm not sure. A few days, at least."

"Then back to Manhattan?"

"Of course."

Time to go, he reminded himself. "Well, I hope I see you around before you leave," he said.

And tried not to feel like he'd lost something as he walked away.

Chapter Two

"You look like you're having a good afternoon," said Angie at the front desk as Hadley walked up.

She was smiling, Hadley realized. It was probably a sad statement on the state of her personal life that it took so little to cheer her up. "Any chance you've got my room ready now?" she asked. "I checked in earlier."

"Let me see." Angie leaned awkwardly toward her computer, trying to shift her stomach out of the way. She looked very pregnant, Hadley realized—like about ten months.

Hadley cleared her throat. "I don't mean to get personal, but should you really be up and around at this point?"

"I know," the receptionist said in amusement. "I look like I'm ready to drop any minute. Believe it or not, I've got another month to go. The doctor says Trot's going to be our New Year's present."

"Trot?"

"My Hank's a Red Sox fan. I wanted to name him Milo but I didn't have a chance."

"Maybe he'll be a distance runner," Hadley said.

Angie laughed. "Maybe." She set the room folio on the polished maple counter. "So let's see, you're up on the third floor." She passed Hadley a key on an ornate brass disk the size of a coaster and gestured at the wall of numbered pigeonholes behind her. "Just drop the key here on your way out and pick it up when you're ready to head back to your room. Any questions?"

It was a quaint arrangement that Hadley had only seen in the older hotels of Europe. Something about it made her feel connected, cared for. "I'm all set," she told her. "Good luck with Trot."

Angie smiled. "The elevator is behind you. Enjoy your stay."

Next to the elevator, the broad grand staircase swept down, all rich carpeting and curving elegance. Hadley could imagine couples descending for dinner back in the old days, the women's gloved hands on the arms of their tuxedoed escorts, their silken skirts trailing behind them as they made their entrance.

And she found herself wishing she had someone to see it with.

The polished brass doors of the elevator opened to reveal a spare-looking elderly man. "Good afternoon, miss," he said, pulling back the accordioned metal gate. "My name's Lester. Where can I take you?"

"Third floor, please." Hadley stepped on and watched him shut the gate. The control panel had no buttons, just a lever, right below the inspection certificate. "So just how old is this elevator?"

"Original to the building." He beamed. "Mr. Cortland wanted all the modern conveniences when he built the hotel. Got his friend Tom Edison to wire it for electricity." The car began to rise smoothly. "Hot and cold running water and fire sprinklers in all of the rooms, even. That was a big deal back then."

"How long have you worked here?"

He considered. "Oh, about fifty years. I started when she was in her prime and saw her through some dark times before Mr. Stone bought her and started turning things right."

She should have expected it, but the name still jolted her. "You mean Whit Stone?"

"The same. Top drawer, a prince of a guy. He spent a week here every summer for almost as long as I can remember. Course, when he started, I was on outside staff." He gave a raffish smile. "These days, I have to take it easy a little." The car stopped at her floor and Lester opened the gate. "Enjoy your stay, miss. I hope to see you again."

A prince of a guy. Top drawer. Not exactly the way her father described Whit. Hadley crossed the octagonal elevator lobby, her mind buzzing, and went through the double doors that led to her wing. Even the third floor boasted ten-foot ceilings and hallways twice as broad as any she'd seen at a hotel before. Antique fixtures on the walls cast a soft light over the striped wallpaper and rich floral hall runner. Brass plates engraved with room numbers in curling script adorned the doors.

Hadley unlocked hers to a spill of golden sunlight through the windows that ran across nearly the entire wall. The room was enormous, bigger than the living room in her loft at home. She caught the scent of freesias from a small clutch sitting in a little vase on the bureau. A feather duvet covered the bed. Again, attention to detail. Someone cared about the guests. And in some obscure way she felt comforted, and some of her soul-sickness ebbed as she settled into one of the overstuffed wing chairs by the window.

Gabe sat at his computer. The screen displayed the previous month's occupancy charts, but he stared into space, re-

membering a pair of sober gray eyes sparking into laughter
Sometimes a small taste stuck with a person longest. Amid the
quiet of snow and winterscape he'd talked with her just enough
to know he wanted more.

And then there was that instant when her eyes had darkened
and something flashed between the two of them....

He blinked and shook his head. What he needed was to fin
ish preparing for his department heads' meeting, not think about
guests. Off-limit guests, he reminded himself firmly. And unless his little winter faerie had some pixie dust that would help
bolster his midweek occupancy, she needed to be off his mind.

The project to winterize the hotel for cold weather business
five years before had cost a bundle. With Whit's agreement,
Gabe hadn't tried to pay it off all at once, but continued to do
the kind of necessary renovations a century-old building required. Whit had happily plowed most of his profits back into
upkeep, hoping to rescue the Mount Jefferson from the decay
it had been in when he'd bought it.

Who knew what the new owners had planned?

"Mr. Trask."

Gabe glanced up to see his administrative assistant at the
door. "Yes, Susan?"

"I just wanted to see if you needed anything before I go
home."

He glanced at his desk clock, stunned to see it was already
after seven. "You were supposed to be off two hours ago."

"What about you? You were here when I got in."

Twelve hours and counting, to be specific. "Goes with the
territory," he said with a shrug and rose. "Anyway, I'm just
about finished here. I'm going to do a quick walk-through and
head out myself."

"Mr. Trask?"

He turned in inquiry.

"You've lost your badge again."

Gabe glanced down at his lapel and bit back a mild curse. He'd gotten the magnetized name tags to save wear and tear on clothing, especially his own. Unfortunately, they didn't stick so well to jacket lapels if a person wasn't careful about putting them on. And that afternoon, he'd been a little bit rushed and a little bit distracted by a pair of gray eyes. "Looks like the magnet flipped off again."

Susan clicked her tongue and looked around the floor of the office for it. "Want me to see if the shop has another?"

"If no one's turned it in by Monday. No sense in worrying about it now, though. I'm not likely to forget who I am. It's Saturday night. Go home and relax."

"Yes, sir."

Someone had once said that the octagonal dining room was big enough that each end was in a different area code. It was Gabe's last stop every night. There was something about the glow of the pale salmon walls in the soft light of chandeliers and candlelight, the semicircular Tiffany windows ringing the upper gallery where the orchestra had played back when the hotel was first open. When Gabe looked at the unapologetically opulent room, he forgot his ongoing struggle to find plasterers who could restore the complicated capitals of the pillars and the ornate ceiling medallions. He just appreciated the reminder of a more gracious time.

"Good evening, Mr. Trask," said the maître d'.

"Good evening, Guy. How's everything going? Full house?"

Guy's Gallic shrug was expressive. "Eh, if I had a roomful of tables by the window, everyone would be delirious. As it is, they are merely very happy."

"That's the way we want to keep them."

In the background, a four-piece combo played a complicated, syncopated tune to an empty dance floor. It wasn't an easy composition; a tune more likely to inspire indigestion. Gabe looked over. "What exactly is that?"

"Miles Davis, I think."

Gabe frowned as the trumpet player wandered off into a spiraling solo. While he could appreciate it as a music aficionado, he wasn't crazy about it as a manager. "No one's going to dance to this."

"Just as well. Dancing…" Guy sniffed in disapproval. "People getting up, sitting down, complaining about overcooked meals because of the rewarming. We should stop it, you know."

"Not a chance. There's always been a dinner orchestra at the Hotel Mount Jefferson." And there was nothing like walking in to the sound of soft music to make a guest truly feel transported, he thought.

He crossed to the bandstand as the combo finished its song and stepped down to take a break. "Richie," he called to the trumpet player, "can you hold up a minute?"

"Sure, Mr. Trask," said the ponytailed redhead. "We just thought we'd take five."

"Sure. How's it going?"

Richie shrugged and looked across the dining room. "Not too many takers tonight. They like the music, I assume—I hope—but it would be nice to get some people on the floor."

Talented, Gabe thought. A bit temperamental and insecure, as all good musicians were. "Then you need to play dance music."

He flushed a little and straightened his tie. "We started out with the usual. No one came up so we thought we'd just get a little of the rust off."

"Do that on your midweek gigs," Gabe advised. "You don't have to play standards, but stick with something that's got a beat people can work with."

"Even if no one dances?"

"They'll dance if you give them the music." Gabe glanced across the room, resigned to working it a little before he left for the night. He'd stop at the tables, chat with the guests, suggest a turn on the floor. "Come back from your break and—" Suddenly he froze, staring at a table by the window.

"Mr. Trask?"

"Play something danceable," Gabe said slowly, absently, staring at a woman with pale hair and gray eyes. "You'll get your dancers. I guarantee it."

"I'm all finished," Hadley told the waiter, gesturing to her nearly full plate.

"Was there something wrong, madam?" he asked.

Hadley shook her head. She'd eaten little, but she chalked that up to her state of mind, not the food or the menu. Dinner had actually been a pleasant surprise. She'd anticipated stodgy French or chophouse surf and turf, not an intriguing fusion menu that would have done any pricey Manhattan restaurant proud. Seared ahi tuna and Thai lobster spring rolls side by side on the menu with pecan-crusted pork loin and duck in huckleberry reduction suggested someone creative was at work. And the guests were tucking in with gusto.

Conversation stayed at a low buzz, a tribute to good acoustics. Women in evening dress smiled and toasted with their escorts. Jackets required. How long had it been since she'd dined anywhere with a dress code? How long since she'd dined in a room so permeated with luxury? Sure, there were plenty of stylish restaurants in New York. None, though, that so vividly brought back the memory of another era.

And the sharp longing for someone to share it with.

Turning her head to ward off the thought, Hadley stared out the dining room window at the snow that had begun drifting down outside. Across the way, the lights of the conservatory bled out into the frozen night. She'd sat in countless hotel restaurants on her own during one business trip or another. It had never bothered her before. Probably it was the romance of the place that was getting to her. The Hotel Mount Jefferson was a haven for romantic getaways, a place where couples could glide across the dance floor and toast to love at their tables.

But she wasn't part of a couple. She wasn't part of anything, just a solo person trying her damnedest to stay out of the funk she'd been fighting for days. She didn't need anyone, she reminded herself. She'd seen what it brought.

So how was it that all she wanted just then was to be held?

"Having a nice evening tonight?" asked a voice behind her.

Hadley turned her head to see not a waiter, but the stranger from the afternoon. And her funk was forgotten.

He'd made an impression in the cold light of afternoon. Now, he jolted her system into awareness. No jeans and sweater this time. Instead, he wore an exquisitely cut gray suit that only made him look taller, leaner. Cuff links gleamed at his wrists. A silver chain made a graceful sweep across his blue patterned tie. He looked as if he belonged in a plush VIP lounge somewhere, swirling a balloon glass of brandy while he talked high finance.

"You've dressed up, I see," she said, wishing for those moments in the afternoon when she'd had him to herself.

"So have you."

She'd worn a drape-necked tank in cream silk jersey. Paired with a narrow black skirt, it had seemed demure enough. Until he stood looking down at her. Goose bumps that had nothing to do with the temperature rose on her arms. She glanced at the windows. "Your snow has started, I see."

"Good thing you decided to come inside. We'd have had to send a Saint Bernard out looking for you."

"With a keg of brandy as my prize?"

"You can get a brandy in here if you want it, with no risk of frostbite."

"The benefits of civilization."

"Indeed."

There was something in his eyes, a light, an invitation to fun.

She felt a little flutter in her stomach and glanced down. She should be more disciplined; she wasn't here to play around and he was probably with someone. But it was so tempting to for once not think about work, to be just Hadley, just a woman.

Too tempting. "Don't you have to get back to your party?" she asked abruptly.

Gabe didn't answer right away, trying to avoid staring at the pale gleam of her throat in the soft light. He'd worked his way across the room to her, stopping at a number of tables to greet the guests, chat a little, charm a lot. And the whole time, he'd been utterly and completely aware of her as she stared out at the night, that wistful look back on her face.

He wanted to wipe it away. He wanted to see the spark of fun again, the spark of heat, the expressions that brought that delicate face alive. Just for a moment he'd stop by her table and chat with her, as he had the other guests. Harmless.

And then he registered the bare tablecloth across from her. "I don't have a party to get back to. I saw you and thought I'd stop by and say hello." And to look at her one more time. In the candlelight, she was luminous, the extravagance of bare shoulders backlit by falling snow. "Mind if I join you?"

She nodded to the bottle of wine on the table as he sat. "Would you like some wine? It's a very good cabernet."

"No. Thank you, though. So how was the rest of your day?"

"All right. I wandered around for a bit, caught up on work. How about you?"

"Wandered around, caught up on work." *Thought about you.*

"Doesn't sound too fun to me."

"You're one to talk. I thought you were here for a break before work heated up. What is it, a business conference?"

She shook her head. "Just some meetings next week."

"But right now it's the weekend. You should be relaxing. I

don't know…going to the spa for a massage." Naked on the table, her back smooth and gleaming.

"No one to play with, I guess."

"That's a tragedy," he said softly. "We really need to do something about that." The candlelight threw shadows in the hollows of her cheekbones.

She swallowed. "Do you have any ideas?"

In the background, there was a thump of bass and the snick of brushes on snare as the combo tuned up. Gabe remembered his assurance to Richie. "I can think of one. Do you dance?"

"Dance?"

"Yeah, like to music." He rose and held out an arm.

It was on the tip of Hadley's tongue to say no. She never danced. On her very rare nights out, she might go to a ballet, but that was about as close as she came. Certainly, she wasn't in the habit of taking to an empty dance floor in front of a room-ful of people. Somehow, though, she found herself pushing back her chair and rising.

She had to look up at him, even in her heels. Amusement flickered in his eyes. In the subdued light, they looked darker than before. Hadley hesitated, then tucked her hand through the crook of his elbow, feeling the fine-weave wool soft against her fingers. She was far more aware of the hard solid-ity of the arm beneath the fabric as they threaded their way between tables. He smelled of something clean and woodsy and completely male.

On the polished wood of the dance floor, he stopped and turned to her. "Do you know how to waltz?"

From somewhere in the distant sands of time, she dredged up cotillion lessons. "I did when I was thirteen."

He laughed and took her hand to pull her into dance position. "It's like riding a bike. Just hold on and go where I lead you."

Heat sang up her arm at the shock of palm against palm. In

defense, she rested her left hand against his shoulder. He was close, so close. Close enough for her to see faint flecks of gold in his green eyes.

Close enough to kiss.

"The count is one, two, three. Back, side, touch, basic box step. Smile," he said. "It'll be fun."

The song was "Moon River," dreamy and slow. His hand pressed against her back; if he pulled just a bit more, they'd be embracing. Suddenly, it felt as outrageous, as daring as dancing must have back in the eighteenth or nineteenth centuries, when women and men barely touched in public.

At first, he counted the steps for her, but with the urging of his hands the old motions came back. The awkwardness evaporated and they began to move, dipping and flowing around the floor. Hadley laughed aloud. "This is wonderful."

"Didn't I tell you? You should trust me." Expertly, he led her into a whirling turn. Then several other couples drifted onto the floor. Aware of the people behind her, she stiffened, stepping forward when she should have gone back, stumbling on his sleek leather shoes.

He stopped for a minute and leaned toward her. His eyes darkened.

Adrenaline sprinted through her veins. A touch? A kiss?

"Look at me," he murmured instead, his mouth just a breath away from hers. "Trust my lead."

This time, when they started again, they moved as one. It was like floating, she thought, anchored by his eyes, the light press of his fingertips at her back. When she'd walked into the hotel she'd felt as if she was stepping into another world. And she had. This wasn't her, this woman being swept around the floor in the arms of a handsome stranger. The rest of the room ebbed away until only his face mattered. The rest of the world—the rest of her life—was irrelevant. In that moment, that glorious moment, all she wanted was him.

She didn't notice when the music ended. She couldn't look away. It was as though she was diving into him, seeing the answer that he wanted as much as she did. When he leaned his head toward her it seemed completely natural. Her lips parted. Just a taste, just a touch. She held her breath—

"You are extraordinary," he murmured. And bowed.

Blinking, Hadley realized the band was on to a new song, a swing tune, and he was leading her off the floor.

It was over.

"You should tell your parents to tip your cotillion teacher," he said as they walked back to her table. "You did well."

"Was that before or after I stepped on your toes?" His arm under her fingertips felt natural now. She didn't want it to end.

"It's always hard with a strange partner. You slid right into it."

"You were pretty good yourself," she said, sitting in the chair he pulled out for her. "Where did you learn all that?"

"During the swing dance craze I dated a woman who wanted to learn ballroom."

"And you indulged her?"

"We aim to please."

"I'd like—"

"Nice moves, Mr. Trask," commented a waiter walking by with a silver-domed tray and Hadley froze.

She knew the name, dear God she knew the name. "Your name is Trask?" she asked, her voice barely audible.

"Gabriel Trask," her dashing stranger confirmed, holding out a hand. "I suppose I should have confessed earlier. I'm not just a dance host. I'm the general manager of the hotel."

Chapter Three

Hadley's feet thudded on the treadmill with metronomic regularity as sweat trickled down the side of her face. *Idiot, idiot, idiot.* The word repeated in her mind in time with her stride. What in the hell was she thinking, flirting with a stranger on a business trip? Losing her focus, getting all doe-eyed over a man she knew absolutely nothing about.

And look where it had gotten her. It was embarrassing, the sort of mistake a rank beginner might make. And on a personal level…

On a personal level it was downright humiliating.

She stifled a groan. That moment at the end of the dance when she'd thought he was going to kiss her, she could only imagine the look on her face. She'd been thinking romance; he'd been the hotel manager attending to a guest dining solo. And now she had to work with him. She was disconcerted, annoyed, mortified.

She'd have crawled over broken glass before admitting she was disappointed.

Of course, if he'd told her who he was up front, everything would have been different. The treadmill chirped, informing her that she was shifting into cool-down mode. Cool down? Not likely to happen anytime soon. A day and a half later, irritation still bubbled through her. There was no way she'd have chatted with him, certainly no way she'd have danced with him if she'd known who he was. All it would have taken was a name badge, something that was standard in every hotel she'd ever been in. Apparently Gabriel Trask was more interested in preserving his Armani than being professional.

Even spending all day Sunday searching out flaws in his hotel and drafting a plan for cuts hadn't salved her pride. She still had to contend with the embarrassment of facing him.

And that would be today, of course. Monday, glorious Monday. Still, the best move was to get it over with. She wiped her face with a towel and headed toward the door. After all, it wasn't as though she'd thrown herself at him or anything. All she'd done was dance.

And wait for a kiss.

She squeezed her eyes shut. With any luck, he'd be the one embarrassed once he found out what was going on—and maybe a little concerned about his job. As well he ought to be. There were big changes in the offing. She needed a manager who could help her implement them, not one with mixed up priorities. She needed a professional who understood how things were done.

And if that meant someone other than Gabe Trask, so be it.

Gabe sat at his desk, finishing his November month-end report. With a few brisk key strokes he sent it to Susan, who would gussy it up and send it off. There had been a time when he hadn't worried about letterhead, just shot quick e-mails directly to Whit or called. These days, he mailed formal documents to the executors of the estate, who presumably forwarded them to the new owners.

Or maybe just tossed them in the round file. Who knew? Almost five months after Whit had died, Gabe hadn't heard a word about what came next or who even owned the hotel. In the absence of direction, he supposed he could have played it safe and socked the profits into an interest-bearing account until the new owners appeared. Instead, he'd stubbornly continued investing in improvements. If no one was going to give him guidance, then he'd continue with the plans he and Whit had laid out in January, as they'd done every year. The old lady deserved as much as he could give her, no matter what happened next.

Clicking on an e-mail from his executive chef, he opened the attachment of menus for the following week. He stared at the list of meals, ingredients and estimated costs, and his thoughts drifted back to the last time he'd been in the dining room.

It had taken willpower to stay away from the hotel the previous day, the one day off each week he granted himself. No one on staff would have thought anything of him doing a walk-through, of course, but Gabe knew why he found himself debating it instead of skiing or heading over to Vermont to visit his family. It had to do with a certain slender blonde laughing up at him on the dance floor, with the feel of her soft, cool hand in his, the lingering memory of her scent.

And that moment at the end when he'd thought only of kissing her.

Off-limits, he reminded himself. Just his luck that when he finally met a woman who knocked him back on his heels, she was a guest. All for the best that he'd been called away—talking with her had been entirely too tempting, and he had no business taking it any further. He knew where the boundaries were.

And he'd thought about them all day Sunday.

Shaking his head, he turned back to the menu estimates and began to crunch numbers. A few changes here and there would bring the costs into line with budget. He was in the midst of sending a reply to the chef when he caught movement out of the corner of his eye. Glancing up to look out the door across from his desk, Gabe saw the head of personnel walk into her office across the hall. Eight o'clock, he realized, wondering how two hours had whipped by since he'd sat down.

One of his first actions after becoming manager had been to unbolt and open that hallway door. Sure, Susan was an efficient interface with the outside world. Visitors still came to him through her office. Staffers, though, were a different matter. If people wanted to talk to him, it was simple enough— walk down the hallway and knock. If he wasn't in a meeting or a telecon, they were free to come in and chat. It meant giving up a little time and privacy, granted, but over the years the communication had paid off. He was wired into the workings of the hotel in a way his predecessors never had been.

And around him the pulse of the hotel quickened.

Hadley headed toward the executive wing of the hotel. The soft, drapey sweater was gone, replaced by a trim taupe suit, matching pumps. Brisk, professional, ready to take care of business, a leather portfolio in her hand. First impressions were everything. If she couldn't have that opportunity back, at least she could start fresh with a show of strength.

As she approached Gabe Trask's office she slowed, looking for his receptionist. Beyond, a man in chef's trousers leaned into an open door, talking animatedly.

And she heard Gabe Trask's voice in reply.

He was there, just inside that room. For an instant, she could only think of his eyes, his smile, his touch on her back as they moved around the dance floor together. And the embarrassment of finding out afterward what was really going on. What must he have thought of her—a poor flower that needed his pity? She needed no one's pity. In fact, that particular shoe was about to be on the other foot.

His, to be precise.

She banked the embers of her anger and walked up to rap on the door. "Good morning, Mr. Trask."

There were people he'd have been more surprised to see standing there, but Gabe couldn't think of any offhand. It was as though he'd conjured her by thinking. One moment she was in his mind, the next she was in his doorway.

And all he could think of was that moment she'd been in his arms.

"Hey," he said, rising to escort the chef out and go to her. "You disappeared the other night."

"Yes, but I'm here now. May I sit down?" she said, crossing to one of his client chairs.

She was different today, he thought. Still cool and blond, but the mischief, the vulnerability, was all but hidden beneath a hard, glossy shell.

"Please. I've got a few minutes." It wasn't strictly true—he never had a few minutes, but no way was he going to let work interrupt. "How are you? Everything all right with your stay?"

"More or less," she said, taking a seat.

He looked at her. Something was definitely off. "Care to be more specific? It's my job to take care of the 'less' part. Has business services supported you all right? You look like you're off to your meetings."

It wasn't quite a smile, more an impression of enjoyment. "That's true, I am." She sat upright with almost military precision. Her hair hung smoothly to her shoulders, her bangs just brushing her brows. Under them, gray eyes stared back at him, as level as a gunfighter's.

"Is your meeting here?"

Definitely enjoyment. "Why, yes." She crossed her legs with a quick whisper of hosiery. "In this office, actually."

That stopped him for a moment. In the back of his mind, suspicion began to brew. "Care to be more specific?"

"Certainly. I'm here to meet with you."

"I don't recall seeing anything on my calendar."

"You wouldn't. However, I'd appreciate it if you'd clear some time for me."

"To discuss what?"

Now the smile did spread across her face—but it was anything but friendly. "You gave me a surprise Saturday night. Now it's my turn." She rose and offered her hand. "I'm Hadley Stone, with Stone Enterprises. We're the new owners of the hotel." She gave him a cool look. "And I'm here to talk about what happens next."

It was just a handshake, a professional gesture she'd made countless times. She'd touched him the night before; the contact now shouldn't have surprised her. But it did, carrying with it an intimacy, a connection that went far deeper than skin. For an instant, she felt laid open to him, thoughts and emotions.

And he was furious, she could feel it.

When he released her, she turned back to her chair without a word, resisting the urge to rub her hand against her thigh.

"And what does happen next?" he asked calmly.

"Changes. We've got to assimilate the hotel into the Stone organization."

"I see."

It was like being out on the water when a squall swept through, changing everything from sunny and warm to blustery wind and churning seas in minutes. It wasn't a surprise to her that he was unhappy about it all. What was a surprise was how deeply the diamond-hard anger in his eyes cut.

Not that what he felt would change anything, of course.

Gabe crossed to the hallway door and closed it, his expression taut. Still, his voice remained even as he returned to his desk. "Stone Enterprises? As in Whit Stone?"

"My grandfather. He left the company to my father, Robert Stone."

"Nice to get that cleared up," Gabe said pleasantly.

"Excuse me?"

"Whit passed away five months ago. For five months, I've been stonewalled by the lawyers every time I've tried to find out just who's responsible for the property besides me. All it would have taken was a letter."

Hadley smiled. Payback for the night before was about to begin. "WSI is a multibillion dollar corporation. This hotel represents a fraction of a percent of the whole. First things first. You were on the list when we could get to you."

"Which is now."

"Exactly. My job is to bring the property up to speed."

That got to him, she saw. "If you'll look at the books, you'll see the property is making a profit and showing revenue growth year over year. We're in good shape."

"Not as far as we're concerned."

"What's the problem? We've been operating in the black for the last five years," he said, a faint edge in his voice.

"That may have been adequate under my grandfather's ownership. Not anymore. We expect double or even triple your profit margins from our holdings." Or Robert did, anyway. "I've looked at your balance sheets. You're not even close to target."

"How about that."

Hadley stared at him a moment. "Don't mistake how serious this is." She opened up her portfolio and pulled out a printed sheet. "Fortunately, we should be able to meet the numbers with the right approach. I've been making notes.

You've got some unnecessary amenities that are driving up costs. They can go."

"Really." Gabe leaned forward with interest, propping his chin on his tented fingers. "And they would be?"

"Flowers in the rooms, for one. It's a nice touch but a waste of money." As a guest, she might want to keep them; as a Stone employee with targets to meet, she couldn't afford to. "Stick with flowers in the public areas only."

"I see. Go on, please."

The other night he'd embarrassed her personally. Now he was trying to do it professionally. "All right. Your dinner portions could probably shrink, you could reduce the menu options," she said, her tone intentionally dismissive. "The food is more exotic than you need. Skip the lobster and seared tuna, stick to lamb and sole. For that matter, your breakfast buffet is far in excess of what it should be."

"What it should be?" He let a beat go by. "I assume you've got hospitality experience to support these directives?"

She leaned forward, resisting the urge to bare her teeth. "Let me make this clear. I have bottom-line experience. As far as you and I are concerned, that's all the experience I need."

"You don't think you need to understand an operation before you wade in demanding wholesale changes?"

Hadley snapped her portfolio shut. "I think some of the changes required are obvious, but to answer your question, I'm not coming in here on the fly. I spent three weeks reviewing major chain hotels and compiling a database. Almost across the board you're spending dollars on services, amenities and staffing that they don't. Your rooms are twice the size of a conventional room, which we can use to double the hotel's capacity once we can afford to spend money on construction."

Gabe straightened, his eyes sparking with temper. "In case you haven't noticed, we are not a major chain hotel. We offer a totally different value proposition to a very different guest. Our client base is about couples and romance."

"At least part of your client base is corporate, particularly during the week," Hadley corrected. "They're not looking for romance, they're looking for value."

"If they wanted that, they'd find a big chain hotel. They're here because of the location, because we offer that something extra, the luxury that the others don't. Your cost-efficiency models don't apply."

"That's what you think. We succeed with new acquisitions because of our skill in finding and applying the right models."

"Stone focuses on light industry and high tech, right? What was the last operation you managed?"

She glared at him. "Becheron Minerals."

"Mining." He nodded. "It's got a lot in common with hospitality."

"You're about to find out how much, Mr. Trask," she snapped. "If you're lucky, that is. I can read a balance sheet and I can formulate a business strategy to address problems. And one of the problems I see here is the manager."

"You think the hotel's exhibiting signs of mismanagement?" His tone would have made anyone he knew take care.

"I think the manager's exhibiting signs of bad judgment. Failing to recognize and deal with new fiscal realities, for one. Getting excessively familiar with the guests, for another." Her voice rose as she spoke. "You have no business running around incognito, playing up to guests. You're the ultimate representative of the hotel. We expect you to act like it."

"Running around incognito?" His tight control slipped a notch. "What about you, coming in here without telling anyone who you are or why you've come? A professional would have called ahead instead of playing games. And as to talking with you, I'm the manager, it's my job to put guests at ease. I saw someone who looked lost and unhappy, and I came up to try to help. I would have done it with anyone. It just happened to be you."

The blood drained from her face. "I'd suggest you curb your friendly impulses going forward, Trask." She fixed him with an icy stare. "And before you say a word about the other night, remember who you're talking to."

He stared right back at her. "And who is that, Ms. Stone—the new manager?"

"No, the head of the transition team."

"And where's the rest of your team?"

"I'll know that when I find people who can get this hotel to stand up to inspection."

"My operation does stand up to inspection and the revenues have always stayed to plan. If we're not up to your numbers it's because your grandfather was happy to put almost every penny of profit back into the hotel, trying to bring it back from where it was when he bought it."

"And that's the first thing that's going to stop until your margins get to where they belong. When we've got money for construction again, it'll go to cutting room size."

"Are you out of your mind?" he demanded, rising to his feet. "You can't stop renovations on a building like this. Do that and she'll be falling apart in a year. This is a national historic landmark. It's a public trust." It was as though a house cat had suddenly transformed into a dark, dangerous panther. If she hadn't been so angry herself, she'd have been alarmed. "This hotel meant more than just profit margins to your grandfather. Do you have any understanding of that?" he demanded. "Is there anything that means more than profit margins to you?"

His eyes blazed at her, green and furious, and for a moment, the words clogged up in her throat. In defense, she rose. "We've got numbers, Mr. Trask, and we are *going* to meet them. The only question is how. If you're not willing to cooperate, I will be more than happy to bring in management with a better appreciation of our objectives."

"Is that a threat?"

"That's up to you. Now if we can continue the discussion—"

"Actually, I've got a telecon right now and meetings throughout the rest of the day. The earliest I can fit you in is tomorrow."

"Fine. Eight o'clock." Stifling her temper, Hadley rose and walked to the door. "Until tomorrow, Mr. Trask."

She didn't shake hands goodbye.

Chapter Four

Hadley stomped up the grand staircase, fuming. Gabe Trask had to go, pure and simple. The man was impossible. She'd come in with a simple list of action items and he refused to even talk about them. And he had the nerve to defend his unprofessional behavior by attacking her for coming in without warning. So what? Plenty of managers would do the same. Why should she have warned them so that they could put on a nice face? She wanted information, and information she'd gotten.

So she hadn't worked in hospitality before and maybe she didn't have any experience with this particular hotel. That didn't mean she couldn't draw conclusions and make business decisions.

And that didn't give him the right to defy her.

Is there anything that means more than profit margins to you? Robert would have laughed at him. And Hadley?

She couldn't go there. Her response didn't matter; only satisfying Robert did. So it pained her to cut away the touches that made the hotel graceful. No matter. Her job depended on meeting the targets. And if Gabe Trask posed an obstacle to that, Gabe Trask would have to go.

She stopped and took a deep breath. She hated getting angry. Irritation was one thing. Irritation could be useful. As Robert had shown her, there was power in controlled emotion, in focused disapproval. Anger, on the other hand, only left her shaky and unsettled. She didn't indulge in the kind of altercation she'd just had with Gabe Trask any more than she'd screamed on the roller coasters the time the twins had badgered her parents into taking them to Disney World.

Feeling jittery, she walked the rest of the way to her room. If she could get rid of the emotion, she could calm down, and the best way she knew of getting rid of emotion was working.

With a grim smile, she unlocked the door and headed for her computer. It was time to write a memo.

Gabe walked through his front door with the pizza box just in time to hear his mother's voice on the answering machine. Cursing, he stepped swiftly into the living room, snatching up the cordless handset just as she was saying goodbye. "Hey, Ma."

"Gabriel." Warm pleasure filled Molly Trask's voice.

"How're you doing?"

"I'm well. How about you?"

Still carrying the pizza, Gabe headed down the hall to the kitchen. "Okay."

"You doesn't sound all that okay. Is something going on with you, too?"

"With me, too?" Setting the box down, he reached into a cabinet and pulled out a plate and a wineglass. "What's that supposed to mean? What else is going on?"

"I don't know, exactly." She hesitated.

"Come on, Ma, you never just go quiet. Tell me what's going on. Is it Jacob? Nick? Or both? I thought they worked things out at Thanksgiving." And for all the times he'd played peacemaker, his mother had never been the one to ask him to do it.

"It's nothing to do with Jacob," she said quickly. "He and Nick have mended fences, I think."

"So what's going on?" Propping the phone against his ear with one shoulder, Gabe poured himself a glass of Chianti.

"I don't know," she said again. "I talked with Nicholas today and he didn't sound right."

"Define 'didn't sound right.'"

"Down. Frustrated."

Frustrated? That made two of them. Gabe took a swallow of the wine. "Did he get the results of the firefighters' exam yet? If he didn't do well, that would be a good reason right there."

"No, I asked him. He says he probably won't know for another week or so. I think he got in a fight with that nice girl he brought to Thanksgiving."

"Sloane? Jeez, they looked like they were on their way to three kids and an SUV. That was what, like a week ago?"

"It only takes a minute or two sometimes. There were a couple of times I was happy as a clam with your father one minute and ready to take a frying pan to his head the next."

Gabe leaned against the kitchen counter and grinned. "You never are going to forgive him for buying you that vacuum cleaner for your anniversary, are you?"

"I suppose I should finally let the poor man off the hook."

He heard the smile in her voice, a smile that had disappeared for so many months after his father had died, and felt a wave of relief. "Generous of you. Anyway, what's the deal with Nick? You want me to give him a call?"

"Would you? I hate to put you up to it, but I'm worried about him."

"It's okay. Just call me Mr. Fix It."

Which he was, Gabe reflected as he hung up. He never set out to take care of people, but somehow he always wound up doing it. Hell, even his job was all about taking care of people. The funny thing was, he didn't mind. Sometimes—lots of times—it made him feel like a world-beater. Then again, sometimes it backfired on him, like helping out Hadley Stone had backfired.

Of course, that hadn't been why he'd approached her, not really. And it hadn't been why he'd pulled her into his arms in the warm glow of the dining room.

He didn't need to go there, though. The last thing he should be thinking about was what it would be like to taste that delectable mouth, to press his lips against her soft throat. It didn't matter that he'd seen both heat and surrender in her eyes that moment on the dance floor. Things had changed. He needed to keep his distance, pure and simple. He needed to get her out of his mind. He definitely didn't need to be thinking about her laughing at him in the candlelight, or the way she'd looked at the end, mouth tempting and full and waiting for his.

With an oath, he carried his dinner out into the living room and sprawled on the couch. With one hand, he dialed his brother's number. With the other, he picked up a piece of pizza.

"Yeah." Nick's voice was flat and exhausted-sounding. Gabe understood, now, his mother's concern.

"Do you have a dog?" Gabe asked.

"What? You know I don't." Irritable, which was at least a sign of life.

"Good. 'Cause if you had I'd have guessed it just died."

"You're cute. How'd you get to be so cute?"

"Just natural, I guess," Gabe said modestly. "Jacob's surly, you're antsy and I'm cute. Except right now you sound like Jacob. What's up?"

"Talking with my brother the great conversationalist always does that to me." In the background, a series of bells sounded.

Gabe took a bite of pizza. "You at the firehouse?"

"Yeah. It's a call for another company, though. What's going on with you?"

"Pizza, right now," Gabe told him, chewing.

"And let me guess, you're drinking some kind of fancy-ass wine with it instead of beer like a normal person would."

"Yeah, so?"

"And with a fork and knife, instead of with your hands."

"No fork and knife, and you'll be happy to know I'm using a paper towel instead of a napkin." Gabe wiped his fingers.

"What, are you turning into a savage?"

"You just can't stand the fact that I have style, can you?"

"So are you calling to dangle your pizza in front of me?"

"Actually, I'm calling up to bitch."

"Don't tell me, you couldn't get the right wine for pizza. What does a guy like you have to bitch about?"

"Stone Enterprises."

Nick snorted. "Why don't you add on Microsoft and Donald Trump, while you're at it?"

"Because Donald Trump didn't just take over my hotel."

"Ah."

"And didn't send in a flunky to take apart everything I've built in the past five years." The frustration that had been simmering in him bubbled up afresh.

"I take it you didn't hit it off with him."

"Her."

"*Ah.*"

"Yeah, *ah.*"

"Our lives may be in sync. What about the her?"

"Besides the fact that she's a corporate shark in the skin of a goddess?"

"Definitely in sync. A goddess, huh?"

"Enough to make me change my religion. Except for the fact that her job is to turn my hotel into a low-end chain joint."

"That is kind of a problem."

"You think?"

There was a short silence while Nick digested the news. "A wise man once told me that the way to get what you want is to help the people in a position to say yes get what *they* want."

"I was the one who told you that," Gabe said.

"Oh, I'm sorry, I meant a wise*ass*. It's true, though. People operate mostly on self-interest. Convince her that it's in her best interest to do it your way. Unless you're a screwup and you're doing it all wrong," Nick added.

"Thanks for the vote of confidence." Gabe's voice was sour.

"Fair and balanced, that's our motto. So why does she want to do this?"

"To meet some bogus profit targets that come from corporate clowns who are clueless about the hotel business."

"And what do you want?"

To bring Whit Stone back. "I want it to be what it is, something special."

"Did you tell her that?"

Gabe smiled faintly. "Let's just say we didn't see eye to eye."

"Lot of that going around."

"Ah," Gabe said. "Goddess trouble of your own?"

"My advice to you is avoid 'em like the plague."

"I'm trying," Gabe said, pushing the image of Hadley out of his mind. "So what, did you and Sloane get in a fight?"

"We broke up."

It explained a lot. "When? You guys looked pretty tight at Thanksgiving."

"I think that was what freaked her out. And if that didn't, the fire sure did."

"Fire?" Gabe sat up straight. "What fire?"

"Oh, we had a big one here last week. Ugly building. A couple of guys got hurt in the collapse."

"One of those guys wouldn't be you, would he?"

There was a pause. "You going to tell Ma?"

Gabe snorted. "How old are you again?"

"I mean it. She doesn't need to be scared, not when she's still getting over losing Dad."

"Okay, sealed shut," Gabe promised, invoking their childhood code.

"I had to go in after one of my guys who got hurt. The building came down on us as we were getting out."

"And what happened to you?"

"Nothing serious," Nick said. "A few burns and bruises. It looked worse than it was—the people on the outside thought we both bit the big one. Sloane bolted."

"Well, you've got to admit, it would give a person pause. If the idea of waking up with you didn't do it already."

"She lost her brother in that Hartford fire a couple of years back. What I do gives her bad vibes, I guess."

"It's not as simple as what you do. It's what you are."

Nick let out a long breath. "That's the problem, isn't it?"

Gabe had never heard Nick sound quite so miserable. "Did she ask you to quit?"

"She says that she knows I couldn't."

"At least she gets it."

"That doesn't really help," Nick said with a little edge.

"I know." Gabe paused. "Do you love this woman?"

"Yes." Nick's answer was calm, immediate, without question.

"Then go after her." Relationships had always seemed simple to Gabe. You were interested in a woman, you asked her out. If it worked, you kept at it until it no longer did. Eventually, you found a keeper.

Unless the one you were interested in was completely off-limits. Gabe shook his head. "Talk to her, change her mind."

"It's not that easy, charm boy. I can't push her into living with a firefighter any more than she would push me into quitting. She's got to come to it on her own. If she ever does."

"While you just sit and wait?"

"While I just sit and wait."

"You're not exactly a waiting type."

"You've noticed?"

Because he knew arguments would be futile, Gabe didn't bother. "That sucks, man."

Nick sighed. "Yeah, it does. What about you—are you stuck with this situation?"

"Unless I want to get another job."

"Do you want another job?"

"I don't know. I love this place. If I left, I'd feel like I'd let down the old owner and the staff. And the hotel itself."

"You ever going to stop trying to take care of everyone?"

"You ever going to stop risking your neck trying to save people?" Gabe asked by way of answer.

"At least I get paid for it."

"I do, too, most of the time."

"So what are you going to do about your goddess?"

"I don't know. Try to do my job. Try to keep her from doing too much damage." Try to erase Saturday from his memory.

"Show her what matters to you about the hotel. Maybe it'll become important to her, too."

What he loved about the hotel was the romance, the history of it. The way he'd felt on the dance floor with Hadley in his arms. The hotel belonged to lovers. If he could make her feel that, really feel it all the way through, maybe they had a chance. "I'll give it a try," he said thoughtfully. "Hey, Nick?"

"Yeah?"

"Why don't you come up and ski next time you're off? Beat

the hell out of yourself on the mountain. It might not make things better, but it'll sure as hell be a distraction."

"Maybe I will," Nick said. "Maybe I will."

Chapter Five

He'd had plenty of relationships in his time. Some had gone fast and furious, starting with a crackle and flaming out within weeks. Others had been slower burns that built and radiated heat long after the fire had begun to go out. He'd orchestrated seductions before, taken pains to give someone he cared about a special experience, a special evening.

He'd never worked to make a woman fall in love with an idea before.

It could work, he told himself. The woman he'd met on the back deck, the one with the fey faerie eyes, would fall for the romance of the Mount Jefferson. The question was whether he could make the businesswoman fall with her.

Gabe glanced at his computer clock. It was after eight, their planned meeting time, and she still hadn't shown. Interesting. He'd have picked her as the sort to be relentlessly punctual. Thoughtfully, he rose to walk across the hall.

And saw her striding toward him over the twining vines of the burgundy carpet, wholly focused on the cell phone clamped to her ear. "Well, if you're not getting a straight answer, I'd suggest flying to Johannesburg," she told whoever was on the line. Today, her hair was swept up, her suit a cool ice-blue.

Her manner, however, belied the calm. Tension tightened her shoulders; her eyes narrowed in irritation. "Eliot, you're head of Becheron now, not me. I got moved to another project, remember? If you've got problems, you'll have to work them out yourself."

Gabe raised a brow as she disconnected.

Hadley stared at the ceiling for a moment and took a deep breath. "Sorry I'm late." Her voice was brisk, but frustration still lingered as she walked into his office.

"Not a crisis." *I got moved to another project, remember?* He'd done his homework the night before. Becheron was the fifth largest division at Stone. How did a corporate hotshot go from heading up a marquee division to running a hotel that represented—how had she put it? A fraction of a percent of their holdings? She was on another project, all right, which might have explained some of the wistfulness. He felt a quick tug of sympathy. But only a small one. "Coffee?"

"Please."

He turned to the coffeemaker that sat on a little table behind his desk, and poured her a cup. "Everybody's got their weakness," he said. "I'm a coffee snob. Cream or sugar?"

She took the mug from him. "Black will do, thank you." She shot him a suspicious look as she sat. "You're all sweetness and light this morning."

"Sounds like you could use it after that phone call."

"It's nothing." But she couldn't quite shrug it off, Gabe saw. No swingy earrings today, but discreet diamond studs to go with the stylishly discreet suit.

"So we've got a problem to solve. Where do we start?"

Hadley opened her portfolio. "I printed out a list of the target numbers for the next four quarters."

Gabe took the sheet and scanned it, resisting the urge to whistle. "You realize, of course, that a healthy business plan lasts longer than four quarters."

"Of course, but the Hotel Mount Jefferson is no longer private. It's part of Stone Enterprises, and the Stone stock price swings with the quarterly financials. We can't afford to ignore them."

The thing to do was to show her that it was in her best interests. "What would you say to a revised business plan that offered less short-term growth but substantially more in the long term?"

"I'd suggest you should update your résumé before you mention it again."

He shot a quick glance at her. "They're that tough?"

"*I'm* that tough." She stared back at him coolly. He thought of the way she'd looked on the dance floor. What would it be like to melt that coolness, he wondered suddenly. To have her heated and gasping in his arms? "The first thing you should understand," she continued, "is that the numbers are the numbers. We're going to meet them."

"Why do I hear an 'or else' in there somewhere?"

"There isn't an 'or else' because it's not going to be necessary. I've been up against aggressive targets like this before. It's not impossible. Management just has to be committed to meeting our goal."

"What I'm committed to is this hotel." Time to draw a line in the sand. "If its survival means meeting your targets, then by all means, let's find a way to do it. I warn you, though, I'm going to fight like hell against anything that's going to turn the hotel back into the shape it was when Whit bought it."

"I'm sure it'll be fine."

"I always did like an optimist."

The sudden, wry glance he gave Hadley sent something skittering around in her stomach. None of that butterfly nonsense today, she thought impatiently. Today was for business.

It would have been easier if he'd been properly dressed. Instead, he sat in shirtsleeves, his suspenders dark and silky against the pin-striped cotton dress shirt, his suit coat hanging over a little rack in the corner. She'd always had a thing for men in ties and suspenders, the kind that buttoned into the trousers with the leather loops. It wasn't him, it was just his clothing.

And then he threw her a glance and she felt the adrenaline rush in her veins. Not him, her ass.

Ignore it, she reminded herself. "Let's get to work. I'd like to go over the books so I know the exact numbers we're dealing with. The only financials I've seen are about six months out-of-date. Can your assistant set up a meet with the CFO?"

"You can set something up with him yourself. Our weekly department heads' meeting starts in about five minutes. I figured it would be a good primer."

"Great. Where's the conference room?"

"Right here." He gestured to the long dining table that filled one side of his spacious office. It took her by surprise. Most managers would demand a separate conference room. Gabe Trask apparently didn't mind having occupancy charts taped up on his walls, and didn't need the status of a pricey meeting table with plush leather chairs. She raised a brow. "Am I looking at vintage hotel furnishings?"

"Vintage as in from the basement. Not particularly valuable, but useful."

"I hope for the sake of your department heads it's a short meeting." The table looked far from new and the chairs appeared only marginally comfortable.

One corner of his mouth quirked as he followed her gaze. "Designed to encourage focus and brevity. Not to mention promptness."

"You ever think about getting a real conference setup?"

"We're short of office space as it is, and I have better things to spend five grand on than furniture. Like meeting my new profit numbers."

The table, in the end, proved just big enough for the meeting, once the client chairs had been pressed into service. Hadley understood the promptness comment when she saw that the first two people through the door grabbed the client chairs, and those who followed them sat in the uprights with aggrieved expressions. Gabe Trask didn't bring over his own comfortable desk chair but sat in one of the same uprights as the rest of the unlucky latecomers. She tried not to like him for it.

"Okay, everyone. Before we get started with the reports, I have a few announcements to make. As you all know, Whit Stone, our former owner, passed away last summer. The Hotel Mount Jefferson has passed into the hands of Stone Enterprises, the company held by Whit's son. I'd like to introduce Whit's granddaughter, Hadley Stone, who's here to help with the transition process.

"I might as well tell you up front that we're going to have to meet some aggressive new financial targets and it's going to take everyone's cooperation to make it happen," Gabe continued in an even tone. "You'll be getting more details on that in the next week or so. For now, I'd like you all to introduce yourselves, with titles, one at a time."

He pointed to the plump man next to him, already balding though he looked to be in his thirties. The man cleared his throat. "Jason Keating, accounting."

The ash blonde next to him gave a professional smile that didn't warm her eyes. "Alicia Toupin, events."

"Pete Mirabelli, sales." Young and slick-looking, Mirabelli gave Hadley a defiant glance.

The three who would play the biggest role in the survival

of the Mount Jefferson, Hadley thought. They were the ones she needed on her side immediately. Keating, she wasn't worried about. Accountants always understood cost cutting. Alicia and Pete might be more resistant to Hadley's changes.

Of course, the one who was the biggest wild card was Gabe Trask. Was he with her or not? She studied him sitting at the head of the table, jacket still off, a sheaf of dark hair falling down over his forehead. Then his eyes flicked up to snare hers, and reaction flashed through her veins. She looked hastily away, but not before she felt the telltale heat of a flush feather over her cheeks.

"…Wheeler, reception and front office."

Introductions finished and Gabe gave a nod. "That's the team," he said. "Anything you want to say?"

Showtime. Hadley rose. "Good morning. I'm sure I'll get to know you all quickly enough, but if you could please repeat your names the first time you speak, it'll help me cement things. As Gabe said, I'm here to facilitate the handover of the hotel." Their expressions ran the gamut from apprehensive to pugnacious to shuttered and cold. Well, she was used to it. In times of uncertainty and change, the easiest thing to do was blame the interloper. She'd faced it dozens of times before. In some indefinable way, though, this time it felt personal.

"We'll want to get the hotel compliant with Stone Enterprises policy and procedure as soon as possible," she continued. "I'll be looking to meet with each of you in the coming week to review department operations with an eye toward economizing. Any questions?"

A thin-faced brunette straightened. "Tina Wheeler, head of guest services and front office. Are we looking at any layoffs?"

It was the part Hadley hated more than anything. "It's impossible to say for sure right now. It really depends on how efficiently the hotel is run." She could see concern flare in their eyes immediately. They couldn't know that she was already losing sleep over the idea.

Wheeler didn't move, but somehow she bristled. "We went through an efficiency review last year on Mr. Trask's request."

And Tina didn't appreciate an outsider questioning what she'd done with her department, clearly. "Can I get a copy of any work-flow or man-hour documents?" Hadley asked.

"Well—"

"Yes, of course." Gabe cut in and looked out over the table. "Just a reminder to all of you, I expect you to extend your full cooperation to Ms. Stone in the coming weeks. She asks for information, you give it to her. If you have questions, talk to me, but I don't want to see any stalling." He looked directly at Tina. "We're all on the same team, so let's act like it."

Wheeler's cheeks tinted and she looked down. Didn't make a friend there, Hadley thought ruefully.

"Jason, we should meet as soon as possible to go over the books," she said, turning to the head of accounting. "I'd appreciate it if the rest of you could e-mail me possible time windows for the next week. I'll be in touch with you to firm up appointments shortly. That's all for now," she added briskly, and sat.

And the meeting went on.

Hadley always found her first management meeting at any new property to be fascinating. It was nearly always the same group of personalities, though with different names and jobs. She could usually judge to a nicety after the first half hour who got things done and who was dead weight, who was high maintenance and who took care of business.

In this particular half hour, her respect for Gabe Trask shot up. He'd assembled a strong management team and listened to what they had to say. More, he held them accountable. True, Tina on the front desk seemed a little too high maintenance, and Mirabelli looked like the type who preferred to go his own way, but everyone knew their job. They'd come to the meeting prepared, with results and, where necessary, solutions rather than excuses. The discussion kept rolling forward, ending as scheduled at ten o'clock on the dot.

"So that's our management," Gabe said after the group had filed out and he and Hadley reseated themselves at his desk. "What did you think?"

"I think you must be one hell of a recruiter."

His teeth gleamed. "I can't claim credit for everyone. Some are homegrown, some I inherited. The way I figure it, you treat the staff right, they treat the guests right. You treat the guests right, they come back."

"It's a nice theory."

"It works."

"Mmm. Tina's going to be a problem."

"Do you blame her? Or any of them? Let's be honest, the way things stand now there are going to have to be cuts, and lots of them, to meet targets."

But it had to be done, no matter how much she might regret it. "It's business."

"It's not the only way."

"What do you mean?"

He shook his head. "Not yet. Tour first, ideas later."

"I've seen the hotel."

"No, you've seen walls and floors and ceilings," he corrected. "The Mount Jefferson is about much more than that. It's about romance, history."

"Romance and history don't show up on balance sheets."

"The hell they don't. Why do you think people come here?" He walked to the valet rack.

"Getaway weekends, I assume."

"And you think that isn't about more than walls and floors and ceilings?" He slipped on his jacket, buttoning it over his tie. If she'd harbored a hope that it would make him safe and unremarkable, she'd been wrong. It only added a layer of polish and style, she thought, watching him shoot his cuffs.

Ignore it.

"Come on," Gabe said briskly. "We can talk while we walk."

Tina passed them in the hall with another desk clerk, both of them stony faced. Only to be expected, Hadley reminded herself. To them, she was the enemy. That was all right. It didn't matter, so long as she satisfied Robert's numbers.

She tried to believe it.

Gabe stopped her at the end of the executive wing, where it branched into the lobby by the front desk and the grand staircase. "The builder was a railroad baron named Richard Cortland." Gabe pointed to a portrait of a hawk-nosed, gray-bearded man. "He met his wife, Clara, at a boating party on the Hudson. Bolt from the blue, or so they said. She was barely a third his age. New York society had a fit."

Clara had been a beauty, Hadley saw, dark-eyed and slender. "Why did they care? Was she a fortune hunter?"

"Worse. She was from Chicago. The New York society dragons were furious that an out-of-towner stepped in and snapped up a very eligible bachelor from under their noses."

"It must have made their daughters very unhappy."

"Maybe. But they couldn't ignore her. Cortland made the hotel *the* place to be. All of New York society came up in the summers, at least the ones who didn't have houses in Newport. And Clara loved to rub it in. Look up." He pointed to a balcony over their heads. "She used to stand behind the curtains of that balcony and watch the women come down the grand staircase on their way to dinner. If she saw anyone whose dress or jewelry outdid hers, she'd go change. Once everyone was seated, she and Cortland would make a big entrance, put them all to shame."

"I don't think that was it." Hadley spoke without thinking,

looking at lovely, dark-eyed Clara. "She was a woman. She wanted to be sure he saw only her."

"Perhaps you're right."

She glanced over to find Gabe Trask's eyes on hers, and this time there was no distraction, only that unsettling green, deep enough and dark enough to dive into. Hadley swallowed, her throat suddenly dry. "And do you think he did?"

"I think a man in love always does," Gabe said softly.

Time stretched out, how many moments, she couldn't say. Then he looked back at the painting, releasing her. "Cortland died only a couple of years after the hotel was built. Clara ran it for the next thirty." He turned toward the lobby. It took Hadley a stride or two to catch up.

"Morning, Angie," Gabe said as they entered by the front desk and the grand staircase.

Angie's smile brightened. "Good morning, Mr. Trask." She looked at Hadley and her expression became tentative, wary. "Good morning, Ms. Stone. I hope you're having a pleasant stay."

It hurt, Hadley discovered, to have become the enemy. And it wasn't nearly as easy to shake off as it should have been. She followed Gabe toward the great, glassed-in, semicircle of the conservatory, but she found herself drifting to a stop in front of the gleaming inlaid wood grandfather clock near the entrance.

"It's beautiful," she murmured, resisting the urge to brush her fingers over the smooth wood.

"Original to the hotel," Gabe told her. "The first guest to check in each spring started the pendulum moving and the last guest to check out in the fall stopped it."

She tried to imagine the heavy weight of the pendulum in her hands. "The hotel was closed in the winter?"

"For decades. We only winterized about five years ago. It was the first major initiative on my watch. Winter's a good time for couples. Think about it—sleigh rides, ice-skating, snow angels. Our Winter Carnival is already sold out."

"What did the winterizing cost?"

"Almost two million dollars."

She raised her eyebrows. "I guess you're not a cheap date."

The wolfish grin took her by surprise. "I'm worth it, though. Besides, it paid its way in a year and a half. I told you, the hotel makes money. We've just made a conscious choice to reinvest. You've got to in a place this old."

"No question, but you've also got to pick and choose."

"Trust me, I pick and choose every day. It's like being the parent of a dozen kids. Never enough to go around."

He wasn't joking, she saw. It wasn't just about satisfying the balance sheets for him, it was about taking care of things. And people. And caring made everything harder.

She knew that from personal experience.

"I think the conservatory's my favorite room," he said, walking onto the fresh spring-green carpet. The room was glorious, all light and open and airy, with a sweep of windows overlooking the woods and the mountains beyond. Greek pillars stood in a semicircle, wound with plaster garlands. In the center of the room, a recessed parabolic cutout in the ceiling looked like nothing so much as the inside of a Fabergé egg, all curves and pastels, with trompe l'oeil vines circling the interior. "We had a wedding here this weekend."

"Do you host them a lot?"

"I told you, romance is our business. People get married, come for anniversaries. We had a guy pop the question in the restaurant last night. There's something in the air here, maybe because Cortland was in love when he built it."

Hadley tried to imagine it, starting a new life amid the garland-draped columns, before the grand sweep of mountains. How could you help but believe it would work, that all the history of the hotel would somehow imbue it with a special magic?

But she'd seen over and over that magic didn't matter.

"I think we're all done here," Gabe said. "Next stop, the ballroom."

Chapter Six

Gabe led Hadley back out into the lobby, down the row of stately pillars. At the far end, a broad hallway led between pairs of sitting rooms en route to the grand ballroom.

"During World War II, the secretary of state's daughter got married here. So many dignitaries and heads of state were invited that they had to block off the highway, wouldn't let anyone in without a badge, not even the Brazilian ambassador."

"Imagine that. What did he do?" Hadley asked in amusement.

"Got the vice president to vouch for him."

"I know it always works for me."

On the walls, photographs showed a young woman in white lace and a nervous-looking groom with a boutoniere. "How nerve-racking to have the president of the United States and the prime minister of Canada looking on as you say your vows," she murmured.

"I guess it made them take them seriously. They were here

in '94 to celebrate their golden anniversary. Still holding hands," he added, pointing to the photograph of an elderly couple beaming at the camera.

"There's a rarity," she said.

He studied her for a moment. "We've got some other old photos you might want to see. Come on." He led her farther down the hallway, to the vestibule of the ballroom beyond. On the wall, photographs showed the half-built hotel, with the workers clustered around the foundation stones, incongruous in their vests and bowler hats.

"Cortland brought stone masons and master carpenters over from Italy," Gabe said, pointing to the workers. "And look, Cortland and Clara." In the sepia-toned print, Cortland had the sober sternness that you so often saw in old photographs. Clara's eyes held a flicker of mischief, a hint of the woman who'd reveled in tipping society on its ear.

"She was really quite beautiful," Hadley murmured.

"She was," he agreed. "According to what I've read, they were truly in love. It wasn't just for money. She practically went into seclusion after he died." He pointed to another photograph. "That's Harold Masterson. He was the head of a Massachusetts syndicate that bought the hotel from the Cortlands after World War II. His group held on to it to the mid-sixties. It went briefly to a property management company that went belly-up after about ten years and turned it over to a savings and loan."

"No pictures of them?"

"No real people, just corporations. That was when things really began to go south. They couldn't take care of it and had problems of their own. They got caught out in the S and L scandal and wound up having to put it on the block. That was when your grandfather bought it." He pointed to a photograph of a laughing couple holding a toddler and pointing to the camera.

"That's Whit?"

Gabe nodded. "He spent a month here the summer his son was three. Made quite an impression on him, I guess."

The laughing woman in the dark lipstick and the circle skirt was her tight-lipped, resentful grandmother, Hadley realized in shock, and the chubby toddler at Whit's feet… "My father," she said faintly.

"Whit gave us this picture to put up here. Said it was the happiest time in his life. That was why he wanted to buy the hotel and bring her back."

Hadley stared at the photo, at the three faces frozen in time, frozen in joy. Whatever had happened after, they had been happy once.

"Are you okay?" Gabe asked, watching her closely.

Snap out of it. "Of course," she said automatically, studying Whit's face in the image. He didn't look like the miserable SOB she'd heard about. He seemed kind.

"You look like you haven't seen this before. We could probably make you a copy of the shot, if you like."

Hadley gave herself a mental shake. Now wasn't the time to be obsessing about the past. She had problems enough in the present. "That won't be necessary," she said, and turned from the photos. "What's next?"

"The ballroom is in through here, though it's a little torn up at present. This year's project," he elaborated, and opened the French doors into the cavernous room.

"This year's project?" Her voice echoed.

"Every January, Whit and I sit down…sat down," he corrected with a little shake of his head, "and made a list of what we were going to do for the year. He spent the first decade after he bought the place just paying off the bank loan and doing basic facilities upgrades. By the time I came on board, he was ready to start real renovations. He didn't take a dime of profit out of the place the whole time I was running it," Gabe added.

Hadley frowned. It didn't fit. None of it fit. Whit had a reputation for being ruthless when it came to financials. Why would he dump all of his profits into a hotel that wasn't one of his core businesses? Why acquire it in the first place—as a hobby? She shook her head, mystified.

"I think it really made an impression on him when he was first here, and he just wanted to bring it back so that other people could enjoy it, too," Gabe said as though he'd heard her.

"You liked him."

"Yeah, I did. He was a decent person. Tough, but decent. He gave me a chance in this business."

"You got to know him running the hotel?"

Gabe gave a laugh. "No, we go further back than that. Whit used to spend a week here every summer. I met him the first year I worked at the golf course here, as a caddy. He didn't own the place then and all the other caddies hated getting stuck with him. You know how he'd look at you with those bushy eyebrows if you screwed up," he said with a quick smile that invited her to remember.

Except that she couldn't.

"None one else wanted him and I was low man on the totem pole."

"So you got stuck with it."

"I got stuck with it," he agreed. "And I don't know why, but we hit it off. He asked for me every day. The next summer I moved to lifeguard, then bellhop, but whenever Whit came he wanted me to caddy for him. And then one day he invited me to play." This time, the smile was private.

"You still miss him, don't you?"

Gabe nodded. "It's hard to get used to. Something will happen and I'll pick up the phone to call him and then I remember he's not there anymore. You know what it's like."

But she didn't. She'd never had a chance to.

Glancing up, she found him looking at her quizzically. Abruptly, she remembered the feel of his arms around her on the dance floor, and in that instant all she wanted was to be held, just held by someone who cared for her.

The targets, she reminded herself. That was what she needed to be focusing on, not fantasies. "So what was your idea about upping revenues?"

For moment, he didn't reply. Then he shook his head. "Come outside, I'll show you."

The day was crisp, cloudless, the sun throwing blue shadows onto the snow. Water dripped from the icicles that lined the roof like crystal trimming. "A perfect location," Hadley murmured, walking to where the veranda curved around the end of the wing and began its return along the back side of the hotel, toward the conservatory. "The mountains, they're everywhere you look."

"This was Whit's favorite place in the whole hotel. Mountains as far as the eye could see, he used to say." And while she took in the view, Gabe could look at her. So sleek, so polished, but it wasn't the polish that attracted him. It wasn't the gloss he found hard to ignore, it was the delicate mouth that softened when she thought no one was looking, the gray eyes and the shadows they held. It was the fragility that popped out when he least expected it, and hand in hand with it the force of will to keep going.

He'd shown her the photo of Whit, hoping to make her connect to the hotel. The unfettered joy in the image always made him feel good. He hadn't expected it to put the sadness back in her eyes. "He used to talk about you," he said now. "He was so proud of what you'd accomplished."

Of all the reactions he'd have expected, shock would have been the last. "He talked about *me*?"

"Of course. Grandparents do, you know."

"But I…he never—" She broke off helplessly.

"Sometimes it's easier to tell someone else," Gabe said softly. Hadley shook her head and stared out at the mountains.

"It's…complicated," she said at last. "So tell me about your idea."

"You're looking at it." Gabe pointed to the ridge on the other side of the road, just down from the hotel. "The Crawford Notch Ski Resort."

"Ski packages? That's it?"

"We already have ski packages. I want to buy the resort lock, stock and barrel, run it together with the hotel. The property already has a couple of inns. We could expand them, add Nordic skiing down here, drive our winter occupancy way up."

She gave him a stare of exasperation and moved along the veranda. "The goal here is to cut costs, not incur more."

"I'm not talking about incurring cost, I'm talking about buying revenue centers."

"Which are going to need a whole lot of money dumped into them. Gabe, this isn't helping."

"That ski area is incredibly run-down. We could double, even triple the revenues with a moderate investment. Think about it, winter romance packages with skiing, sleigh rides, après ski parties…. The corporate clients will like it, too, and regardless of whether they stay here or there we get the money."

"You're out of your mind," she said impatiently. "The board will never stand for it."

"I've crunched some numbers. We could be looking at making our investment back in a year, maybe two. You want to see a big jump in hotel revenues, this is the way to do it."

"And for no money down, I suppose. Targets, remember?"

"Yeah, yeah, targets. But this has long-term upside. I don't know firm numbers yet. I did a little sniffing around in the spring, but when we lost Whit…" He gave a helpless shrug. "My guess is we could get it for six million, maybe seven. The value's mostly in the land. There's money to be made there but it'll cost. Whit would have been behind it. Will Stone?"

Hadley shook her head. "Even if you're not out of your mind

it'll be a tough sell. We'd have to work up the numbers, convince my father, Robert, and the directors."

"Look at the golf course. It just sits there all winter when it could be producing revenue. Same with the bridle paths. You want higher profits, we need to get every square foot of this property earning."

"Okay, I can see that argument, but why buy it? Why not work with the resort to create some bundled offerings?"

Gabe snorted. "That place is so badly managed right now a chimp could probably bring in more money. It would hurt us to be associated with it. They've got historic inns on the property that they're letting fall apart. It would take an investment, but it would pay for itself pretty quickly."

He could see it taking shape as he talked. "Imagine it. You want to get away with your lover. You can't afford the Mount Jefferson but you can come to the Crawford Arms and get a room in a historic inn with world-class skiing right outside your front door, a quiet brandy tucked up in front of the fire at the end of the day, then a long, hot soak in the room's Jacuzzi tub or a massage with complimentary massage oil." He saw her eyes darken and had a sudden image of her stretched out on a bed, naked skin gleaming with oil. What would it be like to work some of the tension out of her shoulders and see her relax for once—before he gave her an entirely different type of tension?

For a moment, she didn't answer him. Then she swallowed. "But I...we need numbers."

Gabe resisted a grin. The businesswoman was trying to come back but she was fighting a losing battle. "Between the benefit to the hotel and the increased revenue we could get at the ski area, I'm guessing it would pay for itself in a couple of years and drive revenues for the overall resort."

"Pie in the sky isn't going to do it for you, Trask," Hadley said more firmly.

"It's not pie in the sky. I can back it up. And that's not even counting what we could do with a cross-country program. The golf shop would be our Nordic center. The bridle paths are already there. We just need a grooming machine and some rental equipment and the right staff and we're ready to print money."

Hadley stared off toward the white stripes of the ski runs, watching the green lift chairs, toylike at this distance. "Do you really think my grandfather would have gone for it?"

"He liked the idea. Like you, he wanted to be convinced. I was working on the package when he had his stroke."

A line of sunlight fell over her shoulder and along the edge of her cheek, lighting up her hair. She was beautiful, he thought, pure and simple. Something had started on the dance floor, like the pendulum of the clock, with an inexorable rhythm of its own. It had no place in what they were doing and yet it hovered over every conversation, the elephant in the room. The manager in him knew to keep his distance.

The man only knew he wanted her.

"So show me what you've got," she said. "And then let's go take a look around."

They were heading back to Gabe's office when the normally smooth and unflappable Alicia hurried up, looking harried. "We have a problem," she blurted.

Gabe looked at her in concern. "I had a feeling. What's up?"

"Balloons."

"Balloons?"

"Purple balloons. It's Jeremy Potter's birthday party today."

And he understood at least the magnitude of the problem, if not the particulars. Joan Potter had been the star of their events planning discussions for three weeks running, ignoring deadlines, making constant demands, presenting a steadily rising head count. But Joan was also the president of the Montpelier Ladies' Auxiliary and in a position to pass a lot of good word about the hotel if she were satisfied with her son's birthday party.

"She asked for purple and white balloons, I have it on paper, but now she insists on red. Jeremy seems to think purple is a girl's color."

"Jeremy's right," Gabe said. It earned him a slight smile. "Do we have red balloons?"

"I bought a giant bag of all colors a month ago, before she started demanding purple. We could sift through for the red ones but we need a hundred of them and there's no time." The normally calm Alicia was practically vibrating with frustration. "Joan's going to be here any minute and we'll have fifty kids and their mothers here half an hour later."

"Don't worry about it," Gabe said mildly. "Take care of Joan. I'll take care of the balloons."

Alicia's eyes shone with gratitude and more than a bit of hero worship. "I knew you'd fix it," she said in a rush of relief. "Thank you."

She hurried off toward the main doors, presumably to wait for Joan Potter. Gabe turned to Hadley. "It looks like our little outing is going to have to wait. Can we do it tomorrow? I've got some balloons to fill."

"Yourself? Why don't you get a staffer to do it?"

"Because they're busy, and getting this party right is important. It could mean a lot more business. Besides, filling balloons is trickier than it looks and we don't want any of those babies getting loose." He glanced at his watch. "I might not be done quite by showtime, but I'll be close."

"Would another pair of hands help?"

It surprised him that she would offer. "Don't you have things to do?"

"Doesn't matter. I want to help."

So it begins… "All right then. Step this way."

* * *

Hadley couldn't believe she was spending a workday filling balloons with helium. If Robert could only see her now. It was one step away from running off to join the circus.

They stood in Gabe's office, the helium tank on one side, a reel of string on the other. More and more she realized his office was the triage center for the hotel. Against the wall, a cardboard box held a pair of silver water pitchers with broken handles. Another box looked to be filled with retired prints from the guest rooms. Plastic-wrapped tubes leaned against the wall.

"What are those?"

"Carpet samples for the ballroom. I'll show you later. We've got to make a decision in the next day or two."

"We?"

"If you're on the hot seat for target numbers, the least I can do is give you a vote." He turned a dial on the tank, and with a hiss, the small rubber pouch pressed over the nozzle expanded to a gleaming red sphere.

Any other man would have looked ridiculous standing there in business clothes, filling balloons. She could say a lot of things about how he looked, but ridiculous wouldn't have been one of them. He'd taken off his suit coat and rolled his sleeves up so that his forearms showed, hard and sinewy. His shoulders, accentuated by the suspenders, looked very wide and solid above the narrowness of his hips. He'd loosened his tie a bit and unbuttoned his collar. He looked just about good enough to eat.

Sexy, hot, magnetic. Any of those would work. Ridiculous? Absolutely not.

Gabe pulled the balloon off, tying shut the neck and holding it out for Hadley to tie on the string. Their fingers brushed and she jerked back.

Gabe raised his brow. "If you're afraid of balloons, now's the time to tell me."

"I'm working on getting over my phobias," she told him. And one of the things that she needed to get over was Gabe Trask, but she didn't seem to be making much progress. She fastened the balloon to the back of one of the conference table chairs, with several dozen others.

He just smiled. "You're getting pretty good at this. Ever consider a job at an amusement park?"

"If we don't hit our targets, I might be looking for one," she said without thinking.

He gave her a sharp glance. "Your father would fire his own daughter?"

She shook her head. "Just joking." It was an idiotic thing to say. The last thing she needed to do was show any sign of weakness. "You find yourself doing this kind of thing often?"

"Among a few thousand other things," he said, watching her far too intently. "One thing I don't find myself doing very often is yawning." The tank hissed as he filled another balloon. "I might wind up doing some odd things but time never drags. It's never predictable."

"And you don't like predictable?"

He handed her another balloon. "I grew up with predictable."

"Where was that?"

"On a farm."

Hadley gave him a long, slow survey, from his cordovan leather shoes to his silk tie. "What did you grow, Armani?"

"Maple syrup. In Armani."

"Seriously?" She tied on the cord. "You really were a farm boy?"

"You bet." He inflated the last balloon. "Fifty acres outside of Montpelier. Sugar maples as far as the eye can see."

It was about as far from her world as anything she could

imagine. "How on earth did you wind up in the hotel business?"

"I was on a Cub Scout trip to the cog railway. The driver got lost and we wound up driving by the hotel."

"It made an impression, I take it."

"When you've just spent half your summer hacking down underbrush in the maples, yeah, a white castle on a hill makes an impression." He unfastened the strings of a dozen balloons from a chair back and twisted the cords together, then wrapped them around one of Hadley's hands. "Hold on tight," he murmured, closing her fingers. "Anyway, I was already pretty confident that farming wasn't for me, but when I saw the hotel and the golf courses and people horseback riding, I started thinking about a different kind of life."

Hadley held out her hand to take the next bunch of balloons. "What did your parents say?"

"I didn't exactly come home and tell them that day."

"But you said you caddied summers for a while."

He nodded. "It wasn't the most popular thing I could have done. I sold it to them as being a good way for me to mature."

"So basically you're telling me you were an operator."

"That's a harsh word." He caught another bunch of balloons and wrapped them around his own hand. "It was a good experience. I stayed in the bunkhouse with the other summer help."

"And didn't have any fun or get into any trouble at all," she said dryly, watching him collect another bunch.

"Nothing I got caught for," he told her. "Anyway, it made me into a hell of a bunkhouse supervisor. I know the things they're going to do before *they* do. And it opened some doors."

"With Whit." Five balloons remained tied to the chair. She could get them, she figured, working them with her fingers while she held on to the others.

"With a lot of people. Just by listening, I learned more about business over a couple of summers than I'd ever have learned otherwise. I learned more about the hotel. And one of the things I learned is to that you don't want to do that," he said suddenly as he saw what she was doing.

"What's wrong with—damn," she said as a red balloon slipped loose and drifted up to the ceiling.

Gabe winced. "Did I ever tell you about our smoke detection system?" he asked conversationally. "It works on an electronic eye. You block the eye and it triggers the alarm."

"Triggers the alarm?" Hadley repeated faintly.

"Uh-huh."

"Where's the eye?" she asked with a sinking heart.

He pointed to the matchbook-size box on the ceiling, near where the balloon bobbed. "There."

And out in the hall the fire alarm Klaxon began to whoop.

Chapter Seven

Flakes of snow drifted down from the morning sky, dotting the windshield of Gabe's Explorer as he drove toward the ski resort.

"So do you think we're ever going to get any more business from the Montpelier Ladies' Auxiliary?" Hadley asked, thinking of the previous day's debacle. It was one thing to have an alarm sound for a few minutes. It was another to have the whole Crawford Notch Fire Department come storming in.

"You might be surprised. I don't know how thrilled the parents were but the kids loved it. They're never going to forget climbing all over the fire truck."

"You're letting me off easy."

"No, I'll extract payment one of these days."

His tone was light but there was something in the quick glance he tossed at her that brought the butterflies back. In force. Hadley swallowed. "You don't have to be *that* careful about your revenue targets."

"Sure I do. A favor saved is a favor earned."

And some kinds of favors were too dangerous to contemplate. She coughed. "Wow, look at all those open parking spaces, huh?"

Gabe's teeth gleamed. "Actually, that's the point. What is it, half-full? A third? It's a Thursday morning. We got two inches of powder overnight. They should be packed. Of course, they should also have twice as much parking capacity, but that's another conversation." He turned into an empty spot and switched off the engine. "If we could close on this sale by the end of January, say, we'd have time to plan a rework and get the construction done by the start of the next ski season."

"First we have to decide whether or not to even make the buy," she reminded him. "You might be able to turn the ski area around, but I'm not convinced that will help the hotel."

"You saw the numbers."

"On the ski area. On the hotel, they're speculative. After all, the ski area's available to guests now." Scooping up her leather-bound notepad, Hadley stepped out into ankle deep snow.

"Such as it is. If we can fix it up, we'll be able to offer better packages, tied into the hotel's theme weekends. And we'll have a serious draw for winter occupancy." He rounded the corner of the vehicle and met her at the back. "Romance is our bread and butter, but the corporate business is growing. Right now, we have seventy or eighty percent occupancy on the weekends and only ten or twenty most weeknights. If we could get one good-size company conference or offsite meeting a week, we'd push those numbers way up."

"And you think skiing will do it?"

"Sure. Now we're offering a resort destination. They can ski in the mornings and have meetings in the afternoons. They can get work done and still make the employees or clients feel like they're getting a treat. Everyone's happy."

"You seem awfully con—" Hadley gave a yelp of alarm as her feet shot out from under her. Snaking out a quick hand, Gabe caught her inches before she hit the snow. She righted herself, cheeks burning. "Sorry. I slipped," she said unnecessarily.

He stared at her feet. "I'm not surprised, in those things. What in the hell are you wearing?"

She frowned at the ankle boots she'd paired with her narrow-legged trouser suit. "Boots."

"Boots?" he echoed in disbelief. "Pointy toes and high heels?" He reached down and raised one of her feet to inspect it, as though she were a show pony. "Don't you have anything designed for snow? Your feet have to be freezing."

They were but she wasn't about to admit it. "They're what I wear at home," she retorted.

"I'll refrain from pointing out the obvious. Come on." He took her arm impatiently.

"Where are we going?" All of her attention immediately focused on the pressure of his fingers.

"You're going to need some real boots before we do anything. Those things have about as much tread as a pair of bowling shoes."

"I wasn't planning to take cross-country hikes when I came here." Unobtrusively, she tried to tug her arm loose. The gap, that critical, sanity-preserving gap, had been breached. "I feel like I'm being marched to my room by my father," she complained, though that wasn't entirely true. Being touched by her father had never felt like this.

"Fine, you grab my arm, but hold on somehow or you'll pancake again. There's ice under that powder."

It was cozy—alarmingly cozy—to walk with her arm tucked through his, flurries of snow drifting down around them. Christmas garlands hung from the powder-dusted trees. The bright parkas and pants of the skiers looked like holiday decorations themselves. She and Gabe were working, she reminded herself, but it didn't feel like it. For a moment, they were just a woman and a man, walking through a winterscape together.

A family passed them. One of the sons jostled Hadley, his ski poles coming perilously close to her face. One minute she was ducking, falling toward Gable.

And the next he'd caught her against him.

For an instant, neither of them moved. Just for an instant, she couldn't. A fraction of an inch, just a fraction of an inch and his mouth would be on hers. His breath feathered warm over her lips. She felt his shoulders hard and solid under her fingers. But it was his eyes that riveted her, arrowing through her with a connection she couldn't evade.

The seconds seemed to stretch out like warm taffy. So easy, it would be so easy to lean just a bit closer, to taste him, to see if his kiss was all that it promised to be. So easy…

"Got your footing?" Gabe released her and bent down to retrieve her pad. He looked at her, his face scrupulously clean of expression. "You dropped this."

"Uh yeah, sure, fine, thanks," she babbled, hardly aware of what she was saying. It was frightening how quickly every thought had gone out of her head but him. "The path's just over here. I'll be fine." Tucking her hands protectively in her pockets, Hadley took the last dozen steps on her own.

She'd simply let her guard down, that was all. It wasn't going to happen again. The stakes were too high. The last thing she needed to do was get caught up in Gabe Trask—she could just imagine what Robert would have to say about that.

Hadley dusted the snow off the leather cover of her pad and opened it. First improvement, paths and parking area. No more slipping.

Of any kind.

The narrow path led toward the slopes and the lift. To one

side lay the ski center, first stop. The faux-chalet design was a bit unfortunate, but she doubted people made their decisions about where to ski based on the architecture—or lack thereof. It was what was inside and on the slopes that counted.

Unfortunately, what was inside was no better, she saw as Gabe opened the door for her.

It was warm, she'd give it that. It had probably been the height of hip back when it was built. Unfortunately, a good thirty years had passed, by the looks of things. Now, it merely looked shabby, crowded and outdated, an impression that wasn't helped even a little by the harsh fluorescent lighting overhead. The line to buy lift tickets straggled across the room, intersecting the queue from the ski rental counter.

And all Hadley wanted to do was get back outside. A fairly common response, she was betting. "They haven't even tried to make this place a draw. They should have a window to buy lift tickets outside. Is there any way for people to even to have some food and something to drink after skiing?"

Gabe pointed without a word to a cramped lounge.

Hadley looked around, shaking her head helplessly. "I don't see how you could fix this place up enough to make it worthwhile. It might almost be better to do a complete knockdown. How do they stay in business like this?"

"They seem to be of the philosophy that to increase profit you cut costs. Sound familiar?"

Her eyes narrowed. "Stick to the point, Trask."

"That is the point."

"No, the point is the building. Knock it down or fix it up? We're talking an order of magnitude in cost."

"I'm not sure," he answered thoughtfully. "This ought to be a place people want to come. Think about it—you ski all day and you want to wind down before the drive home. A little music, maybe a brandy Alexander or a cold beer, a cozy nook in front of the fire to hide away with your date. We could bring in twenty or thirty bucks a head easy in just appetizers and drinks."

"That's some hungry people."

"That's based on the restaurant and bar charges at the Mount Jefferson. Remember, breakfast and dinner are included with the room. Most people still drop upward of thirty bucks any given day."

"You track it that closely?"

"I know what goes on on my watch," he said. "As far as this place goes, we could take it a step further. You have races, you've got fewer people skiing and more people eating and drinking. For the skiers, put in a better pro and service shop. They probably pay their way even now. The clothing store might even make a small profit. In fact—" he led her over "—they're about to make some money right now."

Inside, he stopped in front of the shelf of boots.

Hadley looked from Gabe to the row of boots and back again. "Don't tell me you were serious out there."

"Don't tell me you think you're going to walk around the rest of this property in those shoes. You leave this place without decent boots and you're on your own."

Hadley's lips tightened mutinously.

"Be a shame to see you start to go ass over teakettle again," Gabe observed. "One of these times I'm not going to catch you."

"Can I help you?" The salesman appeared at her elbow.

Gabe merely folded his arms over his chest. "Your call."

She'd give him his due, he didn't gloat, and the new boots allowed her to keep her distance. That was important. Robert constantly harped on the need to separate emotions from business, ranting about company officials who couldn't keep their hands off their colleagues or their subordinates. And even if Gabe Trask weren't answerable to her, he was an indiscretion she couldn't afford, not when she was trying to redeem herself in Robert's eyes. Relationships, especially in the workplace, were not worth it.

But it had felt so good to walk with her arm tucked in his.

Hadley moved her head to ward the thought away. "So talk to me about the ski operation."

They stood near the lift, watching the endless line of green chairs going by, only every third or fourth one occupied. "It's like the ski center, outdated, undermaintained." Gabe pointed to the map of the mountain that sat by the side of the lift line. "Look at the layout. You could fit three or four more runs on the parcel without even remotely crowding the existing plan. We'd need a higher capacity lift, but this one's barely holding on as it is. Listen to it."

The lift groaned each time it brought a chair around. She could see the streaks of rust on the superstructure. "So how do you go about designing new runs?" she asked. "I mean, it's like designing a golf course or something, isn't it? You need an expert."

"Someone who knows the sport inside and out." Time to play his trump card, Gabe decided. "I went to high school with J. J. Cooper."

"J. J. Cooper?"

"You know, the guy who took the gold in downhill last Olympics?"

She gave a mystified head shake. "I don't follow sports."

"Careful giving that kind of reaction in a bar around here." Gabe grinned. "J.J.'s a native son. Eastmont, Vermont, but he's been adopted by all of New England. If we could get him as ski director, it would be huge."

"He'd design the new runs?"

"He'd do lots of things. Design the runs, approve the equipment we carry, help choose the lift, plan ski races. It would be a major draw up here. Think about it, Crawford Notch Ski Resort. J. J. Cooper, Director of Skiing. Like having Tiger Woods as your golf pro and course designer."

Gabe could see the idea take hold of her. "That could put a whole different spin on things," she admitted.

"Makes all those numbers we talked about this morning look a little more solid, huh?"

"Don't get carried away. Do you really think he'd do it?"

"Can't hurt to ask," Gabe replied. "It helps that I know where the bodies are buried."

"Blackmail?" Her smile bloomed.

And a class A smile it was, he thought in appreciation. "If necessary. We were pretty much inseparable in high school. J.J. still spends his summers here. It's harder to get him during the season, but I can track him down if I need to. Want me to give him a call, see if we can set up a meet over Christmas?"

"If you can." Robert wasn't going to like this one bit, she thought. Then again, he was always telling her the best managers weren't afraid to take risks.

A pair of what looked like college students passed them, talking animatedly. The boy lost his balance and tumbled into the snow. The girl leaned over to offer him a hand and he pulled her down, squealing, for a kiss.

Gabe turned speculative eyes on Hadley. "I don't know, maybe I should keep you away from J.J. He has this mind-control thing going on with women. One look and that's that."

She rolled her eyes. "My powers of resistance are pretty strong." Except where Gabe Trask was concerned.

"That's what you say now."

And she hoped to God she could keep to it, because it was becoming abundantly clear that Gabe was a problem.

They turned toward the sprawling Victorian inn, the Crawford Arms, opposite the ski center. "This should be part of the hotel property," Gabe told her. "It was built by Cortland a couple of years before the Mount Jefferson."

"How did it get separated from the hotel?"

"The S and L sold it off when the Crawford Notch group bought the property to put up the ski resort. It belongs with us."

Like the ski center, the Crawford Arms had seen better days. It reminded her of a thirties sedan converted to a hot rod and left to rust. Some scary things had been done to it and the elements and time had played their hands. The elegance and clarity of the original design still showed through, however.

It could be brought back, Hadley thought as they walked through. All it would take was work and money. Trading the innocuous furniture for a few fat sofas and throw pillows alone would make a huge change, and she'd bet twenty bucks that there was hardwood flooring underneath the mottled gold shag rug.

For a moment, Hadley closed her eyes and imagined it restored, all warm wood and jewel tones, with a crackling blaze in the fireplace and the scents of cinnamon and apples in the air. The kind of home she'd always dreamed of living in. "It'll need a full renovation but it could be wonderful," she murmured.

"We don't need to do it all at once," Gabe said, thumping a wall to test it. "We'd work it in stages over a couple of years, eventually make an addition to double the number of rooms."

Neither of them noticed as they continued to walk the property when "could" and "if" became "will." Neither of them noticed when they began to talk as partners.

"I met Roderick Miller of the current ownership group at a corporate event in Burlington a couple years back," Gabe said later in his truck as they drove toward the exit. "I still have his card. I can call him, gauge the interest on their end."

"Let's get our ducks in a row and then you can ring him, see what they're looking for."

Gabe pulled back out onto the road.

"So who owns the condo complex down the highway?" Hadley asked.

He shrugged. "I don't know. It's not part of what I have in

mind for the buy, although there's an adjoining parcel here that we could eventually develop as a small condo complex."

"That's not why I'm asking. I need a place to live. I can't keep staying in the hotel."

He flicked a glance at her. "You're with the company. It's not like it's costing you."

"That's part of the point. My room could be occupied by a paying guest. Besides, living in one room is going to make me crazy before too much longer."

This time his glance lasted longer. "How much time are you planning on spending here?"

"Hard to say." When she'd arrived, she'd hoped to set things in motion and be on her way by January, with occasional return visits. Now, with talk about the ski area and renovations, it looked more like months than weeks.

"It'll be tough to find a place this time of year. Everybody's renting by the week for ski vacations and it ain't cheap." He stopped behind a truck that was waiting to make a left turn. "Of course, there's an alternative. I live in the manager's house behind the hotel. You could always stay there."

Before she could help it, her mind conjured up an image of the two of them cuddled cozily together on his couch. Too cozy, too together.

Too dangerous.

"You've got to be kidding me."

"Why? It'll put you right on site."

Because he was already setting up house in her mind? "Where would I sleep, on the sofa?"

Gabe laughed. "I'm not suggesting you bunk down with me. The manager's house has three separate flats. Furnished, even, at least with the basics."

"I don't know." The last thing she needed was to live in the same house, listening to his footfalls, imagining where he was, what he was doing.

"At least take a look at it. Why live three miles away and pay rent when you can live on site for free?"

Because it might be the only way to keep her sanity? "I'll think about it."

"Well, while you're thinking, let me show you something else, just to round out your tour."

"What?"

"The cog railway."

"So Cortland built this, too?"

They stood on a snowy patch of ground outside the Mount Jefferson Cog Railway base station. Around them rose thick pine forest. Behind them, the hotel gleamed white in the sun.

"What do you expect?" Gabe asked. "He was a railroad man. An inventor brought him a way to run a train up to the top of the mountain and he went with it."

"When was that?"

"Around the time he was building the hotel."

Hadley raised her eyebrows. "Busy boy. So what's with the skiers?" she asked, pointing to the forms schussing down the slope next to the rails.

"That was J.J.'s idea. When he's not competing, he does these nutso things like parachuting onto a glacier wearing skis."

"Mr. Extreme Sports?"

"If it's got snow and a fifty percent grade, sure. Starting up the Ski Train was one way to get a piece of the action. We didn't have to do too much to the slope to get it ready—it was mostly cleared for the railway as it was."

Up along the mountain, the train came into view. "When did you open it?" Hadley asked.

"Last season. The railroad used to be open only in summer. This time of year, it only goes halfway. About a forty-five minute trip."

"For five, ten minutes' worth of skiing?"

"It's not the quantity, it's the quality. We get a pretty steady stream of traffic, especially on the weekends. You'd be surprised."

A sharp whistle from the train interrupted them. Chuffing and clacking, it crept toward them, an old-fashioned steam engine with a broad, funnel-shaped smokestack, paired with an equally old-fashioned-looking wooden passenger car. Except it was backward. Instead of the car being hooked on at the end of the train, it pressed against the nose of the engine. When the train was headed up the mountain, the engine pushed the passenger carriage ahead of it. Coming down the mountain, however, it appeared to be backing away from a confrontation with the pushy orange conveyance.

Something else about the engine looked odd. She frowned. "Why is it all tilted down?"

"Keeps the boiler level on the steepest parts. When it's up on the mountain, it's about the only thing that's level."

The engine came to a stop and with a giant chuffing hiss, the boiler released a cloud of steam. Gabe glanced at her. "Want to go say hello to the engineer? He knew Whit."

A bearded man in a navy-blue jacket and a Red Sox cap hopped from the cab of the engine to the ground, stuffing a pair of canvas work gloves into his back pocket. When he saw Gabe, he changed direction toward where they stood. "Gabe Trask. What brings you up here?"

"Got to make sure you're staying out of trouble."

"Never." He shook hands and slapped Gabe on the shoulder. "Who's your friend?"

"Ed, I'd like you to meet Hadley Stone, Whit's granddaughter. Hadley, this is Ed Wallace, engineer on the cog railway for, how long has it been, Ed? Thirty-five years?"

"Thirty-six as of last year, and I knew Whit for thirty of 'em." Hadley found her hand swallowed up in a callused paw as Ed gave her an assessing stare. "Well, damned if you don't have the look of him. Me and Whit spent a lot of years out on the lake fishing for wide-mouths."

"He fished?"

A smile creased Ed's worn face. "That's code for sitting around in a boat and telling lies. Comparing notes about our grandkids. He said you were a world beater."

Gabe watched Hadley. He knew enough now not to expect uncomplicated pleasure. When her expression turned strained, he reached out to take her elbow. She didn't move away.

"What do you remember of my grandfather, Mr. Wallace?" she asked instead, intently.

"Just Ed, young lady." He pushed his cap back. "Whit? I'll tell you about Whit. We used to take him up the mountain with us in the cab every year. One time, a cinder flew out of the firebox, blistered the fireman's hand so bad he couldn't hold anything. Whit didn't even pause, just stepped in and started shoveling coal. Did it all the way up and back down the mountain. Said it was the most fun he'd had in years."

Hadley tried to picture it, the man from the Forbes 400 list cheerfully shoveling coal. Always, she'd obeyed her father's unstated wishes, keeping Whit out of their lives. Now, she was beginning to wonder why.

"He had a gift for enjoying life, Whit did. I always figured to see you up here with him one of these days." Ed shrugged. "But there's never enough time for everything, I guess."

"I guess not," she said softly.

Behind them, the whistle of the engine tooted impatiently.

"That's my cue," Ed said. "It was a pleasure meeting you."

"The pleasure was mine," she said.

"Ed Wheeler's a good man," Gabe said on the ride down the mountain.

Hadley sat mutely, staring out at the passing trees.

"If you want to go up on the railway, we can arrange it."

Hadley didn't answer.

"You didn't know your grandfather, did you?" Gabe asked softly.

The silence stretched out until he began to think she wouldn't answer.

"No," she said finally, her reply almost inaudible. "I only met him once, briefly, at a dinner function."

Gabe tried to imagine it, not knowing family. "I don't get it. He always talked like he knew you, like he was up with what you were doing. What happened?"

"It was an ugly divorce. My grandmother isn't a very forgiving woman. Once she and Whit split, she never had a good word to say. My father never spoke to him after that." Hadley looked out the window again. "She came from a very wealthy New York family. Back then, it was easier to keep the father from having visitation rights."

So much energy put into vindictiveness and in the end the children were the ones who suffered. "Did she ever get past it?"

Hadley shook her head. "All my life I've been told Whit was a miserable human being who didn't care about anyone or anything but making money. He tried, I know he tried in the past five or ten years to get in touch with my father, but Robert always froze him out. He said it was just an old man trying to suddenly wipe the slate clean."

"And you met him only once?"

"At a charity dinner, during cocktails. I don't usually go to those sorts of things but it was a Stone Enterprises event so it was a command performance. I turned around and he was just there." A tap on the shoulder, a turn into shock.

"What did he say?"

"He introduced himself. I knew who he was, of course. I'd seen his face on too many magazine covers." She'd smiled automatically and for a moment his eyes had looked kind. "I shook his hand and then I glanced over my shoulder and my father was behind me." And the tension had suddenly been palpable, like the hum before a lightning strike. "Whit said, 'Hello, Robert,' and my father didn't even answer him. He just took my arm and escorted me away." She took an unsteady breath. "We left him standing there. And now I don't even know why."

Her breath hitched again and Gabe knew she was crying.

"It's foolish to get upset," she said, swiping angrily at her cheeks. "It's done, there's nothing I can do to change it."

"Isn't that the hardest part of all? To discover that you might have wanted to?"

And she did cry then, weeping for the man she'd never known, while Gabe pulled off to the side of the road and just rubbed her shoulder helplessly.

"Loyalty can be a good thing, but sometimes it can be misplaced," he said after the storm had passed. "I don't know what happened with your grandparents and your father, but Whit was a good man."

"I just don't understand. How can the person I grew up hearing about be the same man you and Ed and Lester knew?"

Gabe pulled the Explorer back out on the road. "People make mistakes, they change. Your father did speak to him once after the divorce, by the way."

"When?" She stared at him.

"When Robert was thirteen or fourteen, I think. Junior high. He was being sent away to prep school."

"My grandfather told you about this?"

"When he promoted me to manager. It started out as a cautionary tale over dinner, I think, but it stretched out over a long couple of brandies." Gabe pulled to a stop at the intersection with the highway. "He said it was important to keep success in perspective, that thinking the people he cared about would wait had cost him his marriage."

"Win the battle, lose the war."

"And how. But they were gone and he figured the hell with them, he had empires to build. About twelve years later he was hammering out a deal to merge Aerotech with McCutcheon Aircraft. He was in a conference call with a half-dozen other folks, including the COO and chief legal counsel for McCutcheon. Final negotiations." Gabe let a car pass and pulled out onto the road. "And this kid gets past his secretary and barges into his office. Says he's Whit's son, that he's run away and he wants to come live with him. Meanwhile, the chief legal counsel of McCutcheon is starting to get nasty over the final offer."

The most delicate part of a deal. "God, what did Whit do?"

"Asked Robert to sit down and wait. The conference call took another hour, and somewhere in there Robert left."

"And hated him the rest of his life. He must have gone straight back. I never heard anything about him running away."

Gabe nodded. "It would have been a huge, dramatic deal, especially at that age. He's in a spot he can't stand, he runs to his father for help and Whit blows him off."

"Utter betrayal."

Gabe nodded. "Whit screwed up and he knew it. He made another go at trying to get visitation at that point, but neither your grandmother nor Robert was having any."

"That's how Robert is. Once you blow it with him, you blow it for good. There are no second chances."

"Tough to live with."

"Tough way to live. Whit tried to call me a couple of times after the charity dinner. I…I never took his calls." And it was hard, so hard to know he'd watched her and beamed over her from afar.

Gabe turned onto the long road that led up to the Mount Jefferson. The hotel, she realized, her stomach clenching. And her, with a face all patchy from crying. Embarrassing wasn't the word for it. She reached into her purse for sunglasses.

"You won't need those," Gabe told her as he drove back by the manager's house and parked. "You can come in and see Cortland House now, wash up and get yourself together."

Gratefully, Hadley nodded.

It was very like the Crawford Arms, a big clapboard farmhouse with a broad, wraparound porch and paned windows. He led her through the front door and into the little foyer. "There are flats on the second and third floors, your choice. My place is in through here. Hold on, let me get the keys." He ducked through the door for a moment, then reappeared and nodded toward the stairs. "Come on up, I'll show you."

The baluster felt silky smooth in her hands, softened, she imagined, by the hands of generations of tenants. When Gabe unlocked the door, she saw afternoon sun slanting across wide-planked, golden oak floors and slipcovered furniture. And it felt like coming home.

Impulsively, she turned to him. "When can I move in?"

Chapter Eight

Hadley stood at the bathroom mirror and slipped on her earrings, ruby-and-diamond to match her scarlet suit. She made a face. Suits, suits, suits. She'd never really noticed just how regimented and, well, boring her wardrobe had become. Not that she had time or interest in shopping, but it would have been nice to have some options, something that didn't look quite so obsessive compulsive.

Then again, she thought as she walked out into the hotel room, if the shoe fit…

The space was faultlessly tidy, the bed made when she'd gotten up, her work files and computer neatly stacked on the small table that served as an inadequate desk. She'd always found disorder suffocating, worse now when the sum of her personal space consisted of a single room. It was a good thing the move to Cortland House was happening soon.

Her cell phone burbled and she picked it up off the polished cherry dresser and flipped it open. "Hello?"

"Good morning, sweetheart."

"Hello, Mother, how are you?"

"Fine, fine. A little crazy getting ready for Gstaad."

"You don't leave for two weeks, do you?"

"Well, no, but you know I like to get my packing planned early. And the twins are on about it day and night. We're trying to convince your father that we should stop by Paris on the way for some shopping."

"Good luck with that." Hadley tried to imagine Robert following her mother and the twins along the Champs-Elysées.

"He shouldn't mind. After all, he wants his daughters to have nice things," Irene said lightly. "And the twins are growing up so quickly, I'm only going to have so many opportunities for these sorts of outings with them now. I never could get you to enjoy it."

Hadley hadn't ever viewed shopping as a sport the way her mother and the twins did. The times she and Irene had tried it had left them both feeling awkward and misunderstood. How did you manage closeness when you had nothing in common?

"Speaking of the twins," Irene continued, "I wanted to remind you that we're going to be leaving at the end of next week. Don't forget about those Louis Vuitton bags. I need to get them in time to bring with us."

Patience, Hadley told herself. "Mother, I'm in the middle of nowhere. Why don't you just buy the bags and I'll pay you?"

"It's hardly a gift from you if I do the buying," Irene said tartly.

"The nearest Louis Vuitton store is three hours away in Boston."

"So? You have access to the Internet, don't you?"

"I suppose." Though she wasn't thrilled about spending two grand for a purse online. By phone, perhaps, if she could get them to agree to it. If not… Hadley sighed. "I'll see what I can do."

"And don't forget to wrap them."

"Of course."

"You're a dear," Irene said, sunbeams in her voice. Hadley thought of Robert. The demands, the occasional praise for complying. Irene's style was different but the message was the same. Always the same.

"Now I've got something very special picked out for you. The only problem is that it's being shipped from Austria. They've promised me you'll get it before the holiday, but just in case, I wanted you to know it's coming."

Hadley thought of the collection of antique figurines that Irene had sent her over the years, exquisitely worked and utterly insipid. Irene adored them and if she refused to listen to Hadley's gentle attempts to dissuade her, at least she was trying.

They'd just never figured each other out.

"It's okay if it doesn't get here. It's the thought that counts."

"You're sweet. Now have a good day and don't work too hard. I love you."

"I love you, too, Mother." *Even if I don't understand you.*

"Just give me an average for cost per square foot." Gabe interrupted the real estate agent before he could go into full sales pitch mode by phone. "Just a ballpark figure, land only."

"We have some nice listings."

"I'm sure you do. Right now, I just need information."

When he heard the number, Gabe smiled. Lower, far lower than he'd expected. It would help, he thought as he keyed the number into his spreadsheet and thanked the agent before disconnecting. They had a starting point for discussion. He and Hadley could massage the numbers and see what they could come up with for an offer.

Hadley...

His plan was working. The hotel, he thought, was getting under her skin. No surprise there; it got to everyone sooner or later. The only problem was that she was getting under his skin at the same time. If he could have thought of her as just a corporate shark, he could have held out against her. But she was a real woman, warm and vulnerable, and he didn't have a defense against that.

In time with the thought he heard the tap on his door and looked up to see her standing on the threshold. He should have gotten used to the quick jolt he felt every time he saw her. Instead, it was getting harder to ignore. "Good morning."

"Hello." She walked toward him, all red and gold with her hair swinging at her shoulders. "Ready to get to work?"

"Sure." A hint of her scent drifted over to him, whispering of spring mornings and midsummer nights. He forced his mind to business. "I've got the top line numbers assembled for the ski area. Property value, capital equipment, earning power and so on. All estimated, except for the assessment, but it ought to put us in the ballpark."

She took the sheet from him and sat. "I drafted the proposal for them last night. I just need the numbers."

"I can e-mail you the file."

"Only if it's small. Don't forget, I'm on dial-up. Which is becoming a problem, by the way." She nibbled her lip. "Any chance you can set me up with some office space here? A cubicle, even, as long as it has a T1 line."

"I could if we had any open. Unfortunately, we're crammed for space as it is."

"I suppose I could set something up once I move into Cortland House," she said dubiously.

"You could, but you're not going to have anything better than dial-up there."

"The house doesn't have high speed access?"

He resisted the urge to smile at her surprise. Definitely a city girl. "We haven't routed it that far. Don't forget, you're in the sticks here. Maybe in the spring."

"I suppose I could work out of Cortland House and just bring my laptop to the business center in the mornings to receive e-mail."

"You could. Or you could move in here." The impulse came from nowhere, surprising him as much as her.

Hadley blinked. "You mean here, here? This room?"

Gabe nodded. "We'd be sharing but least you'd have a place to work. We can bring in a desk, hook up a new phone extension and data line."

"I don't think it's a good idea." The look on her face was interesting. Not annoyed, not unhappy. Alarmed. Now why would she be alarmed at the fact of sharing an office with him?

Unless he was getting under her skin, as well.

Interesting indeed, he thought. "It makes sense," he said aloud. "We've got a lot of work ahead of us for the acquisition. We need to have immediate access to one another." And before he could block it, the image bloomed in his mind, vivid and sudden, Hadley, just Hadley and nothing else, no tidy red suit, no silk blouse, just her hair loose and spilling over his cheek, and her naked skin, heating under his hands.

Her eyes darkened as she stared at him, as though the words had worked on her, as well. "But…" She moistened her lips. "What about your privacy?"

He banished the image. "You think I have any privacy now? Look at this place. Go get your stuff and let's try it out."

Try it out, indeed.

Morning dragged into lunch, lunch dragged into early afternoon discussions with Jason Keating, the CFO, as they fought with the numbers, massaging the proposal, struggling to build a coherent offer and strategy. Finally, Gabe looked across the table at Hadley. "So do we think this is a deal that could work?"

"I think it's worth testing the waters," she said. "I'd like to keep the offering price as lean as we can for the board. Is there any way to drop the cost?"

"We can drop it all we want," Gabe told her. "The only downside is that your board will approve a number and then Miller and his friends will tell us to go jump in a lake. We need this resort, Hadley."

"And I'm trying to find a way to make it happen," she reminded him sharply. They stared at each other for a moment, gazes crackling.

Keating cleared his throat. "There is a way, but it depends on us closing the deal by year end."

Hadley looked at him as though he'd sprouted two heads. "Pull off a deal like this in three weeks? With the holidays coming? You're out of your mind. We wouldn't even have time to get the idea cleared by the board in that time, let alone talk to the sellers."

"Our fiscal year closes December thirty-first. Our bookkeeping is on a semi-yearly depreciation cycle. If we can buy the ski area by year end, we get six months' of depreciation on it. The write-off will offset the cost of the acquisition by..." He tapped at his laptop keyboard. "We'd be looking at a real outlay a good ten percent lower than the actual bid."

"Ten percent? That's worth pushing it," Gabe said.

"It'll take a big push," Hadley pointed out. "We'll have to go through due diligence in a matter of days. That's site reviews, checking for lawsuits and liens, everything." And it would mean moving forward with contacting Miller before Robert had approved the idea.

"I think the payoff's worth it. A little hard work isn't going to hurt us."

She'd be taking a chance, a big one. The question was was it one she was prepared to take?

Gabe held her eye. "What do you think?"

Hadley took a deep breath and let it out slowly. Sometimes

it was worth taking a risk. "I think we're ready to contact your friend Miller about a meeting."

Day had slipped into dusk by the time Hadley walked with Gabe toward the lobby, feeling the familiar combination of tiredness and exhilaration she always experienced after working hard to put a deal together. Of course, they were only in the starting phase, but they were in good shape to pull it off.

The area around the fireplace and grandfather clock was more crowded than usual, with people spilling out of the conservatory. "I had no idea Friday nights were this busy," Hadley said.

"They are when we kick off a theme event. This is the welcome reception for the Decadent Desserts weekend. As you might imagine, it's popular."

Ice sculptures glittered in the centers of the refreshments tables, where tiny petits fours, éclairs and truffles formed complicated patterns on doily-covered silver trays. Tureens of hot cocoa steamed, islands of whipped cream floating on the surface. Chocolate scented the air. Hadley couldn't remember what they'd done for lunch, but it seemed a very long time ago.

Gabe raised his eyebrows. "Want some?"

"Well, I don't know if we should…"

"Consider it research," he suggested. "Do you want mocha or straight chocolate?"

"Fully leaded," she said, giving in to temptation.

"Good girl." He handed her a mug and they found a pair of chairs away from the crowd where they could sit and watch. "It's Lynn the pastry chef's recipe," he said as Hadley stirred the cocoa. "I don't know what's in it because she guards it like a state secret."

Hadley took a sip and closed her eyes in bliss as the flavor burst through her mouth. "You should guard *her* like a state secret. This is incredible." She opened her eyes to find Gabe watching her. The warmth that flushed through her had little to do with the temperature of the chocolate.

"I'll tell her you said so. Too bad she couldn't see you enjoy it."

Bring it back to something safe, she thought, and raised her mug. "Here's to a good day's work."

"We make a hell of a team."

A hell of a team.

She was having a harder and harder time keeping her head above water here, Hadley realized. Reminding herself not to get involved wasn't helping. Reminding herself it was work helped even less. Instead, she found herself wondering how it would be if things were different, if they could just try out a relationship like normal people.

Even though she knew where that would lead.

Looking away was no help. Couples dotted the room, standing arm in arm at the windows and staring at mountains in the fading afternoon, holding hands at the bar. The sound of low, liquid laughter came across to Hadley, and she saw a nearby couple nestled close together on a wicker love seat. Like a slave girl with her Caesar, the women brushed back her dark hair and picked up a miniature éclair off a plate to feed to her companion. When he nipped at her fingers, she leaned in to chastise him, her humming chuckle sounding quick and intimate.

"It's your turn now." The man picked up a truffle and placed it on the woman's tongue. An expression of orgiastic pleasure slid over her face and Hadley could practically see the heat leap between them. When the man leaned in for a kiss this time, it wasn't quick and careless but hard and proprietary as though she was what he wanted to consume, not the chocolate.

Hadley blinked.

"Chocolate's an aphrodisiac, or so Lynn swears," Gabe murmured in her ear as they watched the couple rise and walk quickly and single-mindedly out of the room. "I think she might have a point."

Something rolled over in Hadley's stomach. When she turned to Gabe, his eyes were very dark.

She cleared her throat. "It looks like your weekend is a success."

"It's improving all the time. Drink your chocolate." He set aside his mug. "Do you still have those expensive snow boots you got yesterday?"

Hadley blinked. "Yes, why?"

"Put on warm clothes and meet me in the portico in about fifteen minutes. There's something I want to get your opinion on."

"What is it?"

He rose. "You'll see."

"A sleigh ride?"

Hadley stared up at Gabe. Dusk had come and gone. The rising moon cast silver light over the landscape. They stood on the grounds just below the portico, where the big drays picked up guests for sleigh rides. But they weren't looking at a dray.

Before them, a big, dark gelding stood patiently in the traces of a light, two-passenger sleigh, his breath showing white in the air. A red blanket covered his back and quarters, matching the glossy red panels of the vehicle.

"It's for the Winter Carnival next weekend," Gabe explained. "I want to take it for a test ride, see what you think."

"Why not stick with the drays?" Hadley asked as he helped her in. The sleigh was smaller than it looked, the seat soft, the front panel curving up before her.

"Not exactly romantic, with twenty people. I wanted more of a couples thing. We've made it part of one of the packages."

When Gabe slipped in beside her, Hadley had the first inkling that she'd made a mistake. He was far too close for comfort. "Where's the driver?"

"There isn't one, at least not for us. Ernie from the stables will drive the guests next week, but I figured we could just take a spin for ourselves." There was a glint of devilry in his grin. "You don't mind, do you?"

Hadley gave him a suspicious look. "You do know what you're doing, right?"

"Sure. We used to have horses at the farm. I've got lots of experience." He laid the tartan wool rug over their lap, tucking it in around her. There was something far too intimate about the gesture, she thought, stifling a sudden impulse to flee. "I don't have a lot of time," she hedged. "Maybe—"

"This won't take long. It's just a little track through the woods." Gabe shook the reins and clicked his tongue.

"Through the woods?" she squeaked, even as the sleigh jerked into motion.

"It's perfectly safe. Don't worry." Gabe flicked her an amused glance. "I don't bite."

It wasn't biting that she was worried about, Hadley thought as the bells jingled and the hotel slid away behind them.

"So how long is the ride?"

"That's one of the things we have to decide," Gabe said. "There's a short version and a longer version. Quality versus quantity. We're using one of the bridle paths, which runs along the edge of the golf course. I thought it was more atmospheric than the grounds below the portico."

A little more atmospheric. That was the problem. "Wouldn't it be better to do this in the daylight?"

"Oh, we'll offer day rides as well, but I thought the moonlight would be good."

"Let me guess. Atmospheric."

"You have to admit it is."

The nearly full moon cast a wash of light over the snow-covered expanse, making the landscape seem to glow. There was an unreality to the whole scene, as though she'd been taken away to some magical world where nothing truly mattered.

"So what do you think about the trail? A short version so we can get lots of guests through or a long version?"

It was hard to think about much of anything at all with his thigh pressed warm and hard against hers under the lap robe. "What about longer and faster?"

"You think?" The sleigh bells rang out as Gabe immediately shook the reins and the horse broke into a trot, making Hadley laugh in surprise.

"Too fast?" Gabe asked.

The trail whizzed by and she laughed again in exhilaration. "No, it's wonderful."

"What about the sleigh bells? I know they're traditional, but I'm wondering if they're just annoying." He gave her a searching look. "On or off?"

"Let's try off." And maybe if he moved away so that she wasn't feeling his body heat anymore she could remember her priorities and stop wondering what it would be like to have him kiss her mindless.

"Whoa, boy," Gabe murmured to the horse, and pulled up, bringing the sleigh to a stop. He wound the reins around the anchor post and patted her knee. "Don't go away."

There was promise in his quick grin, and mischief and fun. And desire; she could see it. A little rush of adrenaline rippled through her.

Snow-iced trees lined one side of the trail. On the other, a creek burbled and beyond it stretched the broad, glowing white expanse of the golf course. Gabe snapped loose the bells and walked back to the sleigh.

"Now we'll try this again." In the ghostly moonlight, his face was stripped down into light and shadow—dark brows, shadowed jaw, gleam of teeth. When he stepped into the sleigh again, Hadley didn't look away, and she didn't look away when he slid onto the seat beside her.

Something deep within her began to thrum.

This time, their travel was nearly silent, with only the occasional jingle of the harness, the breathing of the horse and the sibilant hiss of the runners over the snow. On the hillside behind them, the hotel glowed with light. Here on the snowy trail, the world shrank down to just the two of them.

Ahead, the path forked, part of it continuing and part of it curving back toward the hotel. Gabe brought the sleigh to a halt. Crystalline silence wrapped around them. The mountains glowed in the moonlight.

"This isn't the part where you say your horse is out of gas, right?"

"I thought he might like a rest. Besides, this is the point where we have to decide what happens now."

He could have meant the sleigh ride. He could have meant something else. She wasn't sure she wanted to know. Instead, she stared across the open whiteness of the golf course. "It's beautiful out here," she said softly.

"And you're shivering. Do you want my jacket?" When she shook her head, he shifted closer to her and tucked in the lap robe more tightly. His hands rubbed her thighs. Even through the thick wool, his touch made her dizzy.

Gabe leaned closer to her. "It's your call. Do we go on or do we stop here?"

She needed to tell him to go back. It was the responsible thing, the sensible thing. But when he reached out to trace his fingertips up the line of her jaw and curl them around the nape of her neck, it was already far too late.

She was sinking, sinking slowly in a thick wash of desire. There was every reason to avoid this; she knew it and couldn't make herself care. It wasn't about all the good reasons to do so. None of them mattered. At this moment in the silent moon-light, with Gabe's eyes dark on hers, it wasn't about business at all. It was about man and woman, and if she didn't find out what it was like to kiss him she was going to die.

Hadley felt his breath before she ever felt a touch. When his mouth fused to hers it seemed inevitable, a kiss begun on the dance floor that only just climaxed in this moment.

His lips were cool at first from the frozen night air, and then she felt the heat, the persuasion. The contact shivered through her as though every nerve in her body were concentrated in her lips. She could have held out against demand but his touch was more a question, an invitation, a temptation.

And it made her want more.

Passion flowed through her as her lips parted against his. She tasted a hint of chocolate and more of the flavor that was purely Gabe. Rushing heat took her over, had her straining against him. Like Pandora opening the box, she'd unleashed a power she had no idea existed.

So sweet. Gabe had never guessed she'd be so sweet, like maple sugar on snow, candy in the cold. It dizzied him. He wanted to feel the warmth of her and he cursed the layers of winter clothing that only left imagination. He'd imagined far too often for days, though all of it paled against the reality of her mouth, mobile and avid against his.

With an impatient growl, he pulled her close and dragged them both deep and hard so that the contact of mouth to mouth became everything. Then, giving in to long temptation, he pressed his lips into her neck and inhaled the sweetness of her scent. The soft noise she made sent a punch of desire through him. He fought for control.

The horse gave a snort and stamped, jingling his harness, making the sleigh shift.

Bringing them back to reality.

Hadley blinked and broke away, trying desperately to stop

the dizzying whirl that had swept her up. What in God's name was she thinking of? She already knew she was in trouble with him. What was she doing coming out here so that he could kiss her mind to mush?

No, she thought immediately, that didn't fly. The inescapable fact was that she'd been as much a part of it as he.

She cleared her throat. "Okay, time out. This wasn't very smart."

"It was fun, though." Gabe reached out to toy with the ends of her hair.

She batted away his hand impatiently. "It was also a dumb move. Look, we were probably both curious—"

"I'm still curious," he interrupted, his eyes intent. "In fact, now I'm more curious than ever."

She wrenched her mind loose from the lure of that dark gaze. "Well, you're going to have to deal with that one on your own," she said coolly. "We're working together and we both know better than this."

"Everybody goes off the clock sooner or later."

"Not me." She couldn't afford to; he'd just graphically demonstrated that to her. "We've got a job to do here. This was a slip, nothing more. Now take me back, please."

Gabe stared at her for a long moment. "All right," he said finally. "I'll take you to the hotel. But you and I both know there's only so far back we can go."

Chapter Nine

Gabe crammed his head deeper into the stylish ash electronics cabinet and cursed. He'd been waiting all week to set up his new home theater system. Too bad he hadn't been thinking straight enough to read the directions before he'd started putting the components of his surround sound system in place.

Of course, his thinking process had been a bit derailed ever since the sleigh ride with Hadley Stone. The frustrating thing was that she was right, they had no business getting involved in a physical relationship, and yet for chrissakes, if they were adults and both interested, why shouldn't they?

Wanting her was becoming a constant companion to his waking hours. She'd drawn the lines cleanly, but increasingly he had the urge to just walk right over them. In the light of day he'd debated whether to go find her. Instead, he'd decided to give them both a chance to think.

Which was why he was currently half twisted inside his stereo cabinet doing a lame-ass job setting up his home theater system. With one final attempt, he managed to make the connection. When he punched the on button, the display glowed blue and the system whirred. It was a matter of putting things together in the right order, making sure all the connections were complete before he tried to turn things on.

With Hadley, it meant letting her make the connections she needed, giving her the time. He could be patient when it was warranted, when the result was important enough.

And Hadley, he was realizing, was nothing if not important.

He put in a DVD and flopped back down on his couch with the remote to program the system. When the phone rang, he picked up the receiver without looking. "Hello?"

"Hello? Hello? Is that all you can say to the man who just won the freaking downhill at the Innsbruck Invitational?"

Gabe grinned at J. J. Cooper's voice. "Put the man who just won the Innsbruck Invitational on the line, because he's got to sound like less of a goofball than you."

"I deserve more respect than that."

"You want respect from someone who watched you eat paste?"

"It was high quality paste."

"Paste is paste. So you won it, huh?"

"I seriously kicked ass. Beat Bremer by two tenths of a second. The World Cup is just a matter of time."

"J. J. Cooper, man of destiny?"

"You know it, man. So what do you want? I had to climb off the rest of the team's shoulders and put down my champagne just to come up and call you."

"What a guy. It's not true all those things they say about you." Gabe squinted at the screen and used the remote to set the clock on his new system. "You going to be here at Christmas?"

"Why, you looking to lose some money at poker?"

"The way I remember it, I was the one who whipped your butt last time, Snow White."

"I felt sorry for you. Yeah, I'm going to be home. Why?"

Gabe set aside the remote. "Remember the day we were skiing Crawford Notch and talking about what we'd change if we could? What would you say about really having the chance to do it?"

There was a pause while J.J. digested the information. "What, did you get a job running the resort?"

"Not exactly. We're putting out some feelers to buy it and I need to have a big name to dangle in front of the money men."

"And you want mine."

"Only if you're interested in the job."

"Who the hell wants a job?"

Gabe leaned forward, elbows on his knees. "We're not talking full time or even half time here. We wouldn't even bug you in winter unless you happened to be around."

"Don't count on it. So what would I have to do?"

"Nothing you couldn't handle. We'd pay you for information and endorsement, pure and simple. What I want is someone who has a good idea what we need to do with the mountain, someone who can work with designers to put in some top snowboarding slopes and upgrade the rest. If you can be around occasionally to spread a little stardust, great. We'll definitely want to use your name in marketing materials." Gabe waited. J.J. wouldn't jump in without thinking, but when he gave his word it stuck.

"How much time are we talking about?" J.J. asked finally.

"Maybe five or six weeks' worth all told, spread throughout the year. Meetings, mostly, maybe some autograph signing if you're up for it, some photographs."

"My agent would want to get involved."

"First, you've got to decide if *you* want to be involved." Gabe settled back. "I'm not looking for an answer today. Give it some thought. When you hit town, we can talk it over."

"Fair enough."

"I'm a fair guy. Now go back to your blondes and champagne. Have a few for me."

"The blondes or the champagne?"

Gabe considered. "Champagne." He had a blonde of his own.

Saturday. Hadley's first day off in a week. The last thing she wanted to do was drive all the way down to Boston for a pair of Louis Vuitton bags that her sisters would use maybe three or four times before they went on to something else. There, the Internet certainly had its appeal. But she had shopping to do for her parents, as well, and she believed in the minimum grief theorem—the easiest way to make sure she got everyone things that they would like and on time was to make the drive.

Besides, it would get her mind off of Gabe Trask.

Hadley stepped into the lobby, nodding at Lester.

"Morning, Ms. Stone."

She gave him a mock frown. "Hadley, remember?"

"Hadley, then," he said, giving her a jaunty little salute. "Have yourself a fine day."

"I'll try," she promised, crossing her fingers that Gabe wasn't around. She could do without running into him, thanks. The night before was still too fresh in her mind. But she couldn't very well go storming off like an insulted virgin. After all, she'd been there, too. She just needed to…chill, she decided. Put it in a box marked D for done.

She was good at that.

Crossing the lobby, she stopped at the front desk. "How's everything going this morning, Bill?" she asked the clerk.

"Fine."

"All the events going smoothly?"

"Fine," he said again. Respectful, polite, nothing she could put her finger on. So why was it she could feel the chill coming off him? Tina, Hadley thought, had clearly been talking.

"I need to get down to Boston. Can you help me with that? The concierge doesn't seem to be around."

He frowned. "We don't really have any maps." He dug around and handed her a brochure for the hotel. "Here are directions from Boston. To get there, I assume you just reverse them."

From 93 north… The next best thing to useless. "Thank you."

"Don't mention it." Bill gave her a thin smile that didn't reach his eyes, and walked off.

Hadley pushed down a little surge of annoyance and turned away.

"Wait, don't go." Angie hurried out. "I can help."

Angie, Hadley thought in gratitude, had decided to trust her.

"I heard you asking about Boston. Hank's brother lives in the 'burbs so we go there pretty often. Where do you need to go?"

"Someplace called Copley Plaza?"

"That's a piece of cake. Here, let me draw you a map." She pulled out a piece of paper. "It's a beautiful day for a drive," she said as she sketched.

"So how are you?" Hadley took a closer look at the dark circles under Angie's eyes. "You look like you haven't been getting much sleep."

"Trot took his name literally last night. He kept me awake for hours."

"You're almost there, though, right? Only a couple weeks more?"

Angie looked up. "Three, and trust me, I am counting them. Of course, then the fun's just starting." Her eyes glimmered.

"Oh, you'll be a great mom. Is everything all set?"

"I'm working on it." Angie laid down the pen and pressed her hands into the small of her back with a sigh. "I have a few more things to get but it means going to Stowe and I don't like to drive that far at this point."

"Give me your list," Hadley said impulsively. "I'm going shopping today, anyway."

"That's really sweet of you, but please don't bother. Hank's back soon. I'll get him to take me next week."

"He's on a business trip?"

"Sort of. He's a trucker. He's got a regular run to the West Coast."

A hard arrangement for a couple expecting a child. "He must be gone for a long time."

"Yeah, but he gets four days off between trips. He'll be back Monday. I can't wait."

"Make sure he doesn't make a mistake and wind up in Albuquerque on your due date."

Angie laughed. "Oh, we've got it all arranged. He's taking a long vacation the week before I'm due so we've got time to get everything all set. Now if I could just get a good night's sleep, I'd be great." She slid the paper across to Hadley. "Anyway, here's your map. You just follow it in to the T—the subway," she elaborated, "and take it in to Copley. Everything's really well marked. You shouldn't have any trouble."

"Angie?" Tina poked her head out of the back office. "When you're done talking with Ms. Stone, the advance registration needs to be done for this afternoon's check-ins."

"Yes, ma'am." Angie gave a helpless shrug.

"Well, I'll let you go," Hadley said. "Thanks for the help. Are you sure there's nothing I can get for you?"

Angie looked down at the mound of her belly. "A new body?"

"You're going to have one in just a couple of weeks."

"That's right, I am." And a smile spread over Angie's face like sunlight.

Angie had been right, the day was beautiful, Hadley thought as she headed down the highway. The mountains rolled along beside her, blanketed in snow and a bristly covering of pines. She glanced at her dash clock. Nearly nine. Robert would have finished his Saturday morning tennis game and be set up in his home office. On impulse, she picked up her cell phone and pressed his speed dial number.

"Yes?" His answer was terse, as always.

"It's Hadley."

"I got your memo." Not "how are you?" Not "how has your week been?" He was her boss first and her father last.

"About that memo," she began. "You might as well toss it. That was provisionary, before I completed a real assessment."

"I don't know, it looked pretty complete. Certainly your rec- ommendations are consistent with my expectations."

Just her luck. When she liked a strategy, he usually wanted her to change it. This time she wanted to change and he was trying to hold her to it. "Now that I've got a better feel for the place, I'm considering some different options. I'll be sending you something more detailed in a week or two, once I've re- ally looked around. The place is in better shape than it appeared at first glance."

"Just needs someone to run it properly, it sounds like."

She changed lanes to pass a slow-moving truck. "I think Gabriel Trask is the right person to run the hotel. He under- stands the revenue stream. He's also come up with some good, innovative ideas."

"Innovative ideas usually cost money."

"Innovative ideas also have a way of making money."

"I'm not looking for you to reinvent anything up there, and I don't want any five- or ten-year plans," he said brusquely. "I just want cuts, pure and simple. You've got your targets."

"Trust me, they're taped to the wall just like you always taught me."

"The first step to achieving a goal is knowing what it is." Robert Stone lecture #541. "Of course," she said wearily.

"Speaking of goals, I understand Eliot Ketchum is running into some resistance at Becheron."

Hadley's hands tightened on the wheel. "Upper management can be a bit touchy. He probably went in a little too strong. I tried to warn him but he didn't want to hear it."

"Coddling management is never a good idea."

Lecture #542. "That's what Eliot said when he called."

"So I understand. I also understand you were not helpful."

"I assumed you pulled me from the project because you wanted a different management style. I've been trying to stay out of the way." She didn't add that she'd guessed Ketchum would make his share of enemies.

"I expected you to be professional enough to pass over the reins in an effective manner."

It was that, finally, that got to her. "I spent nearly three months passing over the reins. There's a point where I have to let go, isn't there?" She found herself running up way too fast on the car ahead of her. Consciously, she eased her foot off the accelerator. "I'm responsible for targets here," she added more moderately. "I need to focus on this operation."

Robert considered. "We'll leave it for now, but I expect you to be available to Eliot on a consulting basis."

Hadley bit back a sigh. "All right."

"Was there anything else?"

"No," she said.

"Good. Then I—"

"Yes." The word was out before she knew she was going to say it. "I saw a picture of you at the hotel. It's you and Grandmother and Whit, on the front lawn."

"What about it?" Robert's voice dropped several degrees toward icy.

"You were about three years old. I thought you told me they separated when you were a baby."

"They did."

She thought of the chubby toddler, grinning in his overalls as he stood at his father's feet. "But you were together."

"It must have been someone else," he said coldly.

"No. It's you and Grandmother. She looks happy. So do you."

"What do you want, Hadley?"

"I don't understand. The way the people around here talk about him it's like they knew a totally different person, and they all have good things to say. It doesn't fit."

"Of course they say good things. You're a relative."

"Didn't you ever wonder what he was like?" she persisted, heedless of the warning tone in Robert's voice. "Didn't you ever think about patching things up?"

"No, I did not. I didn't see the point. And I'm not sure I see the point of this discussion."

"I just wish I'd known him, that's all," she said softly.

This time there was no reply. The silence stretched out for long moments. Finally, her father sighed. "Is there anything more, Hadley? I have work to get done here."

Hadley bit her lip. She wasn't sure what she'd expected. Acknowledgment? She hadn't gotten it, but then again she never had when it came to her family. "All right, goodbye."

With a click, the line disconnected.

"I love you, too," she whispered.

Packing normally appealed to Hadley's sense of order. A place for everything and everything tucked tidily in its place. This time around she mostly had the urge to stretch the process out as much as possible, because when it was done she had to leave her little lair and go to Cortland House.

Which meant finally facing Gabe Trask.

So? It wasn't like facing a firing squad, she thought impatiently, pulling her suits, each swathed in dry cleaner's plastic, from the closet. It wasn't a big deal. It had only been a kiss.

They'd discussed what needed to be discussed that night in the sleigh. Now, they just moved ahead with business as usual.

If there were any such thing.

She tugged at the zipper of the garment bag. The bright clothing disappeared and then the only things in the room were her purse, her two black bags and her. Slinging her purse over her shoulder, she headed out to the elevator.

"You're not leaving us, are you?" There was real regret in Lester's tone as he helped put her bags in the car.

"No, I'm just taking a management flat in Cortland House. I thought I'd leave my room for the paying customers."

Lester closed the accordioned doors and took hold of the control lever. "Real nice place, Cortland House. Wait till spring."

"I may not be here then."

"Oh, there's tulips and crocuses and a whole slew of hyacinths and daffodils. It greens up real nice. I'd hate to see you miss it."

"You're in the minority," Hadley said, and cursed herself the minute the words were out.

"Oh, don't take these folks too seriously. They just get worried when the boat gets rocked. They'll warm up to you. You just give 'em time." Lester stopped the elevator at the ground floor. "Now, do you know how to get where you're going?"

She hadn't a clue, she realized. "Through the employees' exit?" she hazarded.

"You got it. Follow the corridor past the shop and cold storage and you'll come out at a little loading dock with a railing. There's a granite-paved path that leads to Cortland House." He looked at her bags. "You want me to send for a bellhop?"

"I can get it." She paused. "And Lester, thanks for the good words."

He winked at her. "I thought you might need them about now. Seems like the least I could do for Whit."

The walk down the concrete corridor of the employee's area netted Hadley a few more tight-lipped nods. It only made her square her shoulders and keep going until she found herself on the deck where she'd first met Gabe. Only a week before, she realized with surprise. It felt like ages ago.

Gritting her teeth against the knife-sharp wind that blew into her face, Hadley hauled her bags over the granite-block path that led to Cortland House. She understood that management needed a little privacy from the hotel, but it seemed like an unnecessarily long walk in the cold. Then she rounded a small stand of trees and the old farmhouse came into view and a smile spread over her face.

For no good reason, it felt like she belonged there.

Gabe stood with his bare feet apart and then stepped into a tae kwon do kata. This was practice, repeating the moves again and again, drilling them into his muscle memory until he could react without thinking. Though he'd only been taking classes for six months, he'd been moving through the belts rapidly, mostly because he loved the movement. It was as much about grace and speed as strength, as much about philosophy as about force.

Spin and step, kick and spin. He ran through the kata over and over, slowly at first and then faster and faster until his breath rasped and his sweatshirt stuck to his back.

He was preparing to start the sequence again when he heard a loud clunk at the door, followed by cursing sufficiently inventive to have his eyebrows raising. Opening his front door, he saw Hadley struggling up the stairs with a pair of bulky bags. Her purse lay on the landing at the bottom of the stairs where it had fallen.

"You get points for creativity," he told her, picking up the purse and mounting the stairs behind her two at a time to take what he judged as the heavier of the two bags out of her hand. "Why don't we trade?"

She stopped on the landing and turned to face him. "I don't need..." Her eyes widened.

"You don't need?" he echoed helpfully, handing her the purse and taking the other bag just as it dropped from her suddenly nerveless fingers. "I'll just get these upstairs for you while you work out the details of what you don't need."

Sex. It vibrated in the air around him, from his damp hair to the Sunday-morning beard darkening his jaw. A line of sweat trickled down his neck. His gray fleece shirt had lost its sleeves somewhere along the line, all the better for showing the hard swell of biceps and shoulders as he carried her bags the rest of the way up.

Hadley just stood for a second, then her mouth shut and she scampered after him. "I can get those myself."

"No need to." Gabe set them down in front of the door. "Consider it a hand from a friendly neighbor. Got your keys?"

"Uh, yes." She dug into her purse and unlocked the door. "I'm sorry I interrupted you."

"It's all right, I was pretty much done."

So was she. Put it in a box, hell. She'd speculated what he'd look like outside of his suits or chunky sweaters. She had no idea he'd look like this, all hard and rangy and utterly, undeniably male.

"Where do you want these, in the bedroom?"

"Here is fine," she said hastily. The last thing she needed was the image of Gabe Trask in her bedroom looking like sex on a stick.

Amusement danced in his eyes as though he knew exactly the effect he was having on her. "Well, let's see, the heating register is in the living room. There's a washer-dryer in the basement in case you need to do laundry. We also have wood down there if you want a fire. Just don't forget to open the flue. Anything else you need?"

You. Naked. On your back. "Nothing, thanks," she said hastily. Wanting and letting herself have were two different things. "Well, um, thanks for the help."

"Sure." He walked to the door and winked. "Welcome to the neighborhood." Whistling, he turned and headed down the stairs.

Chapter Ten

Montpelier was unassuming at first glance, stacked up on the opposite side of the river from the highway that threaded up the south side of the Winooski Valley. Only the golden gleam of the capitol dome hinted that the town was anything more than a backwater. Then Gabe drove across the iron bridge into town and Hadley saw the shape of it emerge, all gracefully aged brick and stately buildings from the turn of the last century.

They parked in a municipal lot and began to walk toward Roderick Miller's office. Hadley hunched her shoulders and tried to ignore the icy wind whisking up under her skirt.

"Want to stop and get a cup of coffee and warm up?" Gabe asked, nodding at a café. "We're still a little early."

"Sure. We can figure out our strategy."

It was an old-fashioned lunch joint with a serpentine steel counter and a broad, sizzling grill. It didn't look as if it had been built to ride on the nostalgia craze, it looked like the real deal, complete with Thirties-era Coke posters on the walls that had probably been put up when they were new.

Hadley and Gabe slid onto a pair of fixed stools.

"What'll it be?" asked the counterman, a burly guy with forearms like Popeye.

"Coffee," Gabe said.

"For me, as well."

He served them with quick, economical motions and turned to the grill, where eggs and a mountain of hashed browns sizzled.

Gabe raised his mug and took a cautious sip, then reached for the cream and sugar. "So how do you want to handle this?"

"At this point, we're just trying to find out if we've got cause for further dialogue. Friendly discussion. We make a starting offer, see what they come back with." Taking her cue from Gabe, Hadley didn't bother to taste the coffee but added cream right off. "We won't really know anything until we go through the letter of intent and a confidentiality agreement. That'll be when the real work begins—we look over the facility, review their financial and legal records."

"Something concrete to show to your board."

"Exactly. I want to hold off on sending the proposal to them until we can speak authoritatively." And, she crossed her fingers, convincingly.

"How autonomous are we? Can we execute the buy without their go-ahead as long as we hit our numbers?"

She stirred her coffee and braved a sip. "At this point, I need the board's buy-in. Anyway, now's not the time for dickering about specifics. We just want to demonstrate that we're serious and we've got a basis for discussion."

"Don't forget, they tried to unload it five years ago and couldn't find a buyer." Gabe abandoned his coffee, pushing it across the counter. "It's not like the resort's been lighting the world on fire since, so I think we can assume they're in the same spot. The right offer will get them moving."

"And the lower the offer, the better our chances of getting the board to go for it." And she hoped to God they did or else she was sunk. "I think you should do the talking. You were the one who talked with Miller initially. You know the history. You can come in from a position of strength."

"And it's a way to downplay the Stone Enterprises link."

"Well yes, there's that as well. If they think big money's be-hind the hotel, they'll try to push it. Let them think it's just a quiet little property."

"Works for me." Gabe glanced at his watch and threw a few dollars on the counter. "Okay, we ready to go do this?"

Hadley took a deep breath. "Lead the way."

"So you're interested in buying the ski area." Roderick Miller, head of Crawford Notch Partners LLC, leaned back in his chair a little. "What makes you think we're interested in selling?"

"The fact that you took this meeting, for one," Gabe said.

"It never hurts to listen. I might learn something useful."

Hadley had disliked him on sight. Well-upholstered and well-padded, his brown hair just beginning to gray artistically at the temples, Miller was a little too sleek and self-satisfied, like a well-fed cat who savored toying with mice. He clearly saw himself as a money man, conveniently ignoring the small stage he operated on. She got the feeling status and control mat-tered more to him than dollars. She got a very strong feeling that he was a petty despot when the opportunity arose.

He folded his hands and gave a slight smile that didn't reach his eyes. "So you're here. Tell me what you have in mind."

"You had the property on the market five years ago and again three years ago," Gabe began. "No sale, in either case. Presumably you couldn't find a buyer or couldn't come to terms."

"And you're prepared to make an offer?"

"If the property looks right. Obviously, we've only been able to do a limited inspection of the facilities. We'll want to go through full disclosure, due diligence and so on."

"Of course, before going to the trouble of that, we really need to make sure that we're thinking along the same lines."

"Of course." Gabe pulled a sheet of paper toward him and wrote a figure on it. "We're thinking something like this."

Miller snorted. "Before we'd be prepared to go much further, we'd need to see something more like this." He wrote a second, higher figure.

Gabe's mouth curved a little as he shook his head. "No way. Not until we see more information."

"Why should we disclose to you if the offer isn't high enough to be serious?"

"Oh, the fact that we're opening with an offer forty percent higher than your asking price of three years ago?"

Miller snorted. "You noticed real estate prices lately?"

"The property values have held steady and there have been no capital improvements in the facilities. The increase reflects both of those facts. Clearly the resort isn't a viable business proposition for your group or you'd be putting more money into it. We're ready to take it off your hands."

"Don't think you're going to come in here and steal it from us. That property is a good fit with your hotel. You want it."

Gabe stayed cool as ice, Hadley noticed admiringly. "Perhaps. That's what we're here to investigate."

"And if it improves your business, you stand to make a tidy profit. Maybe we should really be talking about a merger."

"No merger," Gabe said flatly. "A simple transaction to augment our holdings—if the price is right. You'll make a profit, trust me."

"We won't make a profit with your offer," Miller blustered. "The place is worth much more than that."

"Show us the books. Give us a concrete assessment of the property and we can talk about perhaps changing the terms."

"I want to see a letter of intent with a higher offer first. If we take your number, we'd still be upside down."

Gabe gave a smile Hadley didn't recognize. It wasn't affable, it wasn't people-centric. It was the smile of a predator. "Your group has owned the resort for ten years and you're still upside down on it? You're a smarter businessman than that, Rod. I know what the resort went for at the time you bought it. I know what you've put into it and I know to a pretty good accuracy what you take out."

"Who've you been talking to on my staff?" Miller demanded.

"No one. I do my homework and I've been watching your operation closely. Now you can be reasonable and we can cut a deal that will benefit both of us, or you can keep chiseling for cash and we'll just walk away."

Doubt flickered in Miller's eyes. "You won't pass on this."

"Trust me," Gabe said evenly, "we will. The resort represents a guest services opportunity to us but it's not a make or break. And we can easily run our shuttle to another ski area in future if you still have problems."

Miller evidently didn't like being pushed. But he clearly wasn't prepared to take the chance that the deal might evaporate. He cleared his throat. "We'll need a confidentiality agreement before we can disclose anything, of course. And a letter of intent."

"Of course. I'll have a letter of intent off to you this afternoon. Send the confidentiality agreement over and we'll have our people review it."

"And then we'll get you some information."

"A lot of information, Miller."

"Send the letter," Miller said brusquely.

"This afternoon." Gabe and Hadley rose. "We appreciate your time and we'll be in touch."

* * *

They walked across the parking lot toward the car, Hadley in high good humor. "That went well."

"It pays to be informed."

"How long have you been watching the resort?"

"Since they bought it ten years ago. I talked with Whit about it at the time but he was still paying off the note and I wasn't really in a position to pursue it much." Gabe opened the Explorer's passenger door for her. "I had an idea the information would be useful someday, though."

"You were good in there," she said as he got in himself.

He grinned. "I watch a lot of movies."

"I'm sure. So how well do you know Miller?"

"I've met him at a few business receptions." His seat belt clicked into place. "I made it my business to be where he was a few times. Never knew but what it might be useful."

"You make Machiavelli look like a piker," she said admiringly.

"It pays to be prepared. I really want this to come through. I think it would be good for the hotel."

"And it's kind of fun, admit it."

His eyes gleamed. "Time of my life," he said, and started the engine.

Gabe drove out of Montpelier along the highway that looped and curved along the river. On their left, water rushed along loose and wild, tumbling between snow-covered, tree-lined banks. Hadley was so busy looking at the scenery that it took her a moment to realize they'd strayed from their outbound path.

"Wait a minute, weren't you supposed to turn back there?" She craned her neck to stare at the stop sign where the highway to New Hampshire peeled off.

"Nope."

"What do you mean, nope? That's the way back to the hotel."

"We're not going back to the hotel, at least not yet. There's someplace I want to show you."

Trask Family Farm and Sugar House read a white sign decorated with maple leaves in fall colors. A post-and-rail fence surrounded the rolled gravel parking lot currently populated by handful of cars. A broad porch ran along the length of the long, low gift shop, which connected to a high-peaked sugar house. In summer, she guessed, people sat outside and ate the maple creams advertised on a sign by the door. Just now, with snow covering the ground and broad patches of the graveled parking lot, all of the picnic tables were stacked off to one side.

Gabe's family. Just the idea made her uneasy. She wasn't big on making conversation with strangers at the best of times. Oh, she could do it for business when she had to, but in a social setting she looked forward to it with about as much enthusiasm as she would a root canal. "Are you here to do an errand or something?"

He gave her a curious look. "No. We were in the neighborhood. I figured I'd stop in and say hello." He got out of the truck.

"It's the middle of the day," she protested as he opened her door. "Aren't they busy making syrup or whatever?"

"Sap only runs in the spring," he said, shaking his head pityingly. "Jacob's not boiling anything right now."

"Jacob?"

"My older brother. You'll probably meet him. Come on in. You might even get a maple candy if you're good."

"How about if I just stay here while you go inside and do whatever? If I try to cross that parking lot I'll die."

He looked across the gravel and snow of the parking lot and glanced down at her needle-heeled pumps. "Ah. I take it you didn't bring your snow boots."

"Nobody said anything about a field trip," she said darkly. And she'd take a cheap excuse. "These are Ferragamos and I'd just as soon not ruin them. You go on. I'll wait."

"Nope. It's thirty degrees today. I'm not having a frozen woman on my conscience. Get out and I'll help you."

"But they're still going to get wet," she protested.

"Out."

With a glower, Hadley stepped out onto the running board, then gave a little shriek of surprise as he swept her up into his arms. Something giddy skittered through her, something that had no business being there. He shoved the truck door closed with one elbow and began walking, his chest warm and hard against her.

"Put me down," she managed to gasp with what breath she had left.

"Stop twisting or you'll make me drop you." Gabe strode matter-of-factly toward the porch. She fit just about right in his arms, the warm weight of her against him as he went up the path. It didn't satisfy his hunger a bit, but that was all right. He was a patient man.

Struggling was undignified, that was why Hadley hooked an arm around his neck. It didn't have anything to do with the fact that he'd hefted her with about as much effort as he'd carried her garment bag, or that the feel of his arms around her reminded her way too much of the sleigh. She wasn't some airhead who got impressed by muscles or by memories of stolen kisses in the moonlight.

Gabe approached the steps. "Well, here we are."

When he lowered her, his arms slipped down to her waist, pressing her lightly against him. The added height of her heels brought them face-to-face. Then he leaned in just a bit and her heart vaulted in her chest.

"I don't suppose you've changed your mind since this weekend," he said conversationally, so close that she could feel the brush of his lips as he said the words. "Be a shame to miss this opportunity."

She felt a flush of heat. And weakness, sneaky weakness began to spread through her. While she could still muster the strength, Hadley shook her head and pushed away from him. "We should get inside."

"We should definitely do something," Gabe agreed.

The gift shop was an Aladdin's cave of treasures—pot holders and hand-milled soaps, dish towels and ceramic teapots, trivets, fancy jellies, recipe books, and everywhere, everywhere maple.

"Gabriel!" A woman's glad voice rang out as they stepped inside. Tall and slender, she ducked out of the little enclosed cashier's island, pushing her short, gray hair out of her face. "What a wonderful surprise!" She pulled him into an enthusiastic hug and bussed him on the cheek. "What brings you here?"

"Business in Montpelier. I thought I'd stop by. This is Hadley Stone," he said, turning her toward Hadley. "We work together at the hotel. Hadley, this is my mother, Molly Trask."

"Nice to meet you, Hadley," Molly said warmly. She'd caught a bit of the parking lot activities through the window, watching with interest. Now she studied Hadley speculatively.

"It's a pleasure to meet you." Hadley put out her hand and found it taken in a surprisingly strong grip. None of those girlie, squeeze-with-the-fingertips holds for Molly Trask. She shook like she meant it. "I can see Gabe takes after you," Hadley said, studying Molly's high cheekbones and generous mouth.

Molly gave a rueful glance at her jeans and flannel shirt. "Not in the clothing department, that's for sure. It's a good thing I work here where people don't care."

"You're still gorgeous." Gabe squeezed her. "You always will be."

"Oh pshaw," she said, but her cheeks tinted in pleasure.

"Is Jacob around?"

"He's up in the Bixley Road sugar bush cutting brush, but he should be down soon. The ice cream machine's gone on the fritz and I need him to fix it." She nodded toward an arch at the end of the room that led to a bright café.

"You want me to take a look?"

"Oh don't. You'll mess up your nice clothes."

But Gabe was already taking off his jacket and rolling up his sleeves. "I'll just lay a towel on the floor. What's the problem?"

"It sounds like the cooling fan threw a screw or something. It started clanking and then it just stopped."

"Let me take a gander." He moved behind the machine.

Molly turned to her. "Can I get you something to drink, Hadley? Coffee? Cider? It's fresh-made down the road."

"Cider would be lovely, thanks."

Molly bustled behind the counter and poured a couple of glasses. "Gabriel, I'm leaving one on the counter for you."

The only response was the clank of tools.

"We might as well sit down. This could take awhile," Molly said, waving Hadley toward one of the oilcloth-covered picnic tables in the café. "So what do you do at the hotel?"

"I'm helping with the transition to the new owners."

"It's too bad about the previous owner."

"He was my grandfather." Whit's death had never mattered to Hadley before, beyond the regret she'd feel for any stranger's death. The quick stab of sadness she felt as she said the words now surprised her.

Quick compassion filled Molly's blue eyes. "I'm so sorry. I know Gabriel thought highly of him."

"So did everyone else, apparently. I didn't know him well."

"That's a shame."

"It is," Hadley agreed.

"So you're not from here, I take it. How long have you been in New Hampshire?"

"Just a few weeks."

"It must be hard being away from your family."

"Ma," Gabriel called from behind the counter, "you're grilling."

"I am not grilling," Molly answered. "I'm just being friendly."

"Be friendly in another way."

"I'm not grilling," Molly said to Hadley. "It's just that I know what it's like. My son Nicholas lives down in Boston now. We'd hoped that all the boys would stay around, Adam and I, but things happen."

"You're understanding about it," Hadley said, thinking of Robert and Irene.

"Why wouldn't I be? They've got their own lives to lead. I can't keep them around simply because I'd like it. I'm just happy for the time they make." She raised her voice. "Especially when they fix my ice cream machine."

"Just call me the Maytag Man," Gabe said.

Molly's grin was fond. "Anyway, I know how hard it is to be away from the people you're close to, especially after losing your grandfather. Any time you'd like a home-cooked meal, come on by. For Christmas, even, if you can't get home."

"Ma," Gabe began.

At that moment the door to the outside opened and Grizzly Adams walked in, or a close approximation with black beard and eyes the color of the cobalt glass Hadley had seen in the gift shop. "Is that Gabe's car outside?" the giant rumbled.

"Ten points." Gabe's muffled voice came from behind the counter.

The man pulled off his bulky mackinaw to reveal a running back's physique. "If you make that thing worse, you're paying for it," he called to Gabe.

"Jacob, behave yourself," Molly said reprovingly. "You're in front of a guest. This is Gabriel's co-worker, Hadley. Hadley, meet my eldest son, Jacob."

"Pleased to meet you." Jacob's hand was callused from work. "Gabe, let me in there so I can fix the damn thing."

"I've got it." Gabe reappeared and flipped the front switch on the machine. It rumbled to life.

"Couldn't have been too broken," Jacob muttered as the two men shook hands.

"You're just cranky because you came up here expecting a break and now you've got to go back to clearing brush."

"I like clearing brush."

"No doubt. You can exercise your undeniable charm on the squirrels."

Jacob merely snorted.

"Hadley should see the sugar house while she's here," Molly said. "Can you give her the tour?"

Jacob shifted uncomfortably. "Let Gabe do it. I have to stop by my house and get my gloves, and I want to finish that section I'm working on by nightfall. Nice to meet you, Hadley." He hesitated, nodded and walked out.

"Jacob's the antisocial one," Gabe told her.

"He's not antisocial, he's just shy," Molly said.

"He's antisocial, Ma."

Molly just shook her head. "You have to let people be who they are, Gabriel," she said reprovingly. "I'll take Hadley on the tour if you'll give me just a minute."

Hadley blinked. In her family, Jacob would never have gotten off so easily. If she'd refused a request—or a command performance, really—her parents would have made their displeasure known. Molly just seemed to take it in stride.

Gabe motioned Hadley toward the gift shop. "Come on, we might get some ideas for the Mount Jefferson store," he said, drifting back into Aladdin's cave.

Maple. It was everywhere: maple syrup, maple butter—whatever that was—granulated maple sugar, maple candies, maple pepper… She frowned. "Maple pepper?"

"You've never heard of it? It's great." He picked up the tester and handed it to her. "Try some."

Unable to resist, Hadley shook a little on her palm and touched the tip of her tongue to it experimentally. She glanced up and caught Gabe's eyes on hers as the taste spread through her mouth. Sharp, salty with an elusive hint of savory. She raised her head slowly.

"What's it like?" he asked.

She swallowed, throat suddenly dry. "Sweet. Peppery. A mix."

"Like some people I know."

She moved to dust off her hand but he reached out and caught her fingers. Eyes locked on hers, he raised her palm toward his mouth and deliberately, unhurriedly, licked the last bit of maple pepper off of it.

And lust exploded through her. Warm, wet. The touch of his tongue turned her bones to liquid. She couldn't think, couldn't process anything but the touch, the promise, the desire thudding through her veins.

"Hate to see you waste it," he said, closing her fingers over her palm.

"Are you ready for that tou—" Molly came into the room behind them. "Or maybe later."

"No, come back," Hadley said desperately, turning away from Gabe. "I'd love to see it. We're all done here. Aren't we, Gabe?" She glanced back.

He looked at her with unfathomable eyes. "For now."

Chapter Eleven

Hadley strode up to the Mount Jefferson from the parking area, cell phone clamped to her ear, immersed in conversation with Lloyd Archer, their head of legal. "I left Burke from facilities inspecting the equipment at the ski area. We'll have the contractor and assessor out on Monday."

The previous day had been a whirl of activity as they'd bloody-mindedly pushed through the confidentiality agreement by close of business hours, despite demands for a legal review and a ridiculous number of signatures on all sides. The day had been a blur but at least it had given her no chance to dwell on just what the hell she was going to do about Gabriel Trask.

"So what roadblocks are you running into on your end?" she demanded, happy to keep the previous day's distractive momentum going. "We've got to confirm that they don't have any outstanding lawsuits against the property. That's key."

"We can get them to sign an official disclosure."

"Not good enough," she interrupted. "I don't trust this guy. If they're not letting you at the legal records, go down to county and search the casebooks."

"You're talking about an incredible amount of man-hours," Archer warned. "I'll have to haul in two or three paralegals."

"Money, I've got. Time I don't. Do what you need to to get it done." She disconnected and mounted the stairs to the hotel porch. Just for a moment, she stopped and savored the picture. Familiarity hadn't diminished the spell. Walking through the gleaming white door into the lobby still gave her a charge.

Even more so now. Christmas had come to the Mount Jefferson. A twenty-foot spruce festooned with red velvet bows and antique ornaments perfumed the air of the lobby. Garlands and ribbons twined up the banisters of the grand staircase. Pine boughs draped over the mantelpieces. The lobby columns were swathed with cotton wool and faerie lights. It was like walking into wonderland.

"Beautiful, isn't it?" Angie asked from the front desk.

"Hi, Angie. Yes, it's gorgeous. I can't believe it."

"Alicia is amazing." Angie shifted uncomfortably.

Hadley looked at her in concern. "Are you okay? You're not hurting, are you?"

"What I am is desperate," she confessed, shifting again. "Could I ask you a huge favor? Could you just stand here for two minutes while I go to the bathroom? I am dying."

"Oh God, of course, go."

Over at the elevator, Lester saluted Hadley as she stepped behind the counter. "Part of the team, I see."

The lobby looked different from behind the desk. Just the act of walking behind the polished wood barrier somehow made her feel like a part of things. Then she spotted a man with iron-gray hair walking toward her. Hurry Angie, hurry. She beamed the message desperately. To cover her uneasiness, Hadley gave him a big smile. "Good afternoon, sir. Can I help you?"

He slid his key onto the counter. "Can you tell me where I get the shuttle to the ski area?"

An easy one, thank God. Hadley picked up the key. "Go out the front doors here and wait. The shuttle stops right under the portico, runs every fifteen minutes."

"Great, thanks."

"My pleasure." She turned to the bank of pigeonholes behind her and tucked the key carefully into the correct slot.

"You're a lifesaver," Angie breathed, slipping back behind the counter a few moments later.

Hadley frowned. "You of all people shouldn't be stuck here alone. I mean, what if something happened? Aren't there usually a couple of people assigned here?"

"René and Bill are both out with that stomach flu that's going around. Of all the rotten luck. I mean, Winter Carnival starts today. I don't see how we're going to keep up when the big rush hits. It's going to be a nightmare."

"Where's Tina?"

"She just left for lunch. She had to go to the bank but she said she'd be back as soon as she could."

Angie looked exhausted, with dark circles under her eyes. Formerly, she'd glowed with pregnancy. Now, she just looked tapped out by the load she was carrying.

"You look like you're still having trouble sleeping. Are you running yourself ragged getting ready? Is Hank around?"

"No, that's part of the problem. I never sleep right when he's gone." She grimaced in discomfort.

Hadley's concern was immediate. "What's wrong?"

"I had a maplerito craving at lunch. It's revisiting me."

"*Maplerito?*"

"A bean burrito with maple syrup. I know—" Angie laughed and pressed a hand to her stomach "—it's revolting."

"You pregnant women and your cravings," Hadley said, walking over to the computer and tapping the shift key to bring up the screen. "So how does this thing work?"

"The registration system?"

"Yeah. Show me how to use it."

Angie's brow furrowed. "I can't let you do that."

"Come on, it can't be that hard to do the basics. Then I can watch the desk for a little while and you can take a break."

"But…you can't…this isn't your job," Angie spluttered.

"I'm like Gabe. Anything that happens here is my job."

"Tina will freak."

"Leave Tina to me," Hadley ordered. "Now show me."

The system was fairly straightforward, so long as the guest had a reservation. Angie went through the process twice, with Hadley taking notes, then Hadley tried it out. "Okay, I think I've got it. Now you go in back and get off your feet for fifteen minutes. I'll let you know if I need you."

Angie clutched her stomach for a moment and nodded. "I think I hear the ladies' room calling me again."

A moment later, a couple with a pair of children approached the desk. "Hi, we'd like to check in," said the man.

"I'm Hadley," she replied with a smile. "Welcome to the Hotel Mount Jefferson."

Gabe walked through the lobby, stooping to pick up an errant straw wrapper that had somehow blown over from the bar. He'd checked the prep work in the kitchen, assured himself that rooms for the new check-ins would be ready by three, touched base with Alicia on the events schedule and visited the stable to make sure the sleighs and horses were all set. The next stop was the front desk, and he figured on being there for a while. There was never a good time for people to get sick, but the opening day of the Winter Carnival weekend was worst than most. He stopped at the lobby bar. "Hey, Lorraine."

"Hi, Mr. Trask," the waitress said, tray at her hip.

"I hate to give you one more thing to do, but keep an eye on the check-in line, will you? If you see people having to wait, bring by a tray of sodas for them. We might not be able to speed things up, but at least we can keep them happy."

"Sure, Mr. Trask. So far, it's been moving pretty well. Ms. Stone has been helping them out."

"Ms. Stone?" He leaned around a pillar just in time to see Hadley pick up a guest's credit card with a beaming smile. "How about that," he murmured to himself.

"I didn't think her type would pitch in."

"I think her type gets the job done, no matter what."

Lorraine cleared cups and glasses off of an unoccupied table. "You ask me, we could use a few more like her."

"We could," he agreed. "See you later, Lorraine."

"See you, Mr. Trask."

Hadley Stone, desk clerk. Interesting.

"And here's your key, Mr. Breyer. Have a pleasant stay with us."

Hadley glanced down to clear her screen.

"What are you doing here?" an icy voice demanded.

Hadley turned to see Tina Wheeler. "Hi, Tina. Glad you're back. Angie was having some trouble so I figured I'd help out."

Tina bristled. "This isn't your job."

"I don't mind."

A guest walked up to the front desk, credit card in hand, but Tina ignored him. "Where's Angie? She should be out here."

It triggered Hadley's protective instinct. "She wasn't feeling well. I sent her to the back for a break."

"She can't just leave the desk when we're shorthanded." Another pair of guests drifted up to stand in the line.

"I told her to."

Tina was furious, Hadley could tell, but afraid to push it. "We have a schedule for breaks," she said stiffly.

"When was the last time you saw a pregnant woman keep to a break schedule?" Hadley asked.

Tina paled. "Are you questioning my judgment?"

"I was trying to point out why I stepped in, though now that you mention it, maybe your judgment should be questioned. Next person in line," Hadley called.

"I still don't understand how you wound up back here."

Angie emerged from the back, looking wan and holding her stomach. "Tina—"

"Did you ask Ms. Stone to fill in for you?" Tina demanded.

"I did," said a steely voice behind them.

Hadley spun to see Gabe standing there, his eyes coldly furious.

Tina looked as if she'd swallowed a bug. "You okayed it?"

"We were shorthanded. I asked Angie to train Hadley while you were out at lunch."

Angie stared at the terminal, her face scrubbed of all expression.

"Now, I'm sure you can see the line we've got out here." Gabe's even voice held the snap of command. "Let's skip the discussion and get these guests into their rooms. Next in line, please," he said more loudly.

It was a hard way to make a living, Hadley discovered as the day wore on. She might have faced more pressure and more exhausting hours before, but being on her feet and constantly on show wore her down. How Angie stood up to it, pregnant and heavy, Hadley hadn't a clue. By midafternoon, the flow of guests had increased from a trickle to a flood.

"I need to change the card my room charges to," the guest in front of her said. At a loss, Hadley looked around for help. Angie was occupied, Gabe was gone. That left only…

She bit back a sigh. "Tina, can you help me out?"

Tina gave her a frigid look. "Card, please?" She took it and began clicking keys furiously. "There you are," she said to the guest, handing the credit card back.

"Thank you," Hadley said when she was finished. Tina nodded and walked away without speaking.

Angie nudged Hadley. "Don't feel bad. She gets like that sometimes."

"So I've noticed."

"No, really, she's been great about my pregnancy and stuff. She's just worried about René and Bill being out and the big weekend and all. She's not so bad, really."

"Angie, you're a saint."

"No, I just do my job." She picked up a key a guest had set on the counter, and turned to the pigeonholes. Suddenly, she made a little noise of distress and closed her eyes.

"Are you okay?" Hadley asked immediately.

After a few seconds, Angie managed a faint smile. "The burrito again. Maybe I should go back to the ladies' room."

"You've been going every few minutes since I got here." A suspicion began to grow in Hadley's mind. "Those gas pains wouldn't be regularly spaced, by any chance, would they?"

"I haven't noticed. I…" Angie's head tilted. "You don't mean labor pains, do you?"

"Could they be?"

"I'm not due for two weeks."

"Since when has that mattered to pregnant women? Are you sure they feel like gas pains?"

"Well I…" Angie faltered.

"That's what I thought." Hadley nodded. "I don't think we take a chance. Let's get you to the doctor. *Tina*," she called.

Tina reappeared from the back with a frown. "What?"

"It's Angie. We need to get her to the hospital. I think she might be having labor pains."

Tina's eyes widened, the frown gone. "What should we do?"

"We'll get Mr. Trask." Gabe would know what to do. Hadley snatched up the twin to his walkie-talkie cell phone.

The handset beeped. "Trask."

"Gabe, Hadley. We need you, now. Angie's baby's coming."

"Two minutes," he promised, and hung up.

One thing he could say for the job, life was never dull. Calculating the distance to the nearest hospital as he walked, Gabe flipped open his phone and called the valets to bring the hotel car around. No way would Angie be able to get into his Explorer in her condition.

"Where is she?" he asked as he approached the front desk.

Tina looked completely stressed out. It was Hadley who answered. "In back." She appeared calm but for the line of concern furrowed between her eyebrows.

Behind the partition, Angie sat back in an office chair, looking pale. Crouching down before her, he took her hands in his. "How are you doing?"

She was sweating a little, he saw. "I'm okay. It's probably nothing." She sounded calm but a little shaky around the edges. "My sister went into false labor twice before she had her kids. I'm not due for another two weeks."

"Tell that to Trot." That earned him a brief smile. "Look, I don't want to mess around with this. I'm going to take you to the hospital and we'll put you in good hands."

"But what if it's all for nothing?"

"It's worth it just to find out it's nothing. Anyway, I'm doing this for my own protection." He rose. "Hank would kick my ass all the way through Crawford Notch if I didn't take care of you. Now, they're bringing the hotel car around front. Can you get up with me and make it out to the porch?"

She nodded and he helped her up. She was just a kid, he realized, for all her capable efficiency.

"Okay, we're taking Angie to the emergency clinic. It's closest," he said as he walked her to the front.

"Do they deliver babies?" Hadley asked.

"They do now. I need someone to sit with her in the back in case she needs anything."

Hadley stepped forward. "I'll go."

Getting Angie to the car wasn't quick, delayed by a stop for another contraction. Hoping devoutly that the hospital was near, Hadley laid towels on the back seat of the town car and helped Angie lie back against the pillows, her head in Hadley's lap.

"Everybody all set?" Gabe asked, leaning in the open door.

"Ready to go," Hadley told him. She smoothed the hair off Angie's forehead as the car headed down the long curving drive. "You okay, kiddo?"

Angie managed a wobbly smile. "I guess. I mean, I know I am. It's just a little scary to think it might actually be here."

"Well, you don't need to worry. We're going to get you to the doctor and you're going to have a beautiful baby boy." Hadley thanked her lucky stars again for Gabe's calm, reassuring presence. "So tell me about Trot's nursery."

Gabe turned from the access road to the highway.

"Well, the walls are yellow and we've got a blue crib. I was going to get a mobile for him when Hank got home…." Her voice quivered and she stopped a minute before she continued. "My mama got us one of those intercoms so I'll be able to hear him at night if he—" Abruptly, Angie whitened and began a fast, whistling breath.

Hadley glanced at her watch. "The contractions are getting closer." Her eyes met Gabe's in the rearview mirror and he silently held up five fingers. They were close, at least. She wished desperately that she knew enough about labor to tell whether they had enough time. "Do you want to call Hank or your family to tell them what's going on?"

Angie relaxed again, looking paler. "I don't want to tell Hank. He'll only worry and there's nothing he can do." She rubbed her hands over her belly. "Once we get to the hospital and find out if it's for real, I can call my mom. She's down in Albany, but she can be here in a few hours."

"Is she going to stay with you after the baby comes?"

"She's going to stay for a month, which'll be good. Hank's never been around babies so he's terrified."

That would make two of them, Hadley thought. "Have you?"

"I lived with my sister when she had hers. I've changed my share of diapers. I'm more worried about the delivery."

"We'll be at the hospital soon," Hadley said reassuringly, wiping the sweat off Angie's forehead.

"A couple of minutes," Gabe called.

She hoped he was right. The contractions were getting too close for comfort, and while Hadley had every confidence she could deal with whatever came up, she didn't really care to test herself by delivering a baby.

"So is Hank excited about being a daddy?"

"He's already bought a baseball mitt, even though Trot's going to have to wait about six years to use it."

"I like a man who plans ahead," Gabe interjected.

Angie laughed. "This time he planned too far ahead. He wanted to be around my last week so he switched his schedule. Otherwise he'd be home right now."

"I'm betting he'll get home pretty quick once he hears."

Angie gave a smothered groan and more sweat sprang up on her forehead. Seconds stretched out as she tensed, moving her head in silent pain. Finally, she relaxed.

"A bad one?" Hadley asked.

She nodded. "I'll be okay. Just do me one favor."

"Sure, anything."

"When we get there, tell them to forget the natural childbirth thing. I don't want the breathing and the full beautiful experience. I want drugs."

Hadley laughed. "I'll make sure you get them."

"Okay, Angie, we're here," Gabe said, and brought the car around in an arc under the overhang of the E.R.

Chapter Twelve

Gabe had always figured he'd have kids someday. He'd never particularly thought about the realities of it, though, not until he sat in the lobby of the clinic and listened to Angie cry out.

He wiped his forehead, suddenly hot.

"Getting to you?" Hadley asked.

"Right now, adoption is seeming like a really good option."

"I can't believe how brave she was. I was beginning to get worried we weren't going to make it. If I were her, I'd have been in a panic."

"She had you there with her. You were good," he said.

Looking both pleased and embarrassed, Hadley fiddled with her fingers. "I didn't do much except hold her hand and pray that she didn't have it in the car."

"We'd have done all right. I played catcher in high school." A door opened down the hall.

Hadley laughed. "How good are you at barehanding?"

He looked at her. "The best." Beautiful and fearless. Was it any wonder he was beginning to go nuts for her?

At the sound of a throat clearing Hadley and Gabe looked up to see a nurse standing over them. "Are you Hadley?"

She nodded. "Did Angie deliver?"

"She's close. She's a little scared and a little lonely and she was asking for you. How would you feel about scrubbing up and coming in to sit with her for the last bit?"

Shock, panic and horror chased across Hadley's face. She reached out blindly and clutched Gabe's thigh. "She wants me?" Her voice squeaked. "In the delivery room?"

"She's probably got a little while longer in labor and then we'll take her in." The nurse gave a sympathetic smile. "You don't have to. It just might help her to have some support."

He watched Hadley scrape her nerve together, bit by bit. Finally, she took a deep breath and rose. "No problem. Just show me where to go."

As the nurse led her away, Hadley threw a desperate glance over her shoulder at him. Then she straightened her shoulders and walked through the doors.

"It's a boy." Hadley stood before him in a surgical gown, pulling the cap off her pale hair, a dazed look on her face.

"Is Angie all right?"

An ear-to-ear grin split her face. "She's fabulous. She was so great, she did just what they told her to do and it was the most amazing thing I've ever seen in my life." Hadley sank down next to him. "Oh Gabe, he's beautiful. I've never been much on kids but this baby is gorgeous."

"You wouldn't be just a little biased, would you?"

She gave him a haughty look. "Not in the least. He's fine, but they're going to transfer him to the preemie nursery at the hospital for a couple of days. Angie's asleep. She's wiped, poor thing."

"After an hour and a half in labor, she ought to be. And here we were worried about her having it in the car."

"I know. Actually, it was quick compared to some of the horror stories you hear. Painful." She gave a little shudder. "But you should have seen her face when they held Trot up to her." Hadley blinked a few times and her nose pinkened.

"You need to just sit down and chill for a while?"

She pulled off the gown and gave a dreamy sigh. "I don't think so. There's nothing we can really do here. Angie will probably sleep for a week. I've left a message for her to call me if she needs anything when she wakes up, but that won't be for a while."

"Her mom should be here in a couple of hours. She said she'd leave right away when I talked with her."

"I suppose we can get going, then." Hadley stood, wrapping up her gown and hat and stuffing it into a nearby bin. "We've still got a Winter Carnival to run, don't we?"

"I think we already had our thrill ride for today."

It was disorienting when she returned to realize it was only a little after five. It seemed as though days had gone by since she and Gabe had packed Angie off to the clinic. Instead, the evening activities at the hotel were just coming to a peak and every pair of hands was needed, including hers.

She checked in guests, made dinner reservations, gave directions, assisted at the ice sculpture demonstration, cleared tables in the lounge, guided people down to the jingling sleighs, and took photographs of merrymakers. Seven-thirty found her stapling up the velvet hem of one of the Victorian carolers who roved through the hotel.

After, she ducked into the back to replace the stapler, only to find Tina behind her.

"What are you still doing here?" Hadley asked with an internal groan.

"Same as you. Work to be done." Shifting her feet, Tina stared at the carpet. "How's Angie?"

"Fine. She said to tell everyone hi."

Abruptly, Tina raised her head to stare at Hadley. "I screwed up today." The words were defiant.

"It wasn't an easy situation," Hadley said carefully. "You were juggling a lot of things."

"I shouldn't have left Angie alone." The fight in Tina's voice diminished.

"No," Hadley agreed, "but it was an unusual situation. Everything worked out okay."

"Because you stepped in."

"Tina?" She waited until Tina met her eyes. "We're all on the same team here."

"Really?" The edge was back. "When you can lay off half of us any day? It's kind of hard to be sure whose team you're on."

It was the fundamental question. There was a time when Hadley she would have answered "Stone Enterprises" without hesitation. There was a time when she'd been clear on her objectives. Somehow, the lines weren't as apparent anymore.

Then she thought of Angie, of Lester, of Ed at the railway, of Gabe. Of Gabe. And she realized the lines really were apparent, after all.

"I'm on this team and I'm going to do everything in my power to take care of the hotel and everyone in it. You've got my word on that."

Tina studied her. "Even if your bosses won't like it?"

"I'll convince them they do."

"Somehow I think you can do that," Tina said slowly.

"Count on it."

By the time she was able to finally break away, over an hour later, Hadley was almost staggering. After standing in her pumps for nearly ten hours straight, sliding on her snow boots felt exquisite. Ridiculous, of course, to have to put on boots and an overcoat to make a hundred-yard walk, but it hadn't taken her long to learn to respect winter in the White Mountains.

Skaters whirled around the frozen pond behind the hotel, but Hadley had no eye for them. Instead, she headed down the path to Cortland House. All she had to do was go another hundred yards and when she got there she was going to go dead to the world, at least until the next morning, when she'd promised Tina she'd come back and start all over again.

The porch light shone out like a beacon, guiding her home. So she'd yet to actually stock the kitchen except for a couple of cans of soup. It was still her place, all five rooms.

At least for the time being.

As she neared the house, she heard the rapid crunch of footsteps behind her. "It's a good thing you decided to take off," Gabe said. "I was just about to come in and boot you out." He climbed the steps to the porch with her, pulling out his keys.

"Me? What about you?"

He shrugged as he unlocked the door. "I didn't help deliver a baby today. Besides, it sort of goes with the territory for me. It's not really your job."

"No problem." She stepped in ahead of him. "I was happy to help." And it had made her feel a part of something, essential in a way she never really had.

"Lots of people would have figured it wasn't their business. Thank you isn't nearly enough."

"It wasn't a big deal." She stood at the bottom landing, stifling a sigh at the thought of climbing the stairs.

Gabe looked at her. "Do you even have anything to eat up there?" he asked abruptly.

Minestrone and crackers probably didn't count, she supposed, but it was all she'd been able to find nearby. Making the half hour drive to the nearest supermarket had been more than she'd been able to face. "I'll figure out something."

"Have dinner with me."

"I couldn't...."

"Consider it a thank-you. You were there for Angie today, plus you worked yourself blind. Come in," he invited. "You don't even have to talk to me. Just sit, eat and head upstairs."

Warm light spilled out of his door and suddenly the idea of going up to her cold, empty flat to a can of soup seemed decidedly unappealing. Just once she wanted to have dinner with a live person, someone else across the table to talk with. Or not precisely someone else.

She wanted it to be Gabe.

"Let me get out of these clothes."

His eyes lit. "Great. I'll leave the door open for you."

It was a foolish move, she lectured herself even as she tossed her coat down on her couch. She should take a bath, get some sleep. She shouldn't be playing with fire, and spending the evening alone with Gabe Trask definitely qualified as incendiary. But she was tired of being sensible, tired of doing the right thing. For once she just wanted to do something that felt good, have a relaxing evening with an interesting companion.

She'd deal with tomorrow when she got there.

Gabe stood in front of his open refrigerator, pondering the riddle of dinner. Suave invitation. Too bad the only thing he had for an intimate dinner à deux was a bottle of good meritage. Clearly, the chicken breast he'd gotten out that morning wouldn't do. He had venison medallions in the freezer, but no time to get them defrosted. Pizza? He rejected the idea even as it formed.

"Hello?"

He heard a knock on his hall door. "In here," he called. As he turned toward the hallway, he caught sight of a blue box on his open shelves and snapped his fingers. Pasta. Pasta was the ticket.

When he saw her in the hallway, he smiled. It was the first time he'd seen her in casual clothes. She wore jeans and a fisherman's sweater big enough to hide a small pony. Her hair was soft and loose. She looked about fifteen.

"Is this Gabe's Bar and Grill?"

"Tonight, I think it's Gabe's House of Pasta."

"Beats what I had upstairs."

"Hey, I'm not the head of food and beverage for nothing. Want some wine?"

"Sure." She followed him back into the kitchen. "So why did you take on food and beverage with all you have to do?"

"I like food and wine and it was one way to cut costs. Red okay, by the way?"

"Sure." She took a seat in one of the tall kitchen chairs set up around his peninsula. "It's too cold for white."

Digging out his corkscrew, Gabe opened the meritage. "I'm thinking about carrying this in the dining room. Tell me what you think." He handed a glass to her, then raised his own. "Here's to surviving the first night of the Winter Carnival."

"Don't jinx yourself. It's not over yet."

"I know it, trust me. I'll probably take a walk over in a while, just to see how they're making out."

She propped her chin in her hand. "Some people might call you a workaholic."

"They'd be wrong. I'm lazy, I just choose my times."

"Mmm." She sipped her wine. "This is really nice."

"Isn't it? It'll be a midrange wine, not something that requires a big splurge."

She took another taste. "So what are we having tonight, Mr. Food and Beverage?"

"Watch and find out."

He put a pot of water on the stove to boil for pasta, and started slicing the chicken into cubes.

"Something I can do to help?"

"You can cut up the broccoli."

She took a swallow of wine and rose to wash her hands. She'd taken off most of her makeup but freshened up her scent. There was something essentially female about it, something that spoke of woman, not of girl. And it made him want.

But he'd invited her for company, not a seduction, he reminded himself. And even though his desire for her had grown into an all-encompassing ache, he wasn't going to do a bait and switch. Instead, he schooled himself to ignore it. Placing a cutting board in front of her with a knife and the broccoli, he went to work chopping a clove of garlic.

Hadley poked dubiously at the broccoli with the tip of the knife. "What do you want me to do?"

Gabe grinned and relaxed, turning on the heat under the sauté pan. "Cook a lot, do you?"

She gave him a disdainful look. "No one in Manhattan cooks. We live off restaurants, takeout and the salad bar at the corner grocery."

"I see. We don't have salad bars at the corner grocery here."

"I've noticed."

"We don't have corner groceries. You'll have to learn to fend for yourself. Cut the florets off the top and peel and slice what's left."

"Aye aye, captain."

He added some oil to the simmering water then splashed some in the hot pan. A sizzling filled the air as he added the garlic, tossing it around as it cooked, then the chicken.

"So are you a trained chef?"

"Nah, I just like to eat well. I watch the guys in the kitchen, try to pick up what I can."

"Including leftovers?" Cutting the broccoli became easier as she got the hang of it, she discovered.

"If we're trying out something new. Mostly I try to take care of the hotel, not let it take care of me." He took the chopped broccoli from her and raked it into the pan, pausing in his stirring occasionally to give the pasta a whirl.

"You really love it, don't you? The hotel, I mean."

"It grows on you. Don't forget, I've worked here more than half of my life."

She sank back down on the chair. "You're doing something important. Preserving something."

"I like to think so."

"But then you take care of everybody, don't you?"

He made a face. "Not exactly a dynamic recommendation."

"Why not? It means you stand for the things you believe in, you stand for the people. You came to the rescue today. Tina had Angie in her sights and it was going to get ugly."

He reached in a cabinet to get a jar of pine nuts and threw a handful in with the chicken. "Tina has her moments but she's actually a good person. She's just a perfectionist, and I think she's intimidated by you."

"By the idea of layoffs, maybe. We talked about it. Things are better now."

"Good, I'm glad. But I still think she's intimidated."

"Why? I'm not going to call for layoffs. In fact, I'm specifically going to recommend against it." She rose to get a couple of pasta bowls from his open-fronted cabinets. "I'm not going to mess with her. Why should she be intimidated?"

He snorted. "Let's see. It might be because you're the hotshot from corporate. Or the fact that you dress like something out of a fashion magazine or that you can think rings around virtually everyone." He drained the pasta, releasing a cloud of steam. "Or it could be the fact that you're beautiful."

She stared at him as he tossed the chicken mixture and pasta together in a deep, blue bowl, adding a few dollops of pesto and some black olives from the refrigerator. He gave her a guileless look. "Feel like eating in the living room?"

* * *

It reminded her of a stylish fifties jazz bar, with classic leather furniture and polished wood, neither garishly modern nor slavishly period. The carpet was soft and deep, the shelves held books and pieces of art or things that interested him. The walls glowed a rich teal.

"This is wonderful," Hadley said as she sat.

"I do have a dining table but this is the warmest place in the house this time of year. With the high ceilings, it takes the radiators awhile to get going, but the fireplace heats this room up pretty quick." He moved to the granite hearth and began to wad up newspaper.

"Show me how you do it." She set her bowl aside and rose. "I tried to start a fire the other night and I couldn't get it to light. Now I've got a fireplace full of singed wood."

"Did you use kindling?"

"I took some sticks from the bin but they wouldn't catch. Do you need lighter fluid or something?"

He laughed. "No, you just need to build the fire right. Come on." He patted the carpet beside him. "I'll give you a hands-on lesson."

She hesitated.

"You're not going to learn from over there."

Lighting a fire. How dangerous could it be? Hadley came over and knelt beside him.

"The idea is that you start with lots of stuff that burns easy underneath so that by the time it's all gone, the logs are burning. Okay?"

His hair had flopped down over his forehead. He looked, she thought, endearingly intent. Then his eyes snared hers and she felt that snap of sexuality again. Endearing, hell. The man was dangerous.

"First, you want to wad up bunches of newspaper and pack

them into the grate. One sheet at a time but you want to do seven or eight of them."

Hoping for her system to settle, Hadley began crumpling up sheets of newsprint and laying them in the fireplace.

"Not too tightly." Gabe reached past her to adjust the paper, his arm bumping hers. "Air's got to be able to come up from underneath. Good. Now you add some sticks of kindling on top, laid in a crisscross pattern."

"Do I get a fire-lighting merit badge for this?"

"Only if it works. Now you lay the wood on top." He handed her a piece of split oak from the wood box at his elbow. She wasn't prepared for its weight and it tipped her toward him. He caught her with his hands on her shoulders.

And they were eye to eye as they'd been too many times before. Always, she'd been the one to keep control. This time, she couldn't move away, couldn't do anything but stare. This time, they would come together and it wouldn't be an innocent kiss in the moonlight. This time…

The oak lowered bit by bit to rest on Gabe's thigh and he started, releasing her and giving his head a brisk shake. "All right." He cleared his throat. "Lay it on the kindling with the rough side down." His voice was husky and he didn't touch her as he watched her put the oak in place. "Good. Now light it."

Hadley pulled out one of the long fireplace matches and struck it, then held it to the kindling.

"No, like this." Gabe closed his hand over hers. Reaction flashed through her. He moved the match to the edge of the grate, one arm behind her so that she was almost cradled against him as he touched the flame of the match to the paper again and again, the flame leaping up. When he was finished, he drew the mesh fire curtain across and brought the match back toward his lips to blow it out.

But he didn't look at the match. He looked at her.

The flame danced between their faces, shifting with each

breath they took. His eyes flickered with the reflection. His expression was intent, as though he were trying to look inside her. The breath clogged in her lungs. She wanted to escape and yet somehow she knew there wasn't any escape anymore.

Then with a low curse Gabe blew out the flame and dragged her into his arms.

Heat. It bloomed between them, whether from the igniting wood or from their bodies, she couldn't tell. This wasn't like that night in the sleigh. There was nothing cool or tentative about it. This time, they both knew what they were after and there was no hesitation.

This time, they took.

The rush of desire in her veins was familiar, the pressure of his lips known. When he plundered her mouth, she met him move for move, seeking out the heady flavor of the wine, rediscovering him. It didn't matter that she'd told herself again and again she had no business getting near him. She'd held back before but this time the draw was too strong, the connection too deep.

He nipped at her lip and the fleeting pain had her catching her breath in surprise. Almost before she could react, his mouth closed over hers again, taking her deep, dragging her down into hot passion where only arousal mattered. How could a kiss take her so far? How could a touch of lips become something that involved all of her, something that bound them together?

The slick friction of tongue on tongue shivered through her and set up an answering tension between her thighs. And she sank back on the thick carpet.

Gabe leaned in, his mouth hot and hard on hers. Eyes closed, she could see the orange of the flames through her lids as his hands roved over her body, dragging a moan from her. She felt the warmth of his lips moving down over her throat, tasting, sampling, then roving up over her jaw and along her cheek. The fire in the grate was no match for what burned between them.

He'd tried, Gabe thought feverishly, he'd tried to keep from doing this, kneeling beside her with the scent of her hair tangling his senses, looking into her eyes to see that she wanted as he wanted, and still not taking.

He couldn't release her now. Now, he wanted everything at once, wanted to feel her everywhere, to taste her. And yet he fought back the urge to rush. It was the time to go slowly, to savor. He could feel her body, firm and springy under the sweater, and then he slid his hand underneath just a bit, enough to feel the silky skin of her belly quivering under his fingers. She was so responsive it threatened to take him too far.

Hadley moaned and tightened her arms around him. This was what she'd searched for, this feeling, this wholeness. He was everything she wanted, everything she needed.

Everything she needed?

She broke away and sat up, staring at the fire, shattered. That he was a risk, she'd discovered in the moonlight, but she'd never guessed how big. And now, in a few short minutes, she'd laid herself open to him completely. It would have taken so little to continue, so little to take the next step of discovery that her greedy body demanded.

And God help her then.

"What are we doing?" Her voice was low.

"What we've both been thinking about for days. Don't tell me you haven't because I know better."

"It doesn't matter. I know better than this." She was shivering now despite the fire, arms wrapped around herself. "I must be out of my mind."

"Why? What's the problem?"

"A bad breakup for starters." Inevitable heartbreak because he could do it to her; she'd just seen it.

"I don't operate like that," Gabe said, giving her a level look. "And something tells me you don't, either."

"You don't understand," she said desperately.

"Help me. Why is this so scary?"

Because love didn't last and she was already in way too deep. "I don't do this. I don't get involved."

"Maybe you should."

"I can't." She raised her eyes to his and all the defenses dropped. He saw the confused wanting. And he saw the fear. Desire ground through him but the look in her eyes left him powerless to act on it. He dropped his hands.

"I want you," he said softly.

"And I can't do this." She rose, swaying, and stepped to the door. "I'm sorry, Gabe," she whispered. And she fled.

Chapter Thirteen

Airports looked the same the world over, Gabe thought, as he stood in the arrivals hall in Montpelier. Baggage carousels, luggage carts, the same half-dazed looks on the faces of the travelers whose minds hadn't caught up yet with their bodies.

He had a similar problem, only it was his body that hadn't caught up with his mind. Intellectually, he knew that what had started with Hadley that night in front of the fire was on hold. That didn't keep him from dreaming about her. That didn't keep him from waking with the low, dull ache of desire grinding through him.

The job was just an excuse. It was more than that, whatever held her back. He remembered her body, quivering against his, and he remembered the desperation in her voice after. And the fear. *I can't do this.* Why not? Why was she at risk?

There were too many walls around her, too many secrets. And now they were both supposed to go back to business as usual and pretend nothing had happened? No way. Patient?

Sure, he'd give her all the time she needed. But he wasn't going to back away. Sooner or later she was going to let him in.

He heard throaty female laughter and turned to see J.J. and a pair of neatly dressed flight attendants coming past security. J.J. towed their roller bags gallantly, his own backpack thrown over his shoulder. "Now, you both know where to find me. Come on over to Crawford Notch, I'll teach you how to ski," he promised, then his eyes lit on Gabe. "Hey, wait, here's my friend who owns the maple sugar farm." J.J. waved Gabe over.

The flight attendants twittered and laughed and finally, regretfully, took their roller bags back. J.J. kissed them on their cheeks and waved goodbye.

Blond and outdoorsy, looking more like a California beach boy than a lifelong Vermonter, J.J. stuck out his hand.

Gabe shook his hand and slapped his shoulder. "Man, you never stop, do you?"

"Hey, I just make friends easily. They're here until Saturday and they want to learn how to ski. Maureen, the little redhead, loves maple syrup. You've got an in there."

"Thanks, I'll pass."

"Why? You got some hot babe you're working on?" They started walking toward the luggage carousel.

"Why do you ask?"

"Because you never looked twice at her, and I'd have picked her for just your type."

"Maybe my type has changed," Gabe said, thinking of Hadley.

J.J. squinted at him. "You been up to something while I've been gone?"

"Not nearly as much as it sounds like you've been up to."

"Hey, I've just been spreading goodwill among nations."

"Yeah, France, Sweden, Switzerland, Czech Republic, and, where was the snowboarder from again?"

J.J. got a beatific smile on his face. "Finland."

"You and your Eurochicks." A buzzer sounded and the belt began going around on the luggage carrousel.

"You and your redheads."

"There's something to be said for blondes, too," Gabe said, remembering Hadley, warm and fragrant in his arms.

"Who is she?"

Gabe blinked. "What?"

"The look on your face. Oh man, you've been nailed. Who is she? Someone from around here?"

"Isn't that your bag?"

J.J. reached over to hook the duffel bag as it went past. "Nice try, Trask," he said, throwing it over his shoulder and turned to the oversized luggage window to get his skis. "Spill it."

"Nothing to spill." Gabe turned toward the glass doors.

"You've really got it bad if you won't even talk about her. Is this serious?"

It was the question Gabe couldn't bring himself to ask because the follow-on question was what came next.

And he didn't have an answer to that.

"So what happened in the Toblerone Grand Prix?" Gabe said abruptly.

J.J. stared at him for a long moment. Finally, he shook his head and started walking. "Let me tell you about the Toblerone." The discussion of the error that relegated J.J. to second took most of the trek to the car. The description of the beautiful blonde from Helsinki who'd warmed his bed for a week took the rest. It wasn't until Gabe was on the road out of the airport that J.J. stretched back in his seat and turned to him.

"So," he said lazily. "When do I meet the future Mrs. Trask?"

"He's so tiny." Hadley sat on the couch in Angie's cramped living room and looked at Trot, newly home from the hospital.

"He's nearly eight pounds," Angie said proudly, rocking the little bundle in his blue blanket. "They said he was strong enough to go home yesterday."

There was a sound of a door opening in the kitchen. "Ang," a man's voice called. "I'm back."

"In here, hon," she called. "Come meet my friend Hadley."

A tall, skinny man appeared, wiping his hands on his jeans.

"Hank, I'd like you to meet Hadley Stone. She's the one who took me to the hospital. Hadley, this is my husband, Hank."

Hank crossed the room to Hadley. "Pleased to meet you." He released her hand and balled his own in his pockets, watching his wife and son. "I can't thank you enough for taking care of Angie while I was gone. She told me about you and Mr. Trask and all."

"We were happy to do it," Hadley said.

"Hank didn't get home until last night," Angie added. "Drove like a madman."

Hank shifted in embarrassment. "Not too much. I maybe had a little bit of a lead foot. I wanted to get home to meet my boy."

"He's beautiful," Hadley said sincerely, staring at the little flowerlike face.

"Do you want to hold him?" Angie asked.

Terror spurted through her. "Oh no, I couldn't—"

"Sure you can. Sweetheart, would you pass Trot over to Hadley?"

Now it was Hank's turn to look terrified, even as Angie smiled at him like a satisfied Madonna. "I don't want to drop him."

"You won't," she soothed, passing the baby into Hank's huge hands. "Just be sure to support his head like I showed you."

As though he were carrying a soap bubble that might burst

at any moment, Hank brought the baby to Hadley, transferring him with an audible sigh of relief.

Trot was whisper light, sleeping peacefully, his lashes forming little fans on his perfect, pale cheeks. She remembered seeing him burst out into the world, and a wave of tenderness washed over her. Had she held her sisters when they were this age? Unlikely. Her mother and the nanny had been so protective of them that Hadley wasn't allowed near the crib in case she carried some infection. By the time the twins were two, Hadley was off to prep school.

Trot stirred and yawned, stretching up one tiny fist, then he looked at her. "Oh my God," she said, startled. "Angie, he's got your eyes."

"Do you think so?"

A perfect little being with his whole life ahead of him. Hadley blinked back the sudden sting of tears and carried him back over to Angie. "He's so gorgeous."

"Isn't he?" Angie stroked Trot's cheek. Hank reached over to put his hand on her shoulder.

They were a unit, Hadley realized. Maybe they were fighting to make ends meet and maybe they lived in a rickety little cracker box of a house, but they were bound together, by life and by love. A family unit. Part of each other. The way it was supposed to be.

And memories came flooding back of that night by the fire with Gabe, when she'd felt open to him, connected to him in a way she couldn't block. And she could try to pretend it hadn't happened but she couldn't forget it—it was there every time she saw him. She studied the glow on Angie's face, on Hank's. Was it really possible to trust and not just feel terrified and vulnerable? Did people really love each other or did it inevitably turn into a list of expectations?

"Listen, I should be getting back," she said abruptly. "I just wanted to stop by and see how you were."

"I don't know how to thank you for all that you've done," Angie said. "And the presents you bought for Trot."

Some diapers and a wind-up musical toy, Hadley thought. Little enough. "Oh Angie, thanks for letting me be a part of it. I'm so happy for you." She leaned over and kissed her on the cheek. "If you need anything at all, you let me know, all right?" She turned to Hank. "You make sure she does."

He grinned, looking suddenly boyish. "Yes, ma'am."

It was done, Hadley thought later. She stared at her computer screen, at the proposal that represented the efforts of weeks compacted of necessity into days. Everyone had weighed in, the numbers agreed. It was time to give it a kiss and send it on its way. Gstaad or no, her father would almost certainly be checking e-mail—one thing Robert Stone insisted on above all was connectivity.

At the sound of raised voices in the hall, she rose to investigate. A knot of people filled the hallway, among them Susan, Gabe's assistant.

"Now, we had an appointment with this Alicia Toupin," a man in a business suit was saying. A very irritated looking man.

"I'm sorry," Susan said smoothly. "Pete is at an off-site meeting and Alicia is running a seminar right now. Our master calendar shows you arriving tomorrow."

"We came all the way from Burlington." He pushed his chin out pugnaciously. "Forget about tomorrow. We're talking about bringing a hundred and fifty people in here for a week. Isn't there anyone in this damn-fool place who can talk to us?"

"I can," Hadley said smoothly, walking up.

"The place looks good," J.J. said to Gabe as they stepped into the Hotel Mount Jefferson lobby. "You've been fixing it up." He winked at Tina, who blushed and turned away.

"I'm so glad you approve," Gabe said dryly, moving toward the executive wing.

"What's the rush?" J.J. slowed. "I'm taking in the scenery."

"Who is she?" Gabe asked in resignation.

"The girl of my dreams." J.J.'s voice was reverent.

Gabe glanced across the lobby to see Hadley in a narrow white suit, talking with a small knot of businessmen. He watched with interest as she walked them into one of the meeting rooms, emerging like a tour guide with the procession trailing behind, saying something that had them all laughing.

Then she looked up and saw him and the spontaneous smile bloomed, lovely enough to dizzy him. "Why Gabe, I'm so happy to see you." She turned to the group. "Gentlemen, it looks like our timing is perfect. I'd like you to meet our general manager, Gabe Trask. Gabe, meet Jim Pritchard, Hideo Tanaka and Dean Ballinger from Ness Packaging in Burlington. I've lured them into having their summer sales meeting here. Isn't that right, Jim?"

Pritchard gave an affable smile. "Quite a facility you've got. I've heard good things about the course."

"Eighteen holes designed by Donald Ross."

"And don't forget, we're putting in wireless Internet next month," Hadley added.

Gabe kept his jaw from dropping, just. "Exactly. Thanks for reminding me."

"So I'll get an estimate together based on the numbers you gave me," Hadley continued. "We should have something in your hands tomorrow or the next day. Any questions?"

"Nothing we can think of right now," Pritchard said. "We'll let you know if we think of any."

"You do that." She beamed at him. "Safe travel. We'll be in touch."

Gabe watched them leave, and turned to Hadley with a raised eyebrow. "Wireless Internet?"

"It won't cost much. It's worth doing for the corporate business."

"Weren't you the woman who came here to cut costs?"

"I came here to increase profits," she corrected. "What matters is achieving the goal, not how you do it."

"Here, here. So speaking of achieving the goal, can I introduce you to my buddy J. J. Cooper? J.J., this is Hadley Stone of Stone Enterprises, our new parent company."

Hadley shook his hand. "Nice to meet you."

Dark blue eyes widened suddenly as if a riddle had suddenly been solved. "Oh," he said, breaking into a dazzling smile that held more than its share of mischief. "Oh yeah, it's nice to meet you."

Gabe glanced at his watch. "It's getting on five o'clock. Why don't we just call it a day and meet over dinner."

"Scooter's?" J.J. raised his eyebrows.

Gabe looked pained. "Wouldn't you rather go somewhere quiet where we can get something better than grease stains?"

"I'm not asking for much," J.J. reminded him. "I've been stuck in Europe for the last three months. You're here. You can go anytime you want. You forget that."

Gabe sighed. "All right, Scooter's it is."

Scooter's wasn't exactly the type of restaurant she associated with business meetings. Strains of honky-tonk from the jukebox bounced off the exposed beams and rough pine paneling of the walls. Butcher paper topped the tables. A juice can full of crayons sat in the middle. The menu ran to burgers and pizza, grinders and ribs.

J.J. sat with an expression of bliss.

Hadley turned to them after the waitress had left. "So I take it this was your hangout once upon a time?"

"In the summers when we both worked in Crawford Notch," Gabe said. "It was pretty much our hangout for about six years."

"So you have have been friends for…"

"Let me see," Gabe said. "His parents started paying me in, what, kindergarten?"

"Third grade," J.J. supplied.

Gabe nodded. "Mrs. Ruble's class."

"How could I forget? Times tables."

"Not J.J.'s forte," Gabe explained.

"We worked out an arrangement," J.J. added.

"You mean you cheated?"

"Cheated?" Gabe looked at J.J.

"No." His friend shook his head.

"Nope." Gabe shook his head even more vigorously.

"Definitely not."

"Tutoring." Gabe gave her a guileless smile.

"Exactly," J.J. affirmed.

"I was going to blow him off after high school," Gabe added, "but he got dependent so I hung out summers."

What would it be like, Hadley wondered, to know someone for that many years? To have a friend who remembered you as a gap-toothed kid, an uncertain adolescent, a young adult giddy with freedom? Someone whose sentences you could finish. She couldn't imagine it.

She envied it.

It wasn't like seeing a different Gabe so much as a three-dimensional one. Seeing him with J.J. made her like him even more. Not good, she thought uneasily. The last thing she needed was to like Gabe Trask any more than she already did.

When she saw the waitress approach with their meals, she almost sighed with relief.

"Best greasy burgers around." J.J. pushed his empty plate away.

To her infinite surprise, Hadley found herself agreeing.

Gabe gave a lazy smile. "We've got our claims to fame. This

is one of them. I'd like the Crawford Notch ski area to be another. You give any consideration to what I suggested?"

"I've though about it once or twice since we talked." J.J. folded his arms on the table.

"And?"

"How serious are you about doing this?"

"Very," Hadley said flatly. "If everything goes well, we should close by year end."

"And how soon would you start working on the slopes?"

"We'll start working on plans for upgrades to the lodge and an expansion of the Crawford Arms right away," Gabe said. "How soon we start on the slopes depends on you. We'd want to have a plan in place by late April, which would be when we'd add the new lift. We'd begin construction in early May, aim to open around the end of November."

"Six months." J.J. took a drink of his beer. "That's not much time for what you're talking about."

"We're not going to get everything done the first year. We'll have to stage it, but I want at least two snowboarding slopes in place and half of the ski slopes upgraded for next winter. We can finish the rest after."

"And we'll want you around for the opening," Hadley added.

"If you can work around my race schedule."

"Are you going to be comfortable with your name being used like that?" she asked. Better to have it out now than dance around it.

"If the product is good." He looked from Gabe to Hadley. "It needs to be done right. I don't want Gabe and me out on a limb and have somebody cut it off."

"You've got my word on it," Gabe said. "And the contract will protect you."

J.J. didn't take his eyes off Hadley. "You, I trust. There's a big company behind this, though, with lawyers who can probably get them out of anything. How do I know the agreement will hold?"

"You've got my word." Hadley's voice was calm. "We want you involved. You've skied all around the world, you know what works and what doesn't. We can help you articulate your ideas. We'll make it work."

J.J. looked at her for a moment longer and then nodded. "All right. You guys close on the deal to buy the resort and we can start putting something together."

A cell phone burbled. Gabe pulled his out, scowling at the display. "It's the hotel. Excuse me a minute while I get this." He rose and headed back by the bathrooms.

J.J. and Hadley glanced at one another. With business to talk about, with Gabe around, conversation had been easy. Now, the silence weighed on them. "So." She stirred her martini with the swizzle stick. "It must have been quite a change to go from living up here to traveling Europe on the World Cup circuit."

"No more than leaving Manhattan to come to Crawford Notch."

"I suppose. I'm not uprooting my entire life, though."

He looked at her more closely. "Just a short timer, huh?"

"My job is usually triage and resuscitation. Once an acquisition gets running smoothly, it gets passed on."

"Does Gabe know that?"

What exactly was he asking? she wondered. "He knows the business model. It's not like I'll be completely setting the hotel adrift, I just won't be around for the day to day."

J.J. nodded to the beat of the jukebox. "Kind of slow up here for you, I guess."

"Not at all. I like it better than I thought I would." And Robert would never let her stay, she reminded herself. The pang of regret surprised her in its sharpness. "But we move around in my company. That's the way it's done."

"Maybe you should think about getting a different company.

I mean, are you telling me that if you decide you really like it here you can't stick around and see the results? The whole reason I want to try this director of ski thing is that I want to be here in five years when the runs are all cherry and know that I helped make it happen. I love this area."

"I can understand why."

"But not enough to stick around?" His eyes were steady on hers.

"I'm afraid I don't have a choice."

"Let me tell you something, Hadley," he said, leaning forward to whisper conspiratorially. "There's always a choice. You just have to have the courage to make it."

Chapter Fourteen

Christmas Eve dawned sunny and clear. Compared to the noise and hubbub of the Winter Carnival the weekend before, the hotel felt positively empty as Hadley made what had become her habitual midday walk-through. They had guests, perhaps fifty of them being entertained at various events, but mostly the Mount Jefferson was coasting into the holiday.

"Hey."

She turned to see Gabe behind her, and smiled without thinking. "Hi. How was skiing yesterday? You and J.J. have fun?"

"Fun?" He frowned at her. "That wasn't about fun. That was work. We had to review the whole mountain."

"On skis."

"You bet."

"Multiple times, I assume."

"Of course multiple times. We had to make sure our data

was accurate. It took some doing, I'll tell you. And we went back this morning to get more. On a Saturday, no less."

"Boy, you really are a workaholic."

He grinned. "Just trying to do my best by the hotel."

"Hell of a job."

"Isn't it, though? Happy Christmas Eve, by the way."

"You, too."

"Sure you won't change your mind and come to the farm for Christmas? I know my mom would love to have you."

"No, but thanks, really." Holidays with her own family were bad enough. With strangers? Too awkward to contemplate. She'd rather watch movies and eat the chocolate chunk Häagen-Dazs she'd picked up on her long-delayed visit to the grocery store.

"I'll be thinking of you."

That got to her. She made herself ignore the little twinge of longing. "I'm sure you'll keep busy," she managed to answer lightly.

"More like crazed," he said, but there was affection in his voice. "Listen, I've got to get J.J. back to Montpelier. I figured I'd stop by the farm and make an appearance before tomorrow, but I should be back later. Maybe we can have a Christmas Eve toast. Get the holidays off on the right foot."

For a second, she didn't answer and then she smiled. "I'd like that."

The executive wing was quiet, making it easy for her to immerse herself in the work that still needed to be done on the acquisition. The discussion to negotiate the final offer was scheduled for Monday, the day after Christmas. She didn't expect it to be easy. Then again, few things that mattered were.

Her cell phone rang in the silence, making her jump. She let out a long breath. "Hello?"

"What is the meaning of this?" Robert Stone's voice crackled out of Hadley's cell phone.

Her stomach knotted up. "I guess you got my e-mail."

"What I didn't get was your list of cost-cutting measures. Acquisitions and market analyses and multimillion dollar outlays." The words dripped with scorn. "You were supposed to go up there and sort things out. Instead, you send me this ridiculous document."

"It's not a ridiculous document," she said with a calmness she didn't feel. "It's a business proposal."

"Did I ask you for a business proposal?"

She looked at the clock. It was, she calculated, sometime after eight in Gstaad. After eight on Christmas Eve. "Shouldn't we talk about this another time? I'm sure Mother and the twins would rather you were spending Christmas Eve with them. This can wait until next week, can't it?"

"No it can not. I'm putting a stop to this right now. You are not to begin discussions on this, you understand?"

But she already had. Hadley swallowed. "Is there a flaw in the business model?"

"Excuse me?"

"Is there a flaw in the business model?" she repeated, her voice tight with anxiety. "Is there some reason you don't feel it makes sense to move forward?"

There was a short silence. She'd never stood up to her father before, never done anything but comply immediately with his every wish. She'd certainly never had the temerity to question his decisions.

She wondered what insanity was driving her to do it now.

"Yes, there's a reason—I told you to make cuts."

"We're proposing a scenario that positions the hotel for growth. Granted, it involves an outlay—"

"And I told you I don't want to see outlays. Certainly not, what is it, six million dollars? What are you thinking?"

A cold, hard ball formed in her stomach. He hadn't read the proposal. He couldn't have done more than skim the first sentence of the executive summary or he'd know that the real cost was far less than six million.

"If you read on, you'll see that it's quite reasonable."

"I don't have to read on. You call these kinds of numbers reasonable?"

But he'd spent fifty times that much on a recent acquisition that was ten times as speculative. "The capital equipment and land alone are worth nearly that. Untouched, it would pay for itself within five years."

"Five years? That's pathetic. And that ignores the fact that you're proposing to sink another three million into it. What kind of fantasy world are you living in?"

Two sentences, she amended. If she were lucky, maybe she could get him to read the whole first paragraph by the end of the call. "If we make those changes, the resort will pay for itself—and the upgrades—in two years. In four, we'll double our money. And that's the ski facility alone. That's not counting what it'll do for the hotel. You want your profit numbers, give me three good seasons with the upgraded ski area and you'll have them."

"I don't want to hit our numbers in three years, I want to hit them now. Forget about it."

"Please don't order me to walk away from this." Her voice was low but the anger had begun to flicker. "I can make this into something."

"So far, it doesn't look like you're doing anything but wasting money and time. You've disappointed me before, but this really takes the cake, Hadley."

How could he just sweep it aside without even reading it? Hours—they had put hours into crafting a bulletproof proposal that addressed every conceivable obstacle except one— the possibility that he would never even read it. "How can you tell if you don't even bother to look at my work?" she demanded.

She could practically hear his shock vibrate over the phone lines. "I refuse to waste any more time on this," Robert snapped, recovering. "You are not going through with this acquisition and that is final. I want that list of cost-cutting measures in my in-box by Tuesday, understand?"

"No." Hadley felt strangely calm.

"Now you listen to me," Robert thundered.

"No," she repeated, more forcefully. "Not until you start listening to *me*. Good night, Father."

And hands shaking, she terminated the call.

In movies and books, people had fights and felt suddenly powerful, transformed. Hadley just felt jittery and faintly sick. Putting down the phone, she pressed the heels of her hands to her eyes. What in God's name was she thinking, talking to her father like that? There was no telling what he would do. He'd crush her—and the hotel and Gabe and everyone in his path.

She rose and began to pace. She couldn't go forward with the acquisition now. If the board found out she was countermanding a direct order, she'd be out, Stone or no. And when Robert found out... She shuddered. She was out of her mind to even think about it. What she needed to do was start making his cuts, working to minimize as much as she could the damage she had just caused.

The thing was, she knew they were right about the ski area.

The phone shrilled on the desk. At the sight of the country code, her stomach roiled. She wasn't ready to talk to him, not yet. Not until she'd had a chance to think. The ring repeated, as peremptory as the man on the other end of the line. And with each succeeding ring, her anger grew. When it sounded a fourth time, she snatched it up, ready for battle.

"Yes?"

"What have you *done*?" The furious words hit her with the force of a slap—but not from the person she had expected.

"Mother?"

"What did you say to your father? He's furious."

The voice might have been different, but the tone could have been borrowed directly from Robert. "We…had a difference of opinion about business," Hadley said, her own voice barely audible.

"What on earth would possess you to start a fight on Christmas Eve?"

Are you sure you want to know, Mother? "I didn't start a fight. We were talking about my assignment." Hadley took a breath. "Robert and I disagreed on what to do about this hotel."

"Well, I'm sure you could have done it in a better way." Irene's voice was grim. "I would think you'd have more consideration than to run around making waves, today of all days. I want you to apologize to him right now."

"No."

"*No?*"

Hadley swallowed. "No." For the second time that night, one of the shortest words in the language was the hardest to say.

"How can you do that? You get him in a rage and then sit over there an ocean away and leave us to deal with the fallout? You don't care about us. You've ruined everything."

But it was ruined long ago.

"I'm sorry," Hadley said mechanically.

"How can you be? You don't care. It's always been you and your father off in your own world. It's always what *you* want."

"But it's not." Her voice shook. "That's just the problem. It's always been what *he* wants, what he expects. I didn't start a fight. I just told him no."

"And you picked a perfect time," Irene said bitterly.

"*What?*" It was like being cut with a very sharp knife, so quickly that Hadley barely registered the touch, yet looked down to find herself bleeding.

"Christmas Eve, our big trip," Irene continued. "We had

plans to go to the candlelight processional and the midnight banquet. Now your father's in an uproar and the twins are upset and you're refusing to apologize and everything's ruined." Her voice wavered, and Hadley realized suddenly that her mother really was shattered. In Irene's world of carefully orchestrated effects, this was crisis.

It made Hadley suddenly very sad and very tired.

The line was silent for long moments. "It's Christmas Eve," her mother finally said in a small voice. "It's supposed to be a happy time."

"Yes." Hadley closed her eyes. "It is."

Darkness pressed against the windows. The luminous wash of the full moon from two weeks before had retreated utterly. Daylight was a memory, bled away into the dark of the moon.

As bleak and black as Hadley's mood.

The lobby of the Hotel Mount Jefferson stretched out ahead of her, room to pace without the limitations of Cortland House. No one was around. The guests were in their rooms at this hour, the night clerk snoozing in the back with Hadley's blessing.

Only the Christmas tree continued to sparkle with life, its lights blinking gaily for nonexistent revelers.

And she was alone, achingly alone, in a world that had suddenly broken loose from its moorings. Hadley sank into one of the love seats in front of the dying fire.

The things that had always been important to her suddenly didn't matter, and the ones that mattered had come up on her by surprise—Whit, the grandfather she'd never met. Angie, Lester, even Tina—people at the hotel who'd somehow over the course of weeks come to feel more like family than her own. The hotel itself, quickly becoming the center of a life that seemed to be reshaping itself without her consent. And Gabe, the man who'd wormed his way impossibly deep into her heart.

And if she followed her heart, she'd be at risk, cut off from everything that had mattered to her before, with no hope of going back. On this night, in so many places, families were coming together. On this night, hers had come apart. She remembered her father's scathing words and closed her eyes. And she heard Irene's woebegone voice. *It's supposed to be a happy time*. She dropped her head onto her hands.

"Merry Christmas," Gabe said softly from beside her.

Christmas at the farm was always a production that grew to fit. When he'd driven J.J. home, Gabe had intended just to stop by and say a quick hello before coming back to the hotel. He'd be there for Christmas Day. Christmas Eve, he needed to be other places. His relatives, though, had thought differently and drawn him into dinner and toasting, gifts and endless stories.

And all the while he'd burned to be with Hadley.

The hotel walk-through was salve to his conscience for missing most of the day. He'd planned to take a quick look around and head back to Cortland House. Perhaps Hadley would still be up and they could usher in Christmas with a brandy.

He'd never expected to find her in front of the fire, looking lost and alone and far too fragile.

Now she straightened, squaring her shoulders in a movement that looked somehow valiant. "Hi."

"Hey. I'm back, finally. Sorry it took so long."

"You're allowed. It's Christmas Eve." She gave a reflexive smile that didn't reach her eyes. "Did you have fun?"

"It was fine. Are you?"

Her nod was too quick. "Yes, of course. Just tired. I came over to do a walk-through before bed."

He wasn't going to let the walls go up again, not tonight. Tonight she was going to open up to him. "It looks like more than just tired to me." Gabe sat on the love seat beside her. "What's really going on?"

"You don't want to know."

"Yeah, I do." He touched her hair. "Tell me."

Hadley sighed, not moving away. "It's nothing. Just a fight with my folks. My father, mostly."

"No family gets along all the time. Holidays can be intense. Maybe they felt guilty that they're not with you."

Her laugh ended in a choke. "I don't think so."

Neither of them noticed when he reached over to rub the tension out of her shoulders. "What was it about?"

"My father got the proposal about the acquisition."

"I take it he was less than overwhelmed."

"He was furious." She bit her lip. "I've never heard him like that before. I don't think he even read it. All he wants to do is cut."

"No acquisition?"

"He's forbidden it."

"What does that mean for us?"

"If I play by the rules, it's not good. People lose their jobs, the hotel goes downhill. There's one possibility, but it means going against him completely." She swallowed. "I can cover the cost of the deal until I can find some way to get it in front of the board. They'd approve it if it's treated like any other business deal. It makes perfect sense financially and there are enough of them who believe in responsibility to the shareholders to at least argue with my father if—when—he tries to kill it. The trick is to use one of them to introduce it. After that…" She shook her head.

"Where would you get the money to buy a ski area?"

"I have some of my own. Trust funds."

A different world. "Your dad won't be happy."

"He's not happy now." And Gabe could see her begin to turn inward. "No one's happy now."

"Maybe you just need to give him time."

"Are you kidding? My father's job has always been to set

the bar, and my job has always been to meet it." She began twisting her fingers together. "Or not. I'd jump, he'd move it. I'd jump higher, he'd move it again." For a long moment she was silent and still. "I used to think I'd get it right one of these days," she said finally. "I used to think I could please him. I realized today that that's probably never going to happen."

"I'm sure he's proud of you. Maybe he just can't say it."

She shook her head. "He's always wanted a dynasty and that means a son. When my mother first got pregnant with the twins, he was thrilled. Then we got the news they were girls. So I guess he had to make do with me."

If she'd aroused his sympathies the first time he'd seen her, now she tore his heart.

"I always thought if I could just be good enough, if I just worked hard enough, everything would be all right. I know—" she gave a humorless laugh "—it sounds ridiculous. But when you've grown up with something from the time you could think, ridiculous doesn't matter. It just is. And now all of a sudden I've figured out that that's not going to work. I don't fit, Gabe. I don't fit with my father, and I certainly don't fit with my mother and the twins." She looked at him bleakly. "I don't fit anywhere. I'm thinking about burning the bridge to the only life I've known and I've got nowhere to go after I do it." Unconsciously, her hands tightened into fists.

"It Came Upon a Midnight Clear" played faintly in the background, dreamy and slow. The Christmas tree glittered in a parody of holiday cheer. And Hadley's eyes shimmered with unshed tears.

One by one, Gabe took her hands in his own, pressing the knuckles to his lips until they relaxed, unfolding her fingers and rubbing away the deep grooves left by her nails. "I know someplace you fit." He rose and held out a hand to her. "Dance with me," he said softly. "It's Christmas Eve." And he pulled her into his arms.

Connection. It was in their linked hands, in the warmth of his fingers pressed against her back, his eyes locked on hers, his gaze embracing her as surely as his arms. Once before, ages ago it seemed, they'd danced as strangers. In the days since, they'd learned each other's bodies with hardly a touch. They moved together now in the half-light of fire and Christmas tree, a slow, dreamy dip and float, the steps originating in his body and ending in hers. She looked into his face, looked into hope and promise and comfort. And bit by bit, the bleakness eased.

In the circle of the dance she felt protected, cherished. The warmth of his body reached her like a touch. They rose and fell together in rhythm, turning as one, coming ever closer, moving around in front of the dying fire until at last he brought them to a stop, sliding his arms around her entirely. Lips a fraction of an inch apart, they stood, close enough to breathe one another's air.

And as Christmas Eve slid into Christmas Day, they kissed.

Chapter Fifteen

Soft, gentle, the kiss sent warmth whisking through Hadley, reminding her that there was pleasure, too, in this world, and comfort and caring. It was just a simple pressure of mouth on mouth, but when Gabe shifted slightly and gathered her against him, it resonated through her. They stood still and yet it was as though they still floated together in the dance.

She'd touched him before, but somehow it was different now. The taste of him permeated her senses, working its way into her blood like some exotic liquor. And somewhere deep inside her, the slow drumbeat of desire began.

Moonlight, lamplight, firelight. They'd kissed before. It had rocked her, but somewhere down deep she'd known there would be an end, and she'd taken care not to give herself over to it entirely. Each time, however tenuously, she'd managed to hold on just enough that she could pull herself back. Now she abandoned herself to it. Now she let herself want, gave herself permission to take.

And the power was more than she'd ever dreamed.

Moon glow, fire glow and Hadley. It made Gabe dizzy. Her taste had the complexity of fine wine—a sweetness blending into arousal and urgency. Day by day, with weakening control, he'd held back, given her space until the ache for her had become a constant accompaniment to his life. Now, with her mouth eager against his, he fought back a groan. He wanted to take, he wanted to plunder, but in some dim, sane part of his mind he was aware of where they were. Not here, he thought desperately, even as he was compelled to stroke one hand down the smooth line of her back. Not now. But nearby, and soon.

Then Hadley made a small, incoherent noise and desire sliced through him. "We've got to go," he managed to gasp. "Now."

The walk to Cortland House was a journey of fits and starts, halted over and over for feverish kisses because ten steps were too damn long to go without tasting her. Grabbing a passkey and stealing up to an anonymous room in the hotel might have been more immediate, but Gabe didn't want anonymous. He wanted her in his bed, twisting under him, hot and urgent and wanton.

And then they were in his hallway, tearing off their coats, the need for holding back gone.

Gabe's bedroom was unfamiliar and thrillingly male. They stumbled through the doorway and Hadley pressed him against the wall, driven only to get closer to him, to make her body part of his completely. Impatient, she dived into the kiss without reservation. She felt his hands in her hair, roving down her back, molding themselves around her curves, revealing her own body to her in a way that made it something new. There was something proprietary about the touch. Then she felt him, hard against her, and she made a sound of triumph deep in her throat.

She wanted him, she wanted skin under her hands, she

wanted to explore. Before, she'd never let herself fully want, never acknowledged the driving need that thrummed through her. Now, desire for Gabe was her universe and she wanted it all. She dragged his sweater over his head, running her fingers across his bare chest, laughing in delight at the texture.

When his hands slipped under her own sweater, she moaned. His fingers framed her rib cage, traveling up her spine. She felt her bra loosen, pulled away so that her silky sweater brushed against her nipples. Then his hand slid up to cover her breast in a move almost shocking in its intimacy.

She'd had affairs in the past. Men had touched her naked body. Always it had seemed pleasurable, but not earth-shattering. Arousing, but no more so than the brush of her own hands. Now it was as though she'd grown new nerves overnight, so that the contact of skin to skin was an entirely different sensory experience. His fingers on her nipples sent her arching and gasping against him, starting a coil of tension tightening in her, a sweet ache that made her legs tremble.

Clothing was an impediment, to be thrown aside as quickly as possible. There would be time for patience, but not now. Urgently, she reached for his belt buckle, her fingers clumsy with haste to draw him out, to pleasure him. Silk over steel, pulsing and heavy in her hand. She moved to sink to her knees.

"Don't," Gabe said, pushing her hands away, his voice strangled with the effort of control. "Not now." He pressed her back toward the bed. When he stripped down her jeans, she felt not vulnerable but powerful. She could see what she did to him, feel the shudder as she traced her fingertips down his belly. Then the feel of his hands on her thighs turned her knees to water and she lay back.

He had to taste her or he'd go mad. Her skin was luminous, her body long and narrow. She looked fragile but he knew the strength there; the intensity of her response inflamed him. When he would have gone slowly, she urged him on with hands dragging at his shoulders, fingers tangling in his hair. And with his mouth and his hands he sent her tensing, gasping, half sobbing with pleasure.

Arousal thudded through him as he felt her reaction to every slick caress. Every moan sent a fresh surge of blood pounding into him; the more he gave her the closer to the edge he came himself. Every instinct screamed for him to bury himself in her. Not yet, though. He wanted to take her further, until she was mindless with desire, wanting, knowing nothing but him.

An instant later, she began to quake against him helplessly, flinging her hands out to clutch the sheets, crying out. Gabe moved up her body, freeing himself roughly, grinding his teeth because even that much contact threatened to be too much. And then he was sliding into her in a rush of sensation that exploded through him even as she was still shuddering.

She didn't know if she could bear it. Clinging to him, winding her legs around his waist, Hadley felt the strength and flex and flow of his body surging against hers. And what she thought had ended began to build again. He filled her completely, each stroke a movement in an intimate dance, the movements that originated in his body ending in hers. He stared down at her, his features tight with concentration, and it was as though she could dive inside him, see his pleasure while feeling her own. And it was that that flung her over the edge of climax, her body shuddering with her cries as she fell.

Leaning on his elbows, his hands tangled in her hair, Gabe thrust himself into her, feeling her hot and slick around him. He ground his teeth, trying to slow it down, trying to stretch it out because he wanted to live in this moment forever, with Hadley beneath him, taut and naked and feverish, Hadley beneath him, tight and wet, Hadley beneath him, all the shadows gone for once, eyes clear and open with room for him alone, for him.

Hadley beneath him, his.

* * *

She dreamed of walking down the grand staircase of the Hotel Mount Jefferson, her gloved hand on Richard Cortland's, her long, heavy skirts trailing behind her. "It will be yours one day, Clara," he said, kissing her hand, his beard bristly against her fingers. And then he looked up and he was Gabe, and the dream began to evaporate even as Hadley struggled to live within it.

She drifted toward consciousness, becoming distantly aware of her body, heavy and warm against the smooth sheets. An instant later, she realized that the heaviness in her limbs came in part from a warm, male arm and leg thrown over her.

And at that, she came fully awake. Squeezing her eyes more tightly shut, she resisted the urge to groan as she remembered the night before. She'd been pathetic, weepy, telling him things she'd never told anyone. She'd exposed herself in the most humiliating way possible. *I don't fit anywhere.* She sighed and shifted her weight.

Only to feel the arm tighten around her. "Going somewhere?"

She opened her eyes to find herself practically nose to nose with Gabe, who gave her a sleepy smile. And her first ridiculous thought was to wonder what it was about dark stubble that made a man look so absolutely ravishing. "Merry Christmas." He pressed a drowsy kiss on her.

"Merry Christmas," she muttered. How could she have slept so late, she who woke at six every morning without fail? Of course, she usually spent the night sleeping, not having sex, but still. Even the times she did have sex she normally tried to be the first one up, preferably in clothes or at least a robe. And that was with official sex, not something like this.

Whatever "this" was.

She couldn't classify it as a one-night stand, she thought wildly. God help her, she knew him far too well. She couldn't classify it as anything but temporary insanity. "I should get out of here so that you can get going," she said firmly. She tried to squirm away, but Gabe's arm only tightened further.

"Not quite yet." He pressed his lips against her throat and pulled her closer to his body. Against her hip she felt the velvet stirrings of his erection and froze. One by one, her nerves began to come to attention. Gabe ran the tip of his tongue along her throat and she felt the shiver in her stomach. Oh no, she thought.

"You see," he continued, lowering his head to her breast, "we were in such a rush last night I didn't really get a chance to explore properly." Warm and wet, his tongue circled around her nipple. Arousal shot through her like an electric charge. He took the sensitive point into his mouth and Hadley moaned.

"Of course," he said, switching to her other breast, "you're seeming a little tense. Maybe we can do something about that." Stealthily, his fingers stroked the inside of her thigh in time with the rubbing of his tongue, traveling higher and higher each time until she felt them brush against the first curls of hair, and then higher still. Without conscious volition she began to move her hips. Her arms came up around him.

And then he found her.

Gasping, she jolted against his fingers. "Yep," he murmured, "definitely a little tense. Perhaps we should help relieve some of that." He leaned over her.

And with a growl, she reached up to pull his head down to hers.

Gabe smiled lazily at Hadley, who lay on his chest. "My mother warned me about women like you."

"Really?"

"Yep. She said there would be women who'd just want to use me for my body and leave me weak. Which you did an exceptional job of, by the way." He curved a muscled arm around her that didn't feel weak at all.

It must have been the orgasms, Hadley thought. Somewhere around the second one the shyness had evaporated and she just hadn't given a damn. So she'd made a fool of herself the night before. She'd survived worse. It was Christmas. She could spend time worrying about it or she could just relax and enjoy the day. "I'm glad you approve," she said.

His grin widened. "Oh, I do." He squinted at the clock and rose. "But as much as I'd like to demonstrate, we should probably get in the shower. It's nearly eight and we should be at the farm by ten."

"You should be at the farm," she corrected, getting out of bed and rescuing her clothes from the floor.

"Oh no, you're coming, too. My mother already invited you."

Her mouth dropped open for a minute, then snapped shut. "That was two weeks ago and I declined. I can't just show up."

"Sure you can. She was asking about you yesterday."

Not bothering with the bra, Hadley pulled her sweater over her head. "You can't just bring me without warning. People like to plan, you know? Food? Chairs? Forks? It's a nice offer but I've got a date with the VCR and a frozen pizza."

"If you think I'm going to let you sit alone here all day on Christmas, you're nuts."

"I'm not a stray dog, Gabe," she said with an edge to her voice. "I don't need taking care of. If I wanted to be around people today, I'd have gone to New York."

Not "home," he realized. She never called it home. "Come on, it'll be fun. You already know my mom and Jacob."

She glowered. "I barely exchanged more than two words with Jacob."

"See? He likes you. My mom's a great cook and J.J. might be there. Shoot, you get sick of people, you can go hang out with Jacob and be antisocial together."

A corner of her mouth twitched. "And I should do this why?"

Gabe rose and walked across the room to pick a small box off of his dresser. He shook it. "If you want to find out what's in this you have to come to the farm, because that's the only place you're going to get it from me."

Alarm flickered in her eyes. "Is that a Christmas present?"

"Yup."

"For me?"

"Yup."

"But we...I...but why?"

"Because I wanted to. Because I like to give presents." Because he'd wanted to see that sunburst smile.

"But I didn't get anything for you."

"Having you come to the farm for Christmas is what I want." He shook the box again. "Just think, if you don't go you'll feel horribly guilty, not to mention die of curiosity over what's in the box." He waited, waggling his eyebrows encouragingly.

And she gave in and pressed a smacking kiss on him. "All right, I'll go. Thank you. That was very sweet."

"You don't even know what it is."

"It was still sweet." She picked up her jeans and lacy panties and headed toward the door, without putting them on.

"Where are you going?" he asked. Clad in just the tunic-length sweater, she looked leggy and luscious, and he mentally gauged his chances of tumbling her back in bed. Slim at this particular time, he judged. A wise man picked his moments.

"Upstairs to shower and change."

"Like that?"

"I can get away with it." She paused at the door to give him a bawdy wink, taking him by surprise. "I've got an in with the landlord."

And she was gone.

Chapter Sixteen

No holiday celebration Hadley had ever attended prepared her for the Trask household. "Who's here?" she asked, staring at the collection of cars as they drove up to the big farmhouse, which sat down a gentle slope from the gift shop.

"Oh, my brothers, a few aunts and uncles and cousins, probably a neighbor or two and whoever the cat dragged in." He parked between a Jeep and a bright red Prius and got out. "No grandkids for my mom, so it's sort of an all-day open house." He opened the back door of the truck and pulled out a bulging bag.

Hadley walked up, letting herself enjoy just looking at him. He wore charcoal jeans and a black jacket with a pine-colored cashmere sweater that showed the white of his shirt at the neck. For a change of pace, apparently, he'd trimmed his three-day stubble into a Van Dyke that brought out the strong line of his jaw. "Playing Santa?"

He gave her a wolfish wink and scooped her up against him

with his free arm. "I got a present for you right here, baby," he said in an Elvis voice.

"Stop it." Hadley pushed his hands away. "You don't do this kind of thing in front of your family."

He nibbled at her neck. "That's why I'm doing it now." And then his lips covered hers and every thought slid out of her head. How could a man's mouth be so soft, so clever? How could he know just how to kiss her so that—

"Hey, Gabe," said a female voice with the sound of an opening door. "Merry—" Her words cut off and she cleared her throat. "Well, I see it's already a very merry Christmas."

Hadley looked up to see a woman standing on the steps to the side porch, her arms crossed over her chest. Her sweater matched the scarlet ribbon that tied back her glossy brown hair; her eyes sparkled with devilry.

Gabe released her. "Lainie, this is Hadley. Hadley, this is my cousin Lainie, who's going to forget she ever saw anything."

Lainie came down the stairs toward them. "In your dreams." But she grinned and hugged Gabe before sticking her hand out to Hadley. "Nice to meet you. Smart girl. You picked the one who actually knows how to dress properly."

"I didn't—" Hadley began, but Lainie had already whirled and dashed back inside.

"She's a witch." Gabe winked. "She probably got a funny feeling."

Lainie stuck her head back out. "I am not a witch. I just work at the museum. Stop telling lies." She slammed the door.

He grinned at Hadley's puzzled frown. "See? Now you've got something to talk about."

Warm wood, tantalizing scents, a massive table groaning with food. It was everything Hadley thought a farmhouse kitchen should be. The place was less formal than Cortland House, and even more welcoming, if that were possible. The personality of Molly Trask showed in everything from the violets on the windowsill to the polished copper pots hanging from the overhead beams. It wasn't just a house, it was a home.

A home currently alarmingly full of people.

"Hadley!" Molly took both of her hands and then pulled her near for a kiss. "Merry Christmas. I'm so glad you could come. Merry Christmas, Gabriel."

He squeezed her. "Merry Christmas."

Hadley cleared her throat. "I brought you something." She pulled out the package she'd hastily wrapped, and hoped that Molly didn't notice the fact that the paper was used.

"You shouldn't have," Gabe's mother scolded.

"I wanted to."

"Well, you're very sweet." Molly tore off the paper to reveal a cranberry glass faerie lamp Hadley hadn't been able to resist buying at an antique shop. Molly beamed. "Oh, it's lovely. I know just where it'll go." This time she gave Hadley a long, hard hug.

Gabe stared at Hadley and the lamp. Then he blinked as though remembering himself. "Let's get you introduced to everyone else. So you know Ma, you've met Lainie." Lainie, peeling potatoes, waved. "This is my aunt Carol and my cousin Albie and his sister Debbie and his wife, Susan."

Gabe stopped and stared at the doorway. Hadley turned to see a dark-haired man leading a lovely redhead. A slow smile spread over Gabe's face. "And this," he announced, "is my brother Nick and his friend Sloane."

"Not friend, significant other," Nick corrected, pulling Sloane in close to him.

"Significant other?" She raised a brow.

He kissed her temple. "Very significant. Remind me to demonstrate later."

In the living room, Christmas cards crowded the mantelpiece; what looked like an antique children's rocking horse sat near the hearth. The tree was festooned with a mix of ornaments, some clearly handmade. And it was equally clear that the farmhouse was the center of the Trask universe, drawing the entire extended family back, year after year.

Appetizers and drinks began to circulate. People flowed through the door, every one of whom Gabe seemed to know. At first, Hadley shook hands and repeated the names to herself, trying to keep them straight. Somewhere along the line, she abandoned the effort and stuck with smiles.

After an hour of it, she stumbled into the kitchen for a glass of water and a few moments of silence. They didn't last long; Lainie walked into the kitchen carrying a towheaded toddler. An impatient toddler.

"Down. Alex down," he demanded.

"That's the problem with men," she observed. "They never know what they want. Two minutes ago it was 'Alex up.'"

"Is he yours?"

"Mine?" Lainie gave a bark of laughter. "Oh no. I'd like to think I'm smarter than that. He's Stephanie's kid," she said, relenting and setting Alex on the floor. "My sister."

Hadley had zero recollection of anyone by that name, but she'd long since given up trying. "Sure." She nodded.

"I know, it's a mob scene, isn't it?" Lainie observed sympathetically. "We should have everyone wear name tags now that the Trask boys are bringing their women around."

"I'm not Gabe's woman."

Lainie snorted. "Good luck with that one. Judging by the way he watches you, he's got other ideas."

"Actually, I was just in here looking for a glass of water," Hadley said a little desperately.

"The tall cabinet there. It's well water and it's great."

"You sure know the place," Hadley commented as she got out a glass. "Do you come here a lot?"

"I've come to the farm all my life. My dad grew up here."

Hadley stood at the sink to run the water, idly looking out

the kitchen window at the maple grove beyond. It was beautiful country, even in the dead of winter. She looked at the trees, trying to imagine them with leaves. And saw. "Good Lord," she said without thinking.

"What?" Lainie demanded.

"Nothing." Hadley hurriedly turned away.

"What?" Lainie crowded up behind her at the sink. "Oh my…is that what it looks like?" Out in the maples, Nick took Sloane's hand and dropped down on one knee.

"I don't know. We shouldn't be watching, though," Hadley said. "It's private."

"In this family, nothing's private," Lainie declared, and they both watched, round-eyed, as Nick slid a ring onto Sloane's finger. "*Yes!*" Lainie crowed, and pumped her fist. "Excellent! That gets me off the hook for at least six months."

"Gets you off the hook?"

She rolled her eyes. "My parents. You'd think they didn't have a single married child, let alone five grandchildren. I'm not ready to settle down. I mean for Pete's sake, I'm only twenty-five. I've got a right to date, don't I?"

Fighting a smile, Hadley nodded. Outside, Sloane threw her arms around Gabe's brother, laughing. Something twisted inside Hadley. What would it be like to love someone so much, to know that he loved you so unconditionally, that you'd pledge to spend the rest of your life with him? She thought of the way she'd felt in Gabe's arms the night before. What would happen to her if she let herself believe in that, really believe?

Terrifying. Astonishing. Exhilarating. Swiftly, before a small giddy part of her began to explode with joy, she shut it down. Not now; she couldn't let herself think about this now.

But she'd let the genie out of the bottle and she was very afraid there was no putting it back.

Hadley watched Nick and Sloane walk back to the house,

their hands locked together. The kitchen door opened on their laughter. Nick twirled Sloane around when they got inside.

"So what's with you two?" Lainie demanded, eyes bright.

"Come on, everybody in the living room," Nick called, "We've got something to announce."

If possible, the room became even more crowded. Nick linked hands with Sloane and took a deep breath. "You're my family and friends and I'd like you all to be the first to know that Sloane has agreed to be my wife." A broad grin creased his face. "We're getting married."

A chorus of cheers and hoots erupted. "Oh, Sloane, how wonderful." Molly hurried over. "Welcome to the family."

Sloane had a slightly giddy, dazed look on her face as she hugged Molly, then Lainie, then Gabe, then Jacob, then Nick, who appeared to have gotten in line on general principle.

"Let's see the ring," Lainie demanded.

Sloane held out her hand to show the flash of fire.

"Nice job, Nick," Lainie said admiringly. "I didn't know you had it in you."

"Didn't know he had what in him?" asked a familiar voice behind Hadley, and Lainie's grin turned into an eye roll.

"Well, if it isn't Speed Racer," she said as J. J. Cooper walked in from the kitchen. "Who let you in the country? I thought they had warning posters about you in Customs."

"Hi, Hadley." Ignoring Lainie, he kissed Hadley on the cheek. "What's the celebration?"

"Nick just got engaged," Hadley said.

"Engaged?" J.J. looked alarmed. "Get out while you can. It's not safe. The vibes will be zinging around for hours."

"Wuss," Lainie pronounced, and walked toward the kitchen.

"You gotta be able to do better than that, Lainie," J.J. called as he sat down in an empty chair. "What, have you been getting lazy while I've been gone? She loves me," he added to no one in particular.

"Deluded egomaniac," Lainie called from the kitchen.

"And I love this," he added, as Molly handed him a steaming mug. He buried his nose in the fumes. "The famous Trask hot buttered rum. You gotta try this, Hadley. People have been killed trying to steal it."

"Liar," Molly said affectionately, and handed a mug to her.

The rum was delicious, rich and sweet with just enough kick to send tendrils of heat through her veins. Gabe drifted over and leaned on the arm of her chair, resting a hand on her shoulder. She didn't recognize pure, uncomplicated happiness because she'd never felt it.

"We should go to Albertville for New Year's Eve," J.J. said. "Do a little skiing, go out on the town."

Lainie walked in carrying a tray of stuffed mushrooms she set on the coffee table.

"Count me out," Gabe said. "I've got to work."

"You telling me I have to go alone? Now this calls for desperate measures." He snaked out an arm as Lainie passed by and scooped her onto his lap, ignoring her yelp. "Whaddya say, Lainie? Skiing, gourmet dinners, champagne at midnight?"

She slapped away his hands and rose. "You forget, I listened to you and Gabe practicing your pickup lines out in back of the sugar house."

"Oh really?" Hadley raised her eyebrows.

"A long time ago," Gabe assured her hastily.

"Your cousin's a hard woman, Gabe," J.J. said. "I just offered her the kind of trip women dream about, and she breaks my heart. She could have turned out to be the one."

"You mean not counting half the female population of Sweden, Finland, Norway, Denmark and the Netherlands?" Lainie asked derisively. "Peddle it somewhere else, Speed."

"Cruel." J.J. shook his head sorrowfully and turned to Hadley. "What about you?"

"She's busy, too," Gabe said crisply.

J.J. looked from Hadley to Gabe and grinned. "How about that? Looks like I'm going to have to go solo."

Her empty water glass sent Hadley her back into the kitchen. She looked out at the maples dreamily. Then a touch on her leg had her jumping, and she looked down to see Alex.

"Up," he said, raising his arms.

"Well, aren't you just too cute," she said. She crouched down so that she was eye to eye with him. "You want up?"

"Up."

She folded her arms. "How do I know you're not going to change your mind on me? You know what Lainie says."

"Up," he insisted.

"Well, I guess you know what you want." She stood and hoisted him to her hip.

Gabe stopped in the doorway, looking on as Hadley lifted Alex, laughing in surprise at his weight. She rubbed her nose against his. The little boy giggled.

"That's an Eskimo kiss," she told him.

"Esmo kiss," he repeated.

She leaned in to flutter her lash against Alex's chubby cheek until he squirmed. "And this is a butterfly kiss."

"Bufly!" he shouted enthusiastically.

"And this is an honest to goodness kiss," she finished, leaning in to peck him on the cheek.

And something shifted inside Gabe, like an expanding bubble that threatened to float him off his feet. He should have listened to J.J., he realized. He hadn't gotten out of the room quickly enough.

He'd fallen for her all the way.

There wasn't a sound, but suddenly Hadley knew someone was watching. She looked over to see Gabe, and something about his expression brought her to immediate attention. Mechanically, she let the boy slide to the floor, and straightened slowly.

Gabe beckoned her with a finger. "Come here, little girl."

She walked toward him. "What?"

"A little more."

She frowned and took another step. "What?"

"I've got your present." He reached in his pocket.

The box was small, about the size for jewelry. Flushing, she pulled off the wrapping and opened it. Inside, nestled in cotton, lay a shiny key on a Mount Jefferson key chain. "It's for the office," he said. "I thought you deserved one of your own."

It was simple, it was practical. And it was a statement of more trust and faith than she could have dreamed of.

He leaned in and pressed his lips to hers. For long moments, the kitchen receded and it was only the two of them, together in their own world.

"Gabe." Jacob's voice came from behind them. "Ma wants—oops." He spun and retreated hastily.

Hadley broke away, flushing. "All right, you promised none of this in front of your family. That makes it twice now."

"I couldn't help it." Gabe gave an innocent shrug.

"Couldn't help it?"

"Nope. It's the rules." He pointed to the doorway above their heads. "We're under the mistletoe."

It was dark by the time they headed home, the Explorer's headlights' shining cones of blue-white light through the night. "So did you have a good time?" Gabe asked.

"Outside of being so stuffed I can't breathe, it was wonderful. Your family is great."

"Yeah, I figure I'll keep them. You were a hit. I noticed you even got Jacob talking."

"Hard not to," she told him. "He reads my favorite authors."

"Oh, Jacob's always been a big book guy. What else are you going to do when you're stuck up here in the snow all winter?"

"He's really very nice when you get to know him."

"Jacob? Sure. He just takes his time making decisions about people. Once he likes you, you're in. Until then…" He drove for a few moments. "Not to bring up ugly reality, but what's the plan for tomorrow morning? We've got the meeting to negotiate the final price on the ski area. Are we going through with it?"

Hadley stared out her window and finally turned to him. "Yes. I've thought about it and I say we go ahead just as we would have before I talked to my father."

"And you're confident about the board? We're not going out on a limb here?"

"Of course we're going out on a limb, but it's a calculated risk. I wouldn't be willing to put my money behind it if I thought they'd say no."

He nodded slowly, the dash lights throwing his eyes into shadow. "All right. I'll buy that."

Hadley hesitated. "Gabe, we never really talked about what happened last night."

She saw the gleam of his teeth. "It happened this morning, too."

"Yes, it did."

"I thought we did pretty well at it."

She couldn't quite prevent the smile. "You're right, we did. But we're working together and there's a whole lot more going on than just having a good time." Calm, matter-of-fact, that was the way to deal with it.

"There's a lot to be said for having a good time."

"Yes, but that's not what we're being paid to do. We've got a tough profit bogey to meet. We can't let this affair affect that, especially since we don't know where things go from here."

Gabe was quiet for a moment. "Does that mean where our relationship goes or where you go?" he asked carefully, ignoring the knot that formed in the pit of his stomach.

"My life isn't here, you know that. This is just temporary." It was a fact. So why did it sound defensive? She stared out the windshield at the winding double yellow line.

"Well, let me tell you what I think." Eyes on the road, Gabe reached out and took her hand. "I love…being with you, making love with you. I don't want to let this go. We're both adults. If we start having problems, we should be able to handle it. As far as the staff goes, what happens in Cortland House stays in Cortland House. And I'm hoping it's going to happen a lot." He grinned.

"You make it sound simple."

"It is."

Hadley managed a smile and looked out the window. It was a mistake to take it this lightly, she was certain of it, and yet— and yet it was so tempting to let it go on. The giddy part of her had grown since the morning, harder to subdue, like a large, noisy, happy puppy. It had been such a long time since anything had felt so good to her.

Was it worth taking a chance? She thought of Angie and Hank, of Nick and Sloane. She thought of the hours she'd just spent in a house overflowing with joy, a house full of people who lavished affection without emotional price tags. A house full of people who loved.

And suddenly it felt as if all the blood were draining from her body, leaving her weak. How had she not noticed? How had she not seen? But it had happened so gradually she'd hardly been aware of it. He was the constant in her world, the one irreducible part. In the past weeks the deal had absorbed her days, and at every step of the way was Gabe. The hotel had encompassed her world and at every turn Gabe was with her.

He'd shown her its quirks and its magic, and somewhere along the line she'd fallen in love with it.

And somewhere along the line she'd fallen in love with him.

Chapter Seventeen

They sat around a glossy walnut conference table, Hadley, Gabe, Roderick Miller and a supporting cast of lawyers and accountants. The ice in the water pitchers had melted; the coffee had long since grown cold. It had taken the better part of six hours, but they'd finally negotiated through every discrepancy, and the final offer was on the table.

"Well, ladies and gentlemen, it appears we have a deal." Miller leaned back in his chair, just as self-satisfied and no more likable than he'd been the first time Hadley had seen him. "If we can make all the changes we discussed, we can close whenever the funding is ready."

"The funding is in place," Gabe said. "We'd like to execute on this by the end of the week."

"I'm leaving town Wednesday so it'll have to be soon."

After knowing for nearly two weeks that they needed to close by year end, he picked now to tell them? Hadley took in a deep breath. "Jason, how quickly can we turn it around?"

Keating looked up from where he was consulting with the Crawford Notch accountant. "I'll stay here and work on it as late as we need. It'll be in your in-box by ten tomorrow."

"So we're looking at tomorrow afternoon," Gabe said thoughtfully. "Say, three?"

Miller stirred. "Four would be better."

"Four it is." Gabe rose along with Hadley. "Until then."

"So are you still okay with this?" Gabe asked her as they drove the narrow highway to the hotel.

"Which 'this' are you talking about?"

"Oh, the deal. Using your trust fund, going up against your dad. All of it."

"Sure." In the list of heedless risks that she'd taken in the past week, decimating her trust fund and making a decision that could well amount to professional suicide seemed minor.

The decision to let herself love felt far more dangerous.

Panic—sure, there was still panic, but underneath there was elation, certainty. It was a risk, a risk bigger than any she'd ever taken, but the payoff was a chance to live within an intensity of joy and hope that she'd never dreamed of. It was like being given a stupendous gift, one she'd never for a moment expected.

And what did she do with it now? Savor it, inhabit it, certainly. Did she tell him? Did she wait? It seemed absurd to say anything so soon, and yet she felt as though it were spelled out on her forehead with lights for anyone to see.

"Do you want to come to dinner tonight?" she asked aloud.

"What, you're going to cook?"

She blinked. "I hadn't thought, really. I can get takeout…"

"Salad from the corner grocery? I have a better idea. *I'll* cook and you can supervise."

"All right."

"Naked."

"*Naked?*"

"I'll draw the drapes and turn up the heat," he said with a wicked smile. "I think we deserve a nice long evening together."

And maybe, if it felt right, she'd try to tell him what was in her heart. Maybe tonight she'd tell him how she felt.

And trust to love.

"Lobby," Lester said cheerfully, taking them up from the service level. Gabe glanced over at Hadley. It took his breath away sometimes how beautiful she was. How much he loved her.

When the doors opened, she turned to him, eyes bright. He suppressed the urge to kiss her. "I want to stop by the front desk to see if anyone's heard from Angie," she said. "I can do a walk-through while I'm at it."

"Perhaps you need company on that walk-through."

Her smile was dazzling. "Maybe I do."

He started toward the desk with her just as Susan hurried up behind him. "Mr. Trask, thank God you're back. You're needed in your office immediately."

Concern was immediate. "What's wrong?"

The cool, capable Susan looked desperate and on the edge of tears. "I tried to call you but your phone kept saying you were out of range."

"Hadley," Gabe said urgently, "I'm going down to my office. Hadley?"

But Hadley didn't answer because she was standing stock-still, staring at a thin, brittle-looking woman who'd risen from a sofa in the lobby.

"*Mother?* What are you doing here?"

"That's hardly a way to say hello to your mother, is it?" Irene's smile was a little unsteady.

Their last interchange had hardly been standard fare, either, Hadley thought as she mechanically kissed her mother's cheek and hugged the sullen-looking twins. "I thought you were in Gstaad."

"We were supposed to be," muttered her sister Kaya.

"We thought we'd surprise you." Irene caught Hadley's hands and drew her down to the couch she'd been sitting on. "The hotel is beautiful, but it's no place to be all alone on the holiday. I've been thinking about it ever since our conversation the other night went badly." Irene clasped her hands around her knees. "Your father was obsessed with the idea of coming back early and I thought maybe you and I could clear the air, so we took the Gulfstream back last night."

Which explained the expressions on the faces of the twins. And then her mother's words sank in. "Dad's here? Where?"

"I think he went that way," Irene said, waving vaguely toward the executive wing. "We've only been here an hour or so. We've been waiting for a room."

"And waiting," added Lara.

"Don't listen to her, it's gorgeous here," Irene said.

Robert would have found his way to the nerve center of the hotel, Gabe's office. Where Gabe would be. "Excuse me, Mom," Hadley said, "I've got to go find him."

"Wait," Irene protested. "You can't...I need to talk with you about the other night." Her lips tightened. "I think I hurt your feelings and I didn't mean to."

She'd thrown heedless barbs, barbs that still stung. But her eyes held genuine regret now—and confusion, as though she didn't quite know how to get out of the morass she'd created. She twisted her hands together, hands that were starting to look old, Hadley realized.

And a wave of compassion whisked through her. She leaned over to hug her mother. "We'll talk, Mom, really talk," she promised, and rose. "Don't worry. It's going to be all right."

"Can I help you?" Gabe stood in the doorway to his office, staring at the man responsible for the misery in Hadley's eyes. Robert Stone wore an open-collar white shirt under a navy sport coat. His still-thick hair shone silver at the temples.

"Yes, all right, good," Stone said into the telephone, ignoring Gabe. "Fax the final document here." He hung up. "Who are you, another flunky?"

"I'm Gabe Trask, the general manager." Gabe crossed to the desk. "This happens to be my office."

Stone gave him an indifferent glance. "About time you showed up. I've been here since two."

"So I'm told. I'm also told you've been bullying staff, demanding operational documents and generally stirring up trouble."

"I own this miserable pile of bricks. I don't need anyone's permission for anything I do."

"That doesn't give you the right to come in here and run roughshod over my staff."

"I don't believe in coddling." Stone looked at him coldly. "People are paid to get a job done. And as far as trouble goes, it doesn't need any stirring. Where's my daughter? I expected to find her here."

"She'll be in shortly. She's doing a walk-through."

"You've got her doing your work now?" Sarcasm was ripe in his tone.

Gabe chose to ignore it. "Hadley does what she wants to do."

"Funny, somehow when she got here what she wanted to do turned from operating in the best interests of Stone Enterprises to blowing money and wasting time." He leaned back in Gabe's chair. "You wouldn't know anything about that, would you?"

"Maybe for the first time in her life she's figured out what she really cares about."

Stone's eyes were scornful. "And I suppose you helped her figure that out."

"No, she worked it out on her own."

"I sent her with a straightforward assignment—to get this business running lean."

"Is that what you call it?"

"You watch it. You've been playing it fast and loose with no accountability for far too long. I send in one of my best managers and suddenly she wants to let you keep going, business as usual. She hasn't executed any of her original plan and now I'm hearing about some damn-fool idea plan to buy a ski resort. That's not my daughter."

Gabe thought of Christmas Eve and the desolation in Hadley's voice and fought to hold on to his temper. "Maybe it is your daughter for the first time in her life. Maybe you should start paying attention."

Stone sat up, his feet thumping to the floor. "Don't you sit here and try to tell me about my daughter, you parasite."

"Someone ought to. Your daughter cares about more than just meeting your ridiculous profit targets. What matters to her is this hotel and the people in it. Her priority is taking care of them, not scratching out a pissant three or four percent more profit in the short term that'll end up costing more money in the long run, employees be damned."

Stone's eyes narrowed. "My father might have accepted that load of crap. Don't for a moment think I intend to. I'll take this place apart and sell it off piecemeal if I have to."

"Try it," Gabe invited, slapping his hands down on the polished mahogany and leaning across it. "This hotel is a national historic landmark. I'll have the press and the law all over you so fast it'll make your head spin. We'll fight you all the way."

"'*We'll* fight you'? I suppose you mean you and my daughter. Oh, you're slick," Stone said contemptuously, "I'll give you that. I should have come here long ago. I couldn't understand why Hadley was behaving the way she was but now that I'm here I've got a pretty good idea."

"And that would be?"

"Don't get cute with me," he growled. "I've chased off pretty boys like you before. You smell money, you think you've found yourself an easy ride. Well, I can protect my daughter from people like you."

"Hadley doesn't need protecting, except maybe from you," Gabe snapped back. "She's smart enough to take care of herself. If you'd just let her go you'd wind up making far more than you could ever want from this property. But that's not really what this is about for you, is it?"

Stone rose. "What's that supposed to mean?"

"You interrupt a vacation, take an overnight flight from Switzerland just to deal with a business whose entire revenue is probably smaller than what you pay for jet fuel each year." Now it was Gabe's turn for contempt. "You're not here about the money. You're here because you want to control her, because you can't stand the thought that she might be thinking for herself."

Stone's eyes turned into slits. "I want you out of here," he barked, pressing his hands onto the wood of the desk.

"You're here because of Whit."

"Get out," he snarled.

"*No.*" Hadley stood frozen in the doorway, staring at the tableau in horror. Gabe turned to her and she read fury and relief in his eyes. "What are you doing?" she asked her father desperately.

"What you should have done long ago." He stared at her, his brows drawn together thunderously. "How many times have I told you to go with your gut? Your first instinct was to fire him and you should have executed. Now I'm taking care of it for you."

Out of the corner of her eye, she saw Gabe's head snap toward her. "I didn't know the operation then," she protested.

"It has nothing to do with the operation and you know it. One of the first moves is always to reduce head count and salary overhead. This is a good way to start."

"You can't fire him. He's the center of the operation."

"Don't you dare question me." She'd never in her life seen Robert so angry. "I never dreamed you could be so irresponsible. You've damaged the interests of the company and you've hurt your mother and your sisters because you let your head be turned by some pretty boy. If you want to salvage anything at all you'll sit down and figure out how to get things running right."

"But you don't understand," she said desperately. "I've told you that—"

"You don't tell me anything." His voice cracked like a whip. "You refuse this and you are finished. I'll give you one chance and one chance only. I want this operation on track and I want measures implemented by the end of the week. After that we'll figure out your future. If you have one. You're not the person I thought you were, Hadley."

Obey or else. Perform or be punished. It was the same unyielding rebuke she'd heard her whole life. But how could she defy him? If she did, she'd be walking away from everything she'd ever known. Panic washed through her.

"There are some cuts we can't make." Her voice shook; she could hear it. "The head count has to stay."

"The head count drops by twenty percent. You know the rule."

"The normal rules don't apply here."

"The rules always apply."

"But…"

"Are you going to continue to defy me?" His voice rose. "Twenty percent cuts on staffing and on operating costs. I want a plan together by the end of tomorrow. It shouldn't take long—you've already got a preliminary strategy in your initial memo."

She knew there were reasons to disagree but they dried up in her throat.

"Don't do this," Gabe said urgently. "It goes against everything you've said. You know what he's asking. Are you willing to do that for him?"

Hadley looked from face to face. Her ability to speak had deserted her. It had come to this, the moment of choice. There was no evading it anymore. Not now, she wanted to scream, but it wouldn't matter. Her career, her livelihood, her father, her family against Gabe and the hotel. It was an intolerable choice, an impossible one.

"Are you?" Gabe persisted.

She moistened her lips. "Gabe, I..." Her helpless pause said the words she couldn't.

He nodded slowly. "I see." He stood a moment, his jaw working, then turned and walked swiftly out the door.

"Now about these cuts," Robert said.

The words broke her free from her suspended animation, and suddenly she realized what had happened.

And she whirled to follow Gabe.

She caught him just outside the hotel. It was like being on a capsizing ship, with the world shifting crazily, nothing making sense. "Gabe, wait, please."

He turned to her, his face tight and furious. "What do you want?"

"I'm sorry, he's being awful. Don't go."

"I don't have a choice. In case you didn't notice, I just got fired."

"It was a mistake, you have to know that," she said desperately. "He's angry at me and he's taking it out on you."

"Do you think I give a damn about him?" Gabe demanded. "Don't go. We can figure a way out of this."

"I don't think so."

She felt suddenly cold. "What do you mean?"

"I sat in that office and I watched you turn into someone I don't know. I thought I knew what you stood for. You made a promise to the people here, never mind to me. And now the minute things get tough, you bail. You're betraying everyone."

"I'm not betraying everyone," she said hotly. "I'm dealing with him the only way I know how. Walking away isn't going to help. If I stay, maybe I can minimize the damage."

"Oh, what, like you're suddenly going to stand up to him and tell him where to go? Cross a few names off the layoff list behind his back? Face it, Hadley, you'll do what he wants. You're still trying to top that bar. He says jump, you ask how high." Gabe's words were scathing.

"What are you saying?"

"I'm saying do what you know is right. Tell him no."

"You make it sound so easy." She rounded on him. "That's not your father in there. It's not about your family, your career."

He looked at her grimly. "Not anymore, it's not." He turned toward Cortland House.

She ran after him. "Don't treat me like I'm being a coward here. This isn't the movies. If I tell him to take a hike I walk away from *everything*, Gabe, everything I've ever known."

He spun to face her. "Weren't you the one who was telling me you didn't fit? How much this place means to you? Let me tell you what you're giving up if you give in to him— you're walking away from the place where you finally did fit. And you're walking away from everyone in it, from the people who trusted you, people who thought you meant it when you gave your word," he said furiously. "And you're walking away from me."

The words hit her with the force of a blow. Unimaginable,

impossible. Unbearable. "Don't make this about you and me, Gabe," she pleaded. "It's hard enough."

"It's the same thing, don't you understand? It's about what matters, who you are. What you just turned your back on."

"I'm not turning my back on you." *Say it, just tell him.* She swallowed. "I love you. I'd never betray that."

"You just did," he said coldly.

"Why are you doing this?" she cried.

Because he was desperately hoping that the most important moments of his life hadn't been founded in illusion? He'd thought he'd known her, thought he'd found a partner, someone he could make a future with. And then she'd changed before his eyes. Or been revealed for what she was all along.

He'd known in his gut that eventually she'd leave, that rural New Hampshire wasn't going to be enough for a woman who'd grown up conquering the universe. He hadn't thought he'd lose her because she'd never been there to begin with.

"Go ahead, stay here, work for him. I thought maybe there was more to you than that. I guess I was wrong."

You're not the person I thought you were, Hadley.

She'd bared her soul to him and he hadn't even noticed. She'd taken the biggest risk she knew how to take and it hadn't mattered. Instead, he'd thrown out to her the ways she'd disappointed him, he'd given her a list of failures.

Just like her parents.

It was as though she were walking on the surface of a frozen lake and the ice had broken beneath her feet, plunging her into water so cold it froze her blood. She couldn't breathe, couldn't think of anything except the awful truth—she'd thought it was real love, true love, love the way it was supposed to be. Instead, she'd just walked into a different version of the same situation, like a pet going from one owner to another. How had it happened? How could she have been so blind?

She wanted to rail, she wanted to weep, she wanted to sink

to the ground. Instead, she held on. "So basically you're angry at me because I'm not doing what you decided I should?"

"It should be what *you* decided you should."

And emotion flared into bright, diamond-hard anger. "You're damn right it should. You're just like my parents, all of you, treating me like I'm some little circus dog that only gets a treat when I perform. I've got to turn my back on my family to earn your love? Well, you can go to hell, Gabe. If I'm not the person you thought I was that's your problem. I'm done with trying to jump over the bar, no matter who's holding it."

And turning on her heel, she strode away.

The anger carried her all the way back to the office, where Robert still sat behind Gabe's desk in Gabe's chair.

She stalked through the door and slammed it shut behind her. "How dare you walk in here and fire him without cause."

"You recommended it, back when you were watching out for the company instead of your personal life."

"I sent three different follow-up memos countermanding my initial recommendations and giving detailed reasons why, and you ignored them deliberately."

"I ignored them deliberately? *I* did? What the hell do you think you're doing here?" he asked savagely, shoving a fax of the Crawford Notch confidentiality agreement in front of her. "I explicitly forbade you to turn this deal. *Explicitly*. Do you think that because you're my daughter you can get away with ignoring policy and procedure, that you can pull Stone Enterprises into financial obligations in direct defiance of my orders?"

"I never thought being your daughter brought me any special privileges," she threw back. "All it's ever brought me is grief."

"You get what you earn. You've come up here and been to totally ineffective. You've disobeyed orders, failed to achieve goals and completely compromised your authority by getting involved with the hired help."

"What I do in my personal life is my business."

"Not when it hurts my business," Robert snapped. "I sent you up here to do a job, not dally with the help. Haven't I taught you anything? You keep emotion out of it."

And she lost the slippery grip she had on her temper. "Keep emotion out of it?" she demanded. "It's about nothing but emotion for you. You're not making business decisions here, you're trying to destroy your father."

"I'm trying to get this business operating up to speed," Robert thundered.

There was a roaring in her ears. "This isn't about profits," Hadley said savagely. "It's not the hotel, it's the fact that it's something that Whit loved, something that was precious to him. You want to know why? Go down by the ballroom and look at that picture on the wall. It was precious because it reminded him of a time you were all happy. So he screwed up. He loved you and Grandmother, right to the end. He loved you, and all you could do was block him out because he hurt you."

"The past has nothing to do with this conversation."

"It has everything to do with this conversation," she retorted. "The man's dead and you're still trying to punish him. He made mistakes. People do, and you're supposed to let them get past it. But not you. All you can do is obsess over it. You focus so much on the man who was out of your life that you never have had room for those of us who are in it." She caught a breath. "For years, I've worked myself blind trying to please you. It's never been enough, never. And it never will be. So guess what, it's over. I quit. I'm done."

"What?"

"I said I quit."

"Quit?" Robert stared at her incredulously.

"My entire life you've told me what to do. You've ordered

every part of my existence, taken away my choices, and I've let you do it. Not anymore. It stops now. I am not going to cut this hotel to pieces and ruin people's lives because you didn't like your father. I'm going to get a job somewhere they give you the authority as well as the responsibilit, somewhere they don't micromanage me and reject my work because they can't be bothered to read a five-page proposal. Someplace where I stand a chance."

"You do that and you are out of this family," he roared.

"I want to be out of this family." Hadley flung the words at him. "I'm sick of it, do you understand me? I'm sick of not fitting in, I'm sick of constantly being in doubt, I'm sick of having to look over my shoulder all the time because no matter what I do you'll be disappointed. Well, you know what, Robert? *I'm* the one who's disappointed."

And she walked out.

Chapter Eighteen

He didn't want to be stuck in a car driving, he wanted to be skiing or running or beating the hell out of himself doing tae kwon do—anything to get rid of the anger and frustration that surged through him. But it was also dark and about twenty degrees out, and he needed a place to go. So Gabe drove in darkness through Vermont, his mind chasing the anger because it was easier to focus on that than on the yawning emptiness beneath it. He didn't want to go there, couldn't right now.

It wasn't possible, he thought over and over. How could he have been so stupifyingly wrong about Hadley? One minute he was telling Robert Stone he couldn't run his daughter's life anymore, the next Gabe was watching Hadley accept her father's list of demands. How could it have happened? How could she be one person one minute and then roll over into someone else the next? And what did it say for him that he'd fallen in love with her?

Whoever "she" was?

He almost didn't care that he'd been fired, because what really kicked his gut in was knowing he'd lost her. Knowing he'd probably never had her to begin with.

And the emptiness echoed, as dark as the night outside. Gabe shook his head to ward it off. He was lucky that he had places to go, friends and family nearby. A day, he thought, a day to get his feet under him. After that, he'd get out his résumé, make a few calls, deal with what came next. There were other historic properties in the country; maybe one had an opening. Maybe he could go to the Caribbean and run a resort. Or go to a city and try his hand at a big conference hotel, Boston, maybe, or Chicago or D.C. Not Manhattan, though. Not anyplace he was likely to run into Hadley Stone.

His mind veered away then. It just hurt too damn much to think about. Not now, maybe not ever.

At the moment, he needed a place he could go and just be. He had options, of course, he thought as he neared Eastmont. He could go to J.J.'s condo and ski all day. Or go to his mom's—there was always room at the Trask farmhouse. In either case, people who cared about him would be there to offer him support. It was just a matter of choosing which turn to make.

And when he walked up to the door and knocked, he knew he was at the one place he could get the kind of unquestioning sanctuary he needed.

The door opened to reveal Jacob.

"Hey," Gabe said.

"Hey." Jacob looked down at the grip in Gabe's hand, then back up at his brother's face, and nodded slowly. "Looks like you could use a drink."

And Gabe relaxed for the first time since he'd walked away from Hadley. "I got fired. Can I stay with you a couple of days?"

Most people would have reacted with surprise, well-meant

sympathy, regret, questions. Questions he had no desire or energy to answer just then. Perhaps it all flickered through Jacob's eyes, but the dominant expression was something else entirely—unquestioning acceptance.

And Jacob just nodded and stepped back from the door.

Hadley opened the trunk of the rental car and put her luggage inside. The wind off the mountain bit into her but she didn't notice. Compared to what she'd been through, it hardly mattered.

After the fight she'd fled to Cortland House, knowing it wasn't even remotely a sanctuary, not with memories of Gabe permeating every inch of it. She'd packed in a matter of minutes, recklessly flinging clothing and toiletries in her bag, leaving the little that she'd accumulated in the preceding weeks.

It wasn't her home, it had only been a place to stay. She wouldn't let herself remember, couldn't let herself recall just the night before when she and Gabe had come back from the Trask farm to sit in her living room, toasting to Christmas night and the future. They'd started making love on the couch and her carpet and had worked their way into her bed.

And now his presence was everywhere in the flat. Staying even a moment more was impossible—all it did was taunt her with loss. How could she have thought just that morning that she was in love with him? How could she have been so blind, so unable to realize that he was exactly the same as everyone else? In the end, it had come down to conditions. Always conditions.

For a very short time she'd let herself think that maybe people could love one another no matter what, but that was foolish. It always came down to what people wanted from you and what you could do. She knew that. She'd only let herself forget for a little while.

She'd only let herself hope.

Her face heated. Grimly she slammed the trunk and

breathed in the cold air. She would not cry. She would not. Because if she let herself start, she had a feeling she'd never stop.

What she needed to do was get on a plane and go somewhere far, far away. Somewhere distant. Somewhere foreign. Somewhere that didn't remind her of Gabe at every turn.

If there was anyplace that far away.

Shaking her head, she got into the car and started it up. *The minute things get tough you bail.*

For a moment it stopped her, but then she let out the parking brake. Ridiculous. There was no reason to let it get to her. It had just been something for him to say, something designed to hurt. He was wrong, she thought as she backed up. There were plenty of times she'd stuck with things, stuck with them and done so successfully.

But had they ever really been things that demanded a price more than hard work? Had they ever been things that cost her?

She headed down the drive, coming around the stand of trees to see the brilliantly lit dining room. They would be serving dinner now, carrying silver-topped trays while the jazz combo played in the background.

And everybody working at the hotel would know that the runaway train was coming at them, that no one and nothing was safe from Robert. She pulled the car to a stop.

Escape. The need for it twisted at her. She had only to get away from the hotel and that sense of something tearing inside at every reminder of Gabe would ease. But to do that she'd have to leave them all behind, leave them all to their fate.

And she couldn't do that.

This time when her eyes stung, she didn't fight it, couldn't. And when the tears came, she abandoned herself to them, lowering her head to the steering wheel to weep, just weep.

The dawn spilled through the windows. It didn't wake her; she'd never really slept. The fitful half doze she'd managed had only left her more exhausted than ever. She took time over her makeup, trying to cover the smudged, swollen look of her eyes. Finally, she sighed and abandoned the effort. She would be there; they'd have to settle for that.

Walking into Gabe's empty office was, at first, impossible. She was glad it was 6:00 a.m. and no one was around as she stood staring. They'd filled cheerful red balloons together, laughing. They'd leaned over the conference table and fought through the proposal until late into the night, drinking cup after cup of his exotic coffee. He'd given her the key she now held in her hand, on a Christmas that was more magical than any she could remember. It didn't seem possible that it was over, done.

She wanted to lay her head on the desk and wail. Instead, she hung up her coat, turned on her computer and went to work.

Time drifted by. The noise increased only slightly as staff came in, as though they were subdued by the events of the previous day. Hadley had no illusions of privacy; she was sure that the details of each conversation with Robert had long since ricocheted around the hotel. People murmured in the hall, in Susan's office, but no one dared to bother her. Perhaps, like refugees, they wanted to stay low until the battle was well and truly over. Everyone, she was sure, wanted to know what came next, but none of them seemed ready to ask.

That was all right. She wasn't sure she had an answer.

She'd begun to prepare for the weekly staff meeting when there was a tap at the door. And she looked up to see Robert.

"You're still here," he said abruptly.

She just looked at him.

"Can I talk with you?"

For a moment, she didn't answer. The bright-burning anger of the day before had consumed itself, leaving only the taste of ashes and an emotionless resolve. If they could determine the terms of the handover, if she could ensure that the staff of the hotel was well treated in the event of layoffs, perhaps then she could finally make her escape. Perhaps then she could live away from the shadows of what might have been. "All right."

He shifted uncomfortably. "Someplace more private."

"The veranda?" she asked.

The walk through the lobby was another minefield of memories: Gabe telling her the story of Cortland and Clara, sipping chocolate beside her in the conservatory. Waltzing in front of the fireplace on a Christmas Eve that seemed a part of some distant, golden-hazed past.

Clenching her hands into fists, she focused on the sharp bite of her nails into her palms. She'd given into despair the night before. She wouldn't do it now, no matter what.

As they reached the ballroom vestibule, Robert stopped and turned to the wall. "I came down here and looked at that damn picture last night." He walked slowly over to it. In the photo, his younger self tottered against his father's legs. "I tried and tried to remember being here. I can't." He stared at the photograph, at the family frozen in time, and shook his head. "I don't remember it," he said flatly.

"Then let's go outside and you can say what you came here to say." Hadley's voice was calm. Her hands shook only a little as she pressed open the door and walked out to the curved end of the veranda. She and Gabe had stood here, she remembered.

In another life.

Robert leaned on the railing and looked out at the valley. "Beautiful country up here."

"Yes, it is."

"Your mother and sisters are off skiing. They wanted to stay in Gstaad. I brought them here."

"The twins didn't seem very happy."

"I give in too much. It's always been easy to let your mother spoil them. She never did that with you."

"She never had a chance to."

"You're better off for it." His reply was abrupt.

"Am I?"

"You've got an education, experience. I gave you the best."

"You never asked me if it was what I wanted." She couldn't feel heat over it, merely a need for him to finally understand.

"You don't ask a child how to raise it."

"And when does a child start being an adult?" she replied.

He frowned at her. "When does a man stop being a father?" He looked back toward the mountains. "You said some pretty strong things yesterday."

"I meant them." She wasn't going to take a step backward. There was no point. She'd already lost all she could lose.

"The lay of the land looks different depending on where you're standing. I'm not going to apologize. I've always done my best by you. I was involved, which is more than I can say for my father." He met her eyes. "What's done is done."

"Then maybe we should go inside and discuss the hand-over." Her voice was cool.

"You didn't let me finish. You didn't know my father—"

"You never let me."

"You didn't need to."

"Maybe I did." Even she could hear the edge in her voice. "Maybe it was my choice, not yours."

"I saw him shut people out. I didn't want to give him the chance to do it again, to any of us."

"So you did it for him. And you turned around and did it to me."

He stared at her. "I never shut you out."

"What do you call what you did every time I didn't come through exactly as planned?" Anger flared once more, sudden and hot. "Life according to Robert Stone, no options allowed. Did you think I didn't feel it? Did you think because you didn't yell it was any easier? All these years and you've never once told me you were proud of me or that I did a good job. Never once."

"That's not true," he said hotly. "I've told you lots of times."

"Like when? At my graduation, when you said I could have come of top of my class instead of just summa cum laude if I'd only tried harder? Or when I brought in the StormCo project underbudget and you broke it apart without even telling me? Or when I turned Becheron around?" she finished bitterly.

"I'm not going to sit here and defend my every action," he snapped. "What I did for you I did because I wanted you to be the best you could be."

"Except that the best I could be would be your son."

The feelings that she'd felt so long shivered between them. "Is that really what you think?"

"Yes." Her eyes stung. "I never could measure up for you. And I meant what I said yesterday. I'm through trying."

He looked at her and something about him looked grainy and old. "I can't change who I am, Hadley. I can't go back and alter the past. I can tell that I'm as proud of you as I could be of any child, son or daughter." He hesitated. "I don't want to lose you." He stared over at Mount Jefferson, where the smoke from the railway engine puffed up into the air. Suddenly, he stiffened.

"My God," he breathed.

"What is it?"

"I remember," he said slowly. "I remember that smoke and I remember…I remember standing here." He looked around. "Nothing else, but I remember that." He fell silent. "What I wanted to tell you was that I'll abide by your judgment in regard to the hotel. If you want to follow your plan, I won't object."

"Do you mean it?" Could she trust him?

"Within reason. You've got five years to hit target. In the interim you're free to do what you want. Just keep me in the loop." He gave her a sardonic smile. "I'll give it to you in writing, if you want."

He was serious, she realized. "No cuts?"

He moved as if to say something and then shook his head. "You do what you think is best. You want to buy the ski area, it's your call."

Her eyes flew open. "Oh, dear God," she breathed.

"What?"

"The resort. The closing is at four."

"Today?"

She gave a brief smile. "I went ahead with it."

"Despite the fact that I forbade you."

"You always said think outside the box."

"I meant outside everyone else's box, not mine."

"I applied the concept more liberally. We've got to review changes and confirm the arrangements for the bank transfer. I didn't get a chance to yesterday, with everything that happened. Come on." She spun and headed toward the doors, her father hurrying alongside.

"I still don't understand how you diverted Stone Enterprises funds without letting us know."

"I didn't. I used my trust fund. It was going to happen whether you liked it or not."

Robert looked at her as if she was a stranger. "I don't think I had any idea what I have in you."

"You ain't seen nothing yet. Our CFO was supposed to e-mail me the papers by nine. It takes an hour and a half to get to Montpelier. That gives us—" she looked at her watch "—four hours to get everything done."

"You'd better get to work."

She gave him a diamond-hard, merciless smile. "*We'd* better get to work. With Gabe gone, you get to be my second."

It started, as always, with the rituals of handshakes. Hadley saw the looks on the faces of the Crawford Notch Partners contingent as they recognized Robert. Head it off, she thought.

Face it. "Gabe couldn't be here today," she said smoothly. "Allow me to introduce my father, Robert Stone."

As they all shook hands, she could practically hear Miller cursing for not digging more deeply. They sat and the dance began, as formalized as a minuet.

"The agreements have been amended as discussed yesterday," said Miller, while they reviewed the documents point by point. "Any questions from your end, Robert?"

"Hadley is the one running this deal. Talk to her."

Even though she'd spent most of the last four hours reviewing the agreement, the pages looked strange now, foreign. And it seemed wrong to be executing the deal without Gabe there. There was some comfort in the fact that Robert was watching her back, but mostly it all made her conscious of the fact that something in her world was very wrong.

Hadley folded her hands together. "The changes are complete, I've confirmed them. Everything looks consistent with respect to our discussion yesterday."

"Then it's time to begin signing," Miller said, pulling out a pen.

"Not quite."

Everyone in the room stared at her.

Miller's eyes flickered. "What do you mean?"

"There's the little matter of the lawsuit."

No one on the Crawford Notch side of the table moved. "What lawsuit?" Miller asked.

"Anthony Ricciardi. Ever heard of him? You should have, you pay him a hundred thousand dollars annually to compensate for the chronic back pain he suffers as a result of injuries sustained during a fall from your improperly maintained lift." She raised a brow. "I understand his payments are due January first. Just exactly when did you plan to tell us?"

"There's so much involved in a deal like this," Miller blustered. "I thought legal disclosed it."

"No, legal didn't," she said calmly. "The paperwork for transfer appears nowhere in your financial records. It was lucky for us that Ricciardi's lawyer was around. Anthony himself seems to have gone on a sudden vacation."

"Just what are you trying to imply?"

"I'm not implying anything. I'm telling you that the price drops by two million, now."

"Two million? That's twenty more years of payments. He might not even live that long."

"Either that or I want a legally binding note confirming that the Partners take complete responsibility for Mr. Ricciardi's compensation in perpetuity."

"That's ridiculous," Miller snapped.

"No, it's not. It wouldn't have been so high if you'd disclosed. Now that it's come out, though, I have to wonder what else you're hiding. We have to protect ourselves. Of course, we can call the deal off, if you like."

One of the partners glared at Miller, who shook his head hastily. "No. Give me a day to consult with my team."

"Fifteen minutes," Hadley corrected. "If the deal's going to go, we need to finish by close of business. You were the one who took the gamble, Miller. Deal with it."

In the end, it didn't take them fifteen minutes. In the end, Miller rolled over. The rest of the meeting was a blur of signings and wire transfers, legal checks and exchanges.

Finally, they finished. Hadley let out a long breath. It was done. The day before, she'd anticipated a huge celebration at this moment, the culmination of so many hopes and dreams. Instead, she felt faint satisfaction underlain by emptiness.

Outside, the winter sun shone thin and cold. They walked down the pavement toward where Robert's car was parked; he had, predictably, insisted on driving. "You did a good job," he said, hands jammed in his pockets.

Hadley stopped and stared at him. "Can you say that again?"

"Don't get smart, young lady." He continued walking, leaving her to chase after him.

"Is this because of what I said?" Hadley asked.

"You should know me better than that."

She did. Robert did what he chose, no matter what others thought.

"I've always been proud of you. I would have thought you would know that," he said in mild reproof, shaking out his keys. "One thing clear to me is that it's long past time I promoted you. I'm making you an executive V.P. You can have Becheron back if you want—Ketchum's made a hash of it."

"I don't want to run Becheron again."

"All right, we'll find a different project for you." He unlocked the doors. "What do you want to do?" he asked when she got in the car.

"I want the hotel." The words were out of her mouth before she knew she was going to say them, but she realized suddenly it was true. She didn't want to go back into the corporate arena, fighting tooth and nail each day for companies she really didn't give a damn about. What she wanted was to work on something she loved, to be part of something, to watch it grow.

Robert frowned. "Let me get this straight. You can choose any division of a Fortune 500 company and instead you want to run a three-hundred-room hotel in New Hampshire?"

"That's not what I meant."

"Good." He started the car.

"I want to buy the hotel from you."

"*What*?" He stared at her.

"The language of the will says the hotel has to remain in the family. You can sell it to me. It's what I want. I'm not cut out for the shark tank. It makes me miserable. I didn't really understand that until I came up here. I knew I was unhappy but I didn't realize why. And if things…" She hesitated. "If things are going to be different for you and me, we need to make them different all the way."

He shook his head, utterly at a loss. "But you can't...I'm moving you into the command chain at Stone so that you can take over once I'm gone."

"It's no good for us, you know that," she said gently. "If you want me on the board at some point, okay, but what I want for my life is right here."

"Take some time, think about it."

"I don't need to. I'm sure."

His jaw tightened and she held her breath. This was the first test. Were things going to be different for them or not? His response would hold the answer.

Finally, grudgingly, he nodded. "If that's what you want."

"It's what I want."

He stared moodily out the windshield while the car warmed up. Taking off the parking brake, he was moving to shift into drive when he stopped and turned to her. "You know what I'd really like to do?"

"What?"

"Go up on that cog railway. I'd like to see the valley." He hesitated. "I understand it's part of your hotel. Will you show me the way?"

She bit her lip. "I wouldn't miss it for the world."

Chapter Nineteen

Gabe lifted the machete and chopped brush away from a maple tree. His back and shoulders ached. He'd long since stripped off his parka, despite the snow and near-freezing temperatures. His cheek throbbed a bit where a stray branch had caught him.

He welcomed the distraction.

Maybe Jacob had merely wanted extra labor clearing the sugar bush. Or maybe he'd known to get Gabe out of the house and at work the same way he'd known to offer a couple of fingers of bourbon the night before. It had helped Gabe to stop thinking and drift off for a few hours of sleep. It was his bad luck that he'd woken again before dawn. How was it that after only two nights of sleeping with Hadley, the bed could feel so damned empty?

Getting out into the crisp winter air had cleared his head. It was work that required focus because a man who stopped concentrating when he was swinging a machete was soon walking lame. So he bent and chopped, working until the sweat started trickling down his sides.

Nearby, Jacob kept going like an automaton. Gabe kept himself in shape through tae kwon do and swimming, but his conditioning was no match for this kind of labor. Still, it gave him something else to concentrate on besides Hadley and the inescapable fact that his life had gone to hell in a handbasket virtually overnight. What did it say that fourteen years after leaving the farm he was right back here, clearing brush?

If he concentrated on the loss of the job, the damage to his career, he could just about keep the ache at bay. It was like staring at a point on a piece of paper to avoid letting his peripheral vision register what was around him.

He attacked a tangle of blueberry bushes. Work his body hard, focus on what didn't really matter, and maybe he could teach himself to stop feeling. Great theory, anyway, but it wasn't working very well. Cursing, he swung the machete harder.

Behind him, Jacob said something.

Gabe's movements slowed. "What?"

"I said, we don't have to clear out the entire sugar bush in one morning," Jacob said mildly. "We've been at it awhile. Let's take a break."

Gabe gave him a suspicious look. "You don't need a break. I've never once in my entire life seen you need a break."

"You also haven't worked with me in fourteen years," Jacob replied, setting his machete against a tree. "How would you know?" He turned and headed down the hill toward his truck. After a moment, Gabe followed him.

The truck wasn't heated, but after working for three hours, they didn't need it. Gabe tipped back his bottle of water and drank for a long time. When he'd finished, Jacob nodded toward the lunch box. "Coffee in the thermos and a couple of biscuits."

"I thought you went home to eat."

Jacob shrugged and unwrapped a biscuit. "It's a hassle to turn around and drive back and make food. When I'm working, I'd just as soon stay in the sugar bush."

"I figured Ma cooked for you."

Jacob shot him a look. "Don't you think I'm a little old for that? I go to dinner at her house sometimes and she comes to mine, but we don't live in each other's pockets."

"Sorry." Chastened, Gabe bit into his biscuit and chewed. Egg, ham, cheese. "Hey, is this homemade? It's pretty good."

"You're not the only one in the family who cooks, you know. I would have brought wine but I wasn't sure what went with breakfast biscuits."

"Funny." Gabe took a drink of coffee and squinted out at the maples. "Hey, you know I'm grateful for everything, right?"

"Sure. You're going to have to tell Ma you're here pretty soon, though. If she finds out about it some other way it's going to hurt her feelings."

"I know." But telling Molly would mean talking about it, and talking about it would mean facing it and… "I just didn't want to deal with it for a little while, you know?"

Jacob finished his biscuit. "I figured. You're going to have to sooner or later, though."

"Yeah." Sooner or later he was going to have to deal with all of it.

Jacob downed the last of his coffee and crumpled the cup, tossing it into a trash bag along with the biscuit wrapper. "You know, you work pretty well for a guy who spends most of his time pushing paper."

"You ever need me for anything, like during the sap run, you know all it takes is picking up the phone."

Jacob grinned. "Yeah."

Hadley called the department heads' meeting first thing in the morning. Wednesday. Just two days after her life had fallen apart. She tried to forget she was standing in Gabe's spot, and looked out at a circle of hostile faces. Anger, dislike, frustration, trepidation—Hadley saw it all. What she didn't see was a lick of support. She folded her hands together.

"As I'm sure you're aware, things have been rather chaotic in the past few days. I know everyone must be concerned. I want to have an all-hands meeting later, but I wanted to speak to you as soon as possible." Her fingers tightened. "The first thing you should know is that the hotel has changed hands. As of tomorrow morning, it will no longer belong to Stone Enterprises."

"Who are the new owners?" Tina asked.

Hadley took a deep breath. "You're looking at her." She would have been amused at their expressions if she'd been able to find amusement in anything. At least taking on the hotel and ski area gave her something to concentrate on.

Something besides Gabe.

"I can tell you categorically that there will be no layoffs. I intend to keep benefits unchanged and continue investing as much of our profit as possible back into the hotel. I also plan to start an employee profit sharing plan."

A little stir ran around the table.

"There's a very simple reason for the profit sharing—it's going to take everybody working hard to make the hotel succeed," Hadley stated. And it would work, she thought. "I've just bought the Crawford Notch Ski Resort, as well. It's going to provide a lot of benefits, but we're carrying a note on the hotel, so we'll need to run as leanly as possible."

"What about Mr. Trask?" asked Alicia.

It was the crucial moment. Hadley needed to tackle it head-on if she was going to keep any credibility with them. "As most of you know, Mr. Trask has left the hotel."

"You could bring him back now if you wanted to, couldn't you?" Tina inquired.

Hadley bit the inside of her lip. Would he come back if he knew Robert was gone? Perhaps. Would she want him to? Her heart, of course, would immediately accept him. But she'd finally stood up and said no to the carrot and the stick; she wasn't going to revert to that pattern, even if she loved the man holding them.

A love built on conditions wasn't a real love at all. Even if losing him felt like losing a part of herself.

"No, I'm sorry, Tina," she said calmly. "Mr. Trask is pursuing other opportunities."

"So everything went south," J.J. said, handing Gabe a beer and sitting down on his couch. "I wondered what had happened."

"It's been a rough couple of days."

J.J. studied him. "It shows. So what happens now?"

The sixty-four thousand dollar question. Part of him just wanted to hide out for a while, working in the sugar bush. And maybe if he chopped enough brush, he could stop waking up at night in a cold sweat from shadowy dreams that left him drained and sleepless.

Gabe made himself shrug. "Oh, get some résumés out, make some calls, see what I can shake loose." He took a drink of beer. "Work for Jacob in the meantime. I've got some money."

"Oh yeah? Like real money?" J.J. looked at him closely. "How many digits are we talking?"

Gabe gave him a startled glance. "I've put my share away since I've lived in Cortland House. I can stand to be unemployed for a few months, if that's what you're worried about."

"It's not. I've been thinking, Stone may have turned down buying the ski area but we know the owners still want to unload it."

"Yeah?"

"Well, that credit card endorsement deal paid me pretty well. I've got some money to invest. What about if we bought the place?" His voice was casual; his gaze wasn't.

Gabe blinked. "What, like you and me? J.J., it's six million bucks."

"Yeah, so? If you've got a few hundred grand stashed away and I throw in a chunk, we can get a loan to make up the rest. Why not?" He sat up eagerly. "We could do this, Gabe. You could run it, I'd be the silent partner."

"You're never silent."

"Look, it would give you a job and it would give me something for the future. I'm not gonna be racing forever. Another year or two and I'm out."

It was a ridiculous idea. Unlike Hadley, they didn't have million-dollar trust funds to tap at a whim. But much of the money would be secured by the property, and between the two of them they could come up with the rest.

It just might work.

"Let me give them a call tomorrow, see if we can set up another meeting. After getting this close they're bound to bite."

And he would finally have something to get excited about.

Hadley hurried through the lobby of the Hotel Mount Jefferson, checking her watch. Guests were already beginning to check in for the four-day New Year's extravaganza. In contrast to the quiet of Christmas the weekend before, the hotel pulsed with excitement. The staff moved around laughing and joking, the tension of weeks gone in a flash. Already the suggestion box in her office held entries. Mentally, the staff was already invested in the project. She hoped it would be enough.

As for Hadley, she couldn't quite muster up excitement, only a dull wish to put the year behind her and go on. Maybe with a fresh calendar she could start the process of forgetting Gabe.

And eventually, she'd get there.

Just as eventually she'd pay off the hotel. Robert had offered to give it to her, but she hadn't wanted it on those terms. She'd wanted to do it herself, to work and make it happen, not to be indulged. Market value or nothing, because she knew she'd make a success of it.

Business she could deal with.

It was just her personal life that was in a shambles.

"The ski area's been sold?" Gabe fought to keep the incredulity from his voice.

"Where've you been?" Miller demanded impatiently over the phone. "We did the closing on schedule. You could have told me Robert Stone was part of this whole thing," he added.

Like being slapped in the face with a second wave while he was still gasping from the first. "He's not." Or wasn't.

"Well, he showed up at the closing. Look, Trask, I don't think I should talk to you about this anymore. There's obviously something going on. If you want more information, get it from your company—if you're still a part of it."

With a click, Miller hung up.

They had bought the ski area, or Robert had bought the ski area, with Hadley. And what the hell did that mean? Had they kissed and made up once he was gone? Made a trade-off over his bones? And damned if part of him didn't feel good for her that maybe something was going right, after all.

But he didn't really have a clue what that might be.

And in a cold little place inside himself he began to wonder if he'd made a very big mistake.

Scooter's was dressed up for New Year's Eve. Then again, dressed up for Scooter's merely meant a few balloons tied overhead. Gabe muscled through the crowd at the bar, carried his beers back to where J.J. sat and handed him one.

J.J. raised the bottle and paused. "Here's to a new year."

"It's got to be better than this one."

"This year wasn't that bad."

"Except for the entire last month," Gabe said sourly.

"The *entire* last month?"

Slowly, Gabe shook his head. No, not the entire month. In fact, the month had held some of the best times he'd ever had. With Hadley.

He'd spent the past two days since his phone call to Miller thinking about her more than ever, worrying about what had happened. There were people at the hotel he could have called, he supposed, but it seemed kind of pathetic and more than a little sleazy to be hitting up someone who'd once worked for him for inside information.

But it was New Year's Eve. Why not drop by Scooter's? And if he wound up running into someone from the hotel and getting the update, shoot, that was just being friendly, right?

"To old friends and better times," Gabe said, raising his own bottle to clink it against J.J.'s.

"To new friends and better times," J.J. countered. "There are a couple of lonely looking blond ladies over there. Maybe we ought to wander over in the spirit of the season."

"That's for you, my man."

"Oh come on, there are only two of them, but I'm feeling magnanimous."

"I'd hate to cramp your style." To Gabe, it just seemed like work. All he'd be doing was sitting there wondering why the hell they weren't Hadley. At least the Hadley he'd fallen in love with, not the one he'd seen with Robert Stone.

Then his gaze sharpened and he rose, putting a hand on J.J.'s shoulder. "I'll leave the ladies to you. There's someone I want to go see." And he picked up his beer and walked toward where Pete Mirabelli had just sat down with friends. "Pete, hey, how are you doing?"

Mirabelli squinted at him. It was coming up on eleven o'clock and the salesman was well into the spirit of the season. "Hey, Happy New Year." He raised his highball glass to clink against Gabe's bottle, and drank. After a swallow, though, he seemed to remember that it wasn't entirely a celebration. "I heard what happened, man. That sucks."

News traveled like lightning in the hotel. "I'll get by," Gabe said with a shrug. "How about you guys? You getting by?"

"Ah, you know how it goes. My Porsche is acting up again. My girlfriend's bitching about driving me to work, telling me to get something more practical for up here. But I figure hell, I like it and it works fine in the summer."

"Sure." Gabe fought the urge to tap his fingers as Mirabelli rattled on, oblivious.

"Besides, with the profit sharing and all, I might wind up with a chunk of change at the end of the year."

And Gabe's antennae went up. "Profit sharing?" Definitely not a Robert Stone kind of thing.

"Yeah, profit sharing. The new boss lady's idea."

The new boss lady. "Hadley's the manager?" Could she have faced down her father? Stood up for the hotel?

"No, man, everything's changed around there." Mirabelli took another belt of his highball. "That's right, you wouldn't know, you've been gone. The big corporation is out, man. Your girlfriend owns the place now, lock, stock and barrel."

Bunting and balloons hung from the walls of the crowded dining room. Confetti spilled over the tables and the floor. On the bandstand, the combo played a jazzy version of "La Vida Loca" for the revelers crowding the dance floor, a crowd that included the twins, who'd apparently decided to make the best of things.

And the clock ticked its way toward midnight.

Hadley sat at a table with her parents, resisting the urge to go back into the kitchen and check on preparations for the midnight supper. They'd had all the planning meetings, the staff knew their jobs, and anyway, someone would doubtlessly let her know if there was a problem. There was a balance between being involved and being a pest, one that Gabe had managed effortlessly and she was trying her best to emulate.

The band swung into a waltz tune. Out on the floor, a couple began to dance, whirling around to the soft, slow strains.

As she and Gabe had done once.

And suddenly she couldn't breathe, overwhelmed by a suffocating wave of loss. For a moment, she thought only of escape. She rose.

"Where are you going?" her mother asked.

"I should do a quick walk-through and check that everything's okay," Hadley said, fighting to keep her voice steady. "I'll be back in a minute."

Get out, she thought blindly. The hallway, the lobby, anywhere away from the crush of people. If she could just have a few minutes she could get herself together. She could hold on until she was back home and didn't need to hold on anymore.

She walked out into the dimmed lobby, where the faerie lights glimmered around the pillars. It was deserted, the guests at the party in the dining room or the one downstairs in the Cave Lounge. Sinking down on the love seat in front of the fireplace, she stared at the flames.

He was gone. He was gone and she had no idea how to live with that. Only a week ago they'd sat here and talked. Only a week ago she'd danced in his arms. It seemed like aeons. Each of the days that had passed since those nightmare moments with her father had been an excruciating test of endurance. And the only thing that helped her survive was the hotel.

It was ironic, how the very thing that haunted her with memories of Gabe provided her only escape. Throwing her-

self into learning the day-to-day business of running the hotel
provided some small distraction. Working sixteen-hour days
kept her exhausted enough that sleep eventually came, however fitful.

It would pass, she told herself. Someday, she'd be able to
walk through this lobby and sit at this fireplace and not remember the moment he'd held her in his arms and kissed her.

But she'd never be able to forget that she'd loved him.

She dropped her head to her hands, trying for a moment to
block it out.

"Happy New Year," a familiar voice said softly.

From the moment Mirabelli had told him, Gabe had had one
thought and one thought only: to find Hadley. What he was
going to say, he wasn't sure. Whether the situation could be
salvaged, he couldn't say. He only knew he needed to try.

And when he'd walked in and seen her there, the droop of
her shoulders arrowed through him. If she owned the hotel and
the ski area, she had every reason to be triumphant.

Every reason except for the things that he'd said to her, the
things that he'd done. And as she turned to him, eyes shadowed
with despair, all he could think was that he would find a way
to fix it, no matter what it took.

He cleared his throat. "Mind if I sit down?"

For a moment, all Hadley could do was stare. He wore a
dark jacket over an untucked tuxedo shirt and jeans. He needed
a shave. He'd never looked better to her.

"Um, no. Happy New Year. What brings you here?"

He sat on the love seat beside her. "I heard you guys were
having a party. How's it going?"

"So far, so good. The staff…" Her hand fluttered, finishing
the sentence for her.

Gabe smiled. "I know." He looked away for a moment, then

back again. "Speaking of staff, I ran into Mirabelli over at Scooter's. He told me you bought the hotel."

"And the ski area. I'm a regular takeover artist."

"Well, that's great. It's a great thing you're doing." He looked uncomfortable. "I guess I wanted to thank you for it. I don't know how you managed to pull it off. I can only imagine what it might have cost you, and I'm not talking about money, but...thanks for taking care of the people here."

And he was back, now that she'd done what he wanted. "Is this the part where I get a pat on the head and a Jerky Treat?" At his quick blink, she felt ashamed. "Sorry," she muttered.

"I suppose I deserved that."

The little stab of guilt she felt irritated her. She'd done nothing wrong, she thought, raising her chin. "I made the deal because it was the right thing to do. Because I wanted to. I didn't do it to win your approval."

A spark flared in his eyes and quickly died. "I didn't claim you did. But I hired a lot of these people. I've supervised some of them for five, ten years. You don't stop thinking about that overnight. I was worried about them."

"They're going to be taken care of."

"I know that now." He sighed in exasperation. "Look, Hadley, I came here really to apologize for Monday. After the scene in your father's office I was..." his mouth twisted "...not in a mood to listen."

"No, you were very effective at telling me what was what." And it still hurt, the things he'd said. Not to mention the fact that he'd never once reacted when she'd told him how she felt.

"I'd do it differently if I had a chance to, but I can't."

"What does that mean? You'd be more diplomatic?"

"Maybe I'd do a better job of telling you why I was angry. It wasn't that I wanted you to obey me. It was the fact that it looked like you were going to let all these people go down the drain. That you were going to let your relationship with your father come between you and the person I knew you really were." He hesitated. "The person I fell in love with."

She wouldn't let it snatch the breath from her lungs. They were just words, to be taken away the next time she disappointed him. "So you love me now because I bought the hotel and stood up to my father? You can't really love someone if it's about conditions, Gabe."

"What conditions?" he responded. "I love you, because you're you and not someone else. And you've proved that."

"You and my father would make quite a team," she said contemptuously.

"Hadley, it's not that you bought the hotel from your father. I love you because you had the guts to walk into that delivery room with Angie and because you worked like a dog to fill in for her all Winter Carnival weekend—not because it was your job but because you wanted to help. I love you because you gave up something you really liked to bring my mom a gift on Christmas. Because you figured out a way to make the employees here feel involved, because you saved all of them when you bought the hotel." He stopped and looked at her searchingly. "Don't you understand? I love you. Not unconditionally— only children love like that. I love you because what you do has shown me who you are."

Could it be as simple as that? All she had to do was reach out? But for the first time in her life she was standing alone, wobbly perhaps, but on her own. Could she risk it? What would he do the next time he was disappointed?

Hadley moistened her lips. "I know it looked like I was caving when we were in your office. I was just so shocked to see my father and I couldn't handle the idea of walking away from everything. It was like being torn apart. I wasn't ready." She smiled faintly. "It took getting furious at you to give me the guts to finally tell him off."

"What happened?"

Hadley shrugged. "The sky didn't fall. We yelled at each other. I got a lot of things out I've been holding onto for a long time. And the next day, we talked. I don't think I changed his mind about anything, not really, but things are different with us. I feels like it's going to get better. And I have you to thank for that."

From the dining room came the strains of "Moon River" and Gabe stood and looked down at her. "We danced here before," he said softly. "Dance with me now. It's almost the New Year."

And she couldn't say no. At first, they moved in the steps of the waltz, the slow turns, the rise and fall. It made her want to cry, being so close and so far. It made her want to weep at what a hash they'd made of things. It shouldn't have been ending this night. They should have been celebrating a beginning.

Gradually, their motions slowed until they merely stood together. She pressed her forehead against his chest, feeling the tears gather in her eyes.

"I love you," Gabe said softly. "Whatever mistakes I made, I still love you. And whatever mistakes we might make in the future, I am always going to love you." He raised her chin so that she met his eyes.

And in the dining room, the party erupted in cheers and the clamor of bells and noisemakers as the midnight hit. A new year, a fresh start, and suddenly it was so easy, so clear to say the words and let him back into her life.

"Happy New Year," Gabe said softly.

"I love you," she blurted. And as the band swung into "Auld Lang Syne," their lips met and it was like coming home. Minute stretched into minute as the future opened up, shining and bright.

Gabe leaned back and looked at her. "I want a life with you. I may not always be easy to live with, but I'll do my best. And I'll always believe in you. I'll always be at your side."

"God, Gabe, I love you so much." And she wrapped her

arms around him his neck, throwing everything she felt into what was not just a kiss but a promise.

At the sound of guests walking by, she stirred and broke away. "I suppose we really shouldn't be kissing in front of the staff and everybody else. It's not exactly good for our authority."

"Our authority?"

She blinked. "Well, you're coming back to work, aren't you? I can't run both places on my own, you know."

And he lifted her up and spun her around until they were practically inside the conservatory. "God, you're amazing," he said when he'd finished kissing her silly.

"I still don't think we should be doing this in front of the staff."

"We don't have a choice," he said with a grin. "It's the rules."

"What do you mean?"

He pointed to the arch over their heads. "Mistletoe."

* * * * *

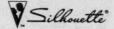
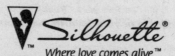

If you enjoyed what you just read,
then we've got an offer you can't resist!

Take 2 bestselling love stories FREE!

Plus get a FREE surprise gift!

Clip this page and mail it to Silhouette Reader Service™

IN U.S.A.	IN CANADA
3010 Walden Ave.	P.O. Box 609
P.O. Box 1867	Fort Erie, Ontario
Buffalo, N.Y. 14240-1867	L2A 5X3

YES! Please send me 2 free Silhouette Special Edition® novels and my free surprise gift. After receiving them, if I don't wish to receive anymore, I can return the shipping statement marked cancel. If I don't cancel, I will receive 6 brand-new novels every month, before they're available in stores! In the U.S.A., bill me at the bargain price of $4.24 plus 25¢ shipping and handling per book and applicable sales tax, if any*. In Canada, bill me at the bargain price of $4.99 plus 25¢ shipping and handling per book and applicable taxes**. That's the complete price and a savings of at least 10% off the cover prices—what a great deal! I understand that accepting the 2 free books and gift places me under no obligation ever to buy any books. I can always return a shipment and cancel at any time. Even if I never buy another book from Silhouette, the 2 free books and gift are mine to keep forever.

235 SDN DZ9D
335 SDN DZ9E

Name	(PLEASE PRINT)	
Address	Apt.#	
City	State/Prov.	Zip/Postal Code

Not valid to current Silhouette Special Edition® subscribers.

Want to try two free books from another series?
Call 1-800-873-8635 or visit www.morefreebooks.com.

* Terms and prices subject to change without notice. Sales tax applicable in N.Y.
** Canadian residents will be charged applicable provincial taxes and GST.
   All orders subject to approval. Offer limited to one per household.
   ® are registered trademarks owned and used by the trademark owner and or its licensee.

SPED04R   ©2004 Harlequin Enterprises Limited

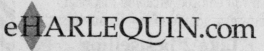

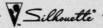

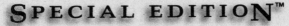

The second story in
The Moorehouse Legacy!

HIS COMFORT AND JOY
by **Jessica Bird**
January 2006

Sweet, small-town Joy Moorehouse knew
getting tangled up in fantasies about political
powerhouse Gray Bennett was ridiculous.

Until he noticed her...really noticed her.

Alex Moorehouse's story will be
available April 2006.

4 1/2 Stars, Top Pick!
"A romance of rare depth,
humor and sensuality."
—*Romantic Times* BOOKclub on
Beauty and the Black Sheep

COMING NEXT MONTH

SPECIAL EDITION

#1729 PRODIGAL SON—Susan Mallery
Family Business
After his father's death, it was up to eldest son Jack Hanson to save
the troubled family business. Hiring his beautiful business school
rival Samantha Edwards helped—her creative ideas worked wonders.
But her unorthodox style rankled by-the-books Jack. They were
headed for an office showdown...*and* falling for each other behind
closed doors.

#1730 A PERFECT LIFE—Patricia Kay
Callie's Corner Café
The divorce was tough enough on Shawn Fletcher—selling the house
and watching her ex remarry *really* stung. So a flirtation with her
daughter's math teacher, Matt McFarland, came as a nice surprise.
But when things with the younger man seemed serious, Shawn
panicked—how would her daughter and the Callie's Corner Café
gang take the news?

#1731 HIS MOTHER'S WEDDING—Judy Duarte
Private eye Rico Garcia blamed his cynicism about romance on
his mom, who after four marriages had found a "soul mate"—again!
Rico's help with the new wedding put him on a collision course
with gorgeous, Pollyanna-ish wedding planner Molly Townsend.
The attraction sizzled...but was it enough to melt the detective's
world-weary veneer?

#1732 HIS COMFORT AND JOY—Jessica Bird
The Moorehouse Legacy
For dress designer Joy Moorehouse, July and August were the kindest
months—when brash politico Gray Bennett summered in
her hometown of Saranac. She innocently admired him from afar until
things between them took a sudden turn. Soon work led Joy
to Gray's Manhattan stomping ground...and passions escalated in
a New York minute.

#1733 THE THREE-WAY MIRACLE—Karen Sandler
Devoted to managing the Rescued Hearts Riding School,
Sara Rand kept men at arm's length, and volunteer building contractor
Keith Delacroix was no exception. But then Sara and Keith had to join
forces to find a missing student. Looking for
the little girl made them reflect on loss and abuse in their pasts,
and mutual attraction in the present....

#1734 THE DOCTOR'S SECRET CHILD—Kate Welsh
CEO Caroline Hopewell knew heartbreak. Her father had died,
leaving her to raise his son by a second marriage, and the boy
had a rare illness. Then Caroline discovered the truth: the child wasn't
her father's. But the endearing attentions of the true dad,
Dr. Trey Westerly, for his newfound child stirred Caroline's soul...
giving her hope for the future.